THE SUMMER SAND PACT

FIVE ISLAND COVE, BOOK 2

JESSIE NEWTON

COPYRIGHT

CHAPTER ONE

Alice Kelton signed the paperwork on the clipboard and handed the keys to the sedan to the man who'd be driving it onto the ship. She tucked her arms into a fold as she watched, the wind coming off the harbor bringing the scent of summer with it. Sunshine, and ice cream, and an easier time was what Alice imagined summer to smell like, and she drew in a deep breath as she pressed her eyes closed.

In her mind, she saw Frank sitting behind his desk in his home office. She'd asked him for a meeting, but he hadn't looked up when she'd entered. Until then, she'd second- and triple-guessed her decision to talk to him about a mutual split.

A *divorce*, she told herself as Charlie stepped to her side. Alice gave him a faint smile and put her arm around his shoulders. "That's almost everything," she said.

Her son said nothing, because the move from the Hamptons to Five Island Cove had been hard on all of them. Alice had spoken with the twins first, and they'd both agreed to move to the vacation home on Rocky Ridge.

"Where's Ginny?"

"Waiting in the office," Charlie said, his eyes focused out on the ship that would take everything they owned across the waters to the cove. "She said she doesn't feel well."

Alice didn't either, and she watched the men on the ship too, thinking they looked remarkably like little dolls among all the huge shipping containers. Until recently, Alice had hosted one of those bright, vibrant shipping containers in her front driveway.

She'd dealt with half a dozen visitors asking questions before she'd texted the most gossipy woman in the community and told her to spread the word that Alice wasn't entertaining visitors, nor did she need any help going through things or packing.

In that moment, Alice panicked, wondering what she was doing here, standing in front of a waist-high wall made of gray stone, watching her life get loaded onto a ship.

Another breath, and the scene in Frank's office played through her mind again.

"Frank," she'd said, settling into the wingback chair in

front of his desk. She placed the agreement she'd put together herself over a two-week time period on his desk and inched it closer to him. "I'd like to talk about splitting our assets."

That had got him to look up from the small tablet he used to do literally everything. "What?"

"I've put together a proposal," she said, staring straight at him. She'd been attending law school when she'd met Frank, and she still knew plenty of people in the industry. She'd worked in a family law firm for two years before the twins had been born. She also knew how to use the Internet, and she had all her facts lined up.

Facts, not emotions. She wasn't stupid, and neither was Frank.

Frank reached for the eleven-page proposal and began to read it. Alice's heart tapped out an extra beat every third second, but she folded her legs like boredom might overtake her before Frank finished reading.

"You're going to move to Rocky Ridge?" He lifted his eyebrows but didn't look up at her.

"That's right," Alice said, knowing the next paragraph down laid out her request for him to either pay off the mortgage or provide the monthly payment to her.

She knew when he'd reached that part of the proposal, because the air hissed out of his lungs. He put the packet down and looked at her. "You write very well," he'd said.

"Thank you." Alice didn't miss a beat, because the time for praising her legal writing skills had come and gone twenty years ago. Of course, Frank was used to charming his way back into her good graces with compliments and gifts, but Alice would not be swayed this time.

"Mom," Ginny called, and Alice pulled herself back to the shipyard. She turned toward Ginny, who approached from the direction of the office. "He said we can go."

"We better do it," Charlie said. "We don't have much time."

"All right," Alice said, turning completely away from the ship that would take a week to arrive at the industrial dock on Diamond Island. Then came the task of moving the cars and her belongings out of the storage container.

She'd paid for six months of storage at the dock, because the vacation home was fully furnished, and she didn't really need anything she'd packed.

"Did they call a cab?" she asked.

"Yes," Ginny said. "He's two minutes out."

Alice joined her, thinking of their tight itinerary. She'd booked their drop-off at the shipyard and their flight close together on purpose, because she didn't want any opportunity for any of them to back out of their plan.

She walked with her children back to the office, through the back door, the office, and then the front door. By the time they arrived, a bright yellow cab waited at the curb. Alice waited for the driver to say her name, and then he loaded the few suitcases where she and the children had packed their immediate needs into the trunk.

He opened the back door, and Charlie slid in first. Alice rode in the middle, with Ginny the last to enter the car. Alice had tried to keep herself between the twins as the split had happened, because they needed her. She needed them.

Honestly, life for the three of them had not changed all that much, and Alice wanted to keep it that way. The only real difference was that everyone now knew Frank wouldn't be coming home from the city. Before, there'd been the hope, the tiny glimmer of hope, that they'd see him in the kitchen on Saturday morning.

Ginny leaned against the window and closed her eyes. Alice didn't, but the memories ran through her head anyway as the cab started navigating the streets farther inland.

After she'd thanked Frank for the compliment on her legal drafting, she'd said, "I'm being very fair. I don't want this house. If you'd like to keep it, that's fine. If you want to sell it, I'm requesting an even split on profit, as outlined on page four."

He hadn't gotten to page four, but Alice didn't care. He was a huge corporate lawyer, but Alice had never gotten below an A in college, and her proposal *was* more than fair—and iron clad for any divorce lawyer.

"I want my car," she said. "And you have the same choices with it as you do the house in the cove. I'd also like the Toyota for the twins." Two cars—one of which no one had driven in months. But the twins would be getting their licenses soon, and the white Camry just collected dust in the expansive garage in the Hamptons. Frank would have no need of it in the city.

"All the other vehicles, you can do what you wish with," she said. She didn't care if she got an even split of the sale of them. She'd also been very careful to leave many decisions like that up to Frank, because he loved making decisions for her and the children. He excelled at it, and he'd already be reeling from her requests for car payments and house payments, child support...and alimony.

Alice had given him several seconds to say something, but he didn't. He didn't move toward the paperwork either, and Alice uncrossed her legs, and put the right over her left. "I'm asking for full custody. The children will move to Five Island Cove with me, and I've already discussed it with them, so you won't have to."

She hated that she'd sounded like she was doing him a favor, but they both knew she was. Frank barely spoke to the twins when he was home, and she couldn't remember the last time he'd called or texted them during the week.

"You'll be free to speak with them whenever you wish," she said. "Texts, calls, video, chat. They have phones, and we'll have the Internet." She wanted to shift, but she remained absolutely still.

"The alimony is an average of payments judges across

the state of New York have awarded in cases like ours, in the past twelve months," she said. "I'm asking for twenty-one years, the same number of years we've been married, as I started supporting you as you finished law school, and then quit everything when the twins were born."

Alice hated the weakness in her stomach, but she did need the alimony. She could do anything, but she hadn't been employed in over fifteen years.

"I'm aware of what you've done," Frank said, his voice icy.

Alice nodded, schooled her face into complete passivity, and reminded herself not to make anything she said sound like an accusation. "The child support is the same as the alimony. The twins are in high school, with the activities, opportunities, and expenses that requires."

Frank tapped the papers but made no effort to pick them up again. "So the beach house, the Lincoln SUV, the Toyota, alimony, and child support."

"Full custody," Alice said. "You can, of course, see them whenever you wish. It's a forty-five-minute flight, and we don't need to be so strict with visitation. We don't need to go through the courts." She stared at him, and he lifted his eyes to hers. Her message had gotten through. She didn't want a nasty divorce, and she didn't want to take him to court. Nothing about this needed to be made public.

"We'll be out of the house by June tenth," she'd said. "If you want to take them to Disneyworld for a week, just text me the dates. I'm sure we can work out those kinds of things."

Frank would want to take them during Homecoming week, or when they had finals, Alice was sure. He didn't pay attention to that kind of stuff, because he'd never had to before.

"And then you'll be free," she'd said. "To move to the city. Sell the house. Keep it. Do what you want."

And she'd be free too, and she'd inhaled and held her breath.

She repeated the gesture in the cab too, pushing the hardest conversation she'd ever had out of her mind.

"What's the first thing you're going to do when we get there?" Charlie asked, looking at her.

Alice smiled at him, her sweet, strong son. He looked so much like Frank, but his square jaw had been softened by Alice's genes. He did sport the same dark hair and eyes, and when he kept the scraggly facial hair that had started to grow in patches along his chin shaved, Charlie was downright handsome.

"Go to the grocery store," Alice said, grinning now. "There's nothing to eat at the house."

"We should get one of those island burgers," he said, returning the smile. "Then we can go to the beach when we get there."

"You and Ginny can go," Alice said, patting his knee.

"We're going to have a great summer," he said, and it sounded like he was trying to convince himself. His phone chimed, and Alice caught the name of the girl who'd texted him. Mandie. No last name, but Alice knew Mandie Grover. Her best friend, Robin, was Mandie's mother.

Alice had sat Charlie down and talked to him about the girl he'd started a little relationship with the last time they'd been in the cove. Charlie had rolled his eyes through most of it, then he'd said he wouldn't "mess with Mandie," and he'd gone to Jessica's.

Alice had been distracted enough by Ginny, who'd needed an extraordinary amount of help getting ready for the prom. Her first. She'd been beautiful in a bright blue dress that had layers and layers of fabric for the skirt. She'd gotten more of Alice's fair features, with skin that would rather turn pink than tan.

When Alice had suggested that Charlie take Jessica to the prom, he'd once again rolled his eyes, and said, "No. We're just friends." He hadn't gone at all, but he had hung out with her that night.

"Friends can go to the prom together," Alice said.

"No, they can't, Mom," Charlie informed her, which hadn't settled her stomach at all about sending Ginny with her date. Not with her shoulders bare and her makeup adding at least five years to her age.

But Matheson Turner had been very gentlemanly when he'd come to pick up Ginny. Afterward, Ginny said she'd had to dodge his attempts to hold her hand and kiss her for the whole night, and Alice had half a mind to march over to Sandra Turner's house and tell her to keep her son in line.

But the shipping container had arrived the next day—a week early—and Matheson stopped texting. Apparently, he was not interested in a long-distance relationship with someone who was moving.

"Mom," Ginny said, and Alice turned her head to see her daughter had gotten out of the car. Everyone had, except for Alice, and she quickly scooted to the end of the seat and stood up. She paid the cab driver, took her suitcase by the handle, and faced the airport entrance.

She'd given up her position on the library board, the HOA presidency, and a prominent fundraising position on the PTA, all with simple texts. Just like that, positions she'd campaigned for aggressively were gone.

With a couple strokes of a pen, Frank had agreed to her proposal. The divorce wasn't final yet, but neither of them would contest it, and she wasn't planning to come to the hearing at all.

"Okay," she said, gripping the handle on her suitcase until her knuckles ached. "Tell me our summer sand pact."

"Not a word about the divorce," Ginny said, facing the doors with the same tenacity Alice felt rising through her. She looked at her son, her eyebrows going up.

"Be good with Mandie," Charlie said, rolling his eyes.

She nodded and squared her shoulders. "Mine is to do something new every day." And today, that thing was leaving behind the life she'd worked so hard to get. The life she'd thought she wanted. The life that had been suffocating her for years.

She took the first step, and the second was easier. The third landed smoothly, and the doors opened automatically, and Alice Kelton moved into a future without a housekeeper, the biggest house on the block, or a husband.

CHAPTER TWO

K elli Thompson saw the man with the light brown hair and freckles across his face sitting in the area for the gate next to hers. She'd seen him at the market yesterday too, and this morning, on her block as she and Parker had left the house to come to the airport.

Her skin prickled, but Kelli told herself not to over-react. She watched a lot of crime dramas, that was all. This man wasn't following her.

She stared at him for several minutes, and he never once looked up from his tablet. Someone bumped into her leg, and Kelli's attention diverted from the man to her son, who had taken off his headphones and opened his backpack to put them away.

"Done?" she asked, reaching over to smooth Parker's loose hair off her forehead. He'd gotten kissed by some of her strawberry blonde hair, but his eyes were much darker than hers, a trait that had come from Julian.

"Yeah," Parker said. "Can we get a cinnamon roll?"

"Yes," Kelli said, some relief moving through her. "Let's go get a cinnamon roll." They shouldered their packs and walked away from the man sitting a few rows over. A slip of unease moved through Kelli to turn her back on the man, but no one grabbed her from behind.

Calm down, she told herself, and she glanced over her shoulder. The man still studied his screen as if his life depended on memorizing whatever sat there.

She bought a cinnamon roll and a bottle of milk for her son, skipping everything except a bottle of water for herself. They walked slowly back to the gate, and it had grown even more crowded as their flight's departure time grew closer.

After scanning the waiting area and the one for the next gate over, Kelli didn't see the man. Further relief seeped into her muscles, and soon after that, she and Parker boarded the plane, found their seats, and settled in.

The flight from Jersey to Five Island Cove only took eighty minutes, and the plane was full this time where Kelli had enjoyed her choice of seat the last time she'd gone. Seven weeks made a big difference on the island, and the summer vacationers had obviously already started to flood the cove.

She disembarked behind Parker, taking his hand in

hers once they could walk side-by-side so they wouldn't get separated among the masses of people making their way to the baggage claim area. "So," she said, smiling down at him. "What did you think? Your first flight."

"It was great," he said, smiling. "I wasn't even scared."

A rush of love for the eight-year-old moved through Kelli, and she led him to the baggage claim only to find other people four deep, waiting for their bags.

Kelli never was one to push her way to the front, so she hung back, waiting for others to get their bags and go. She'd told Robin she could get herself to Rocky Ridge, because she was coming in a day after everyone else.

Delaying her trip by one day had allowed her to finish the week at the gym without having to get someone to cover for her for too long. And Julian had been able to get a huge order out yesterday while Kelli laundered everything she and Parker owned, packed, and scrubbed the townhome from top to bottom so Julian would have a clean house while she was gone.

When Kelli had proposed the idea of a two-week vacation in a luxury home in Five Island Cove for the three of them, Julian had frowned. Actually frowned. Kelli could still see the drawn-down eyebrows, the way small lines appeared on the outer edges of his mouth as his chin drooped.

She pushed the image of her unhappy husband out of her mind. She'd been unhappy when they hadn't taken the vacation he'd promised they would. His mother hadn't known about taking Parker so Julian and Kelli could reconnect.

Parker didn't have school, and other than her few aerobics classes each week, Kelli wasn't tied to New Jersey during the summer. So she'd boldly told Julian she'd take Parker herself, and they'd see him on the twenty-fifth.

Done. Simple as that.

Her phone dinged, and Kelli rummaged in her purse to find it as it continued to chime over and over. Embarrassment heated her face, and she quickly silenced her phone as if the people around her cared that it had made a few noises.

Julian had texted several times, saying he missed her already and he couldn't wait until she got home. A sigh gathered in the back of her throat. She wasn't sure how to interpret the messages. He could simply miss her and wish she'd hurry home. That would be the sweet assumption, the one that made her smile softly at how romantic her husband was.

But Kelli suspected he'd sent them to make her feel guilty for leaving at all. The back of her throat burned, and familiar bitterness gathered there.

Miss you too, she sent back, adding a smiley face emoji to the text before shoving her phone back in her purse. The crowd inched forward, and Kelli looked up to see if she could get closer to the rotating baggage belt.

Her eyes met those of the man who'd been sitting in the airport in Jersey. They were a darker blue than hers, but just as bright and just as...electric. He lifted his hand in a wave, and Kelli turned to look at the people around her. He couldn't be waving at her; she didn't know him.

When she looked back at him, he'd moved, and Kelli frantically searched to find where he'd gone. Who was he? Why was—?

She found him heading out the door, towing a single, black piece of luggage behind him. She glanced around at the others beside her, sure they could protect her. He wouldn't dare try to hurt her or Parker with so many people around.

"That's mine," Parker said, and Kelli blinked her way back to the present.

She said, "Stay here," and went to get his bag. It too was black, with a bright green duct tape turtle on the front of it. She hefted it off the moving belt and took it to him. She turned back and got her own bag, pulling out the handle so she could walk with the bag beside her.

"All right," she said, refusing to scan for the stranger. "Let's go get in line for a car."

Five Island Cove had an amazing summer transportation system, as no one could drive to the cove. At the airport and every ferry station, a station for RideShare could be found, and all she had to do was get in line and say how many people she had and where she was going. They'd drive her there, and if she bought a monthly pass, she could ride as much as she wanted.

Since she and Parker would only be there for a couple

of weeks, Alice had said she had two cars, Eloise had volunteered to rent one so she could go see Aaron whenever she wanted, and Robin said she'd have her SUV, Kelli hadn't bothered with a pass. But she still needed to get to the house on Rocky Ridge.

The line stretched down the sidewalk, and Kelli joined it, noting that it was moving quickly, as cars were lined up to get people already. It was just a matter of loading as quickly as possible, and only a few minutes later, she and Parker had a car headed for the north ferry station.

Parker's eyes stayed round as dinner plates as he took in the island, the ferry, the water that seemed to stretch in every direction. Kelli kept a smile in her heart at the way he wondered and experienced everything, confident in her decision to bring him to the cove this summer. They rarely went anywhere, and she'd taken him to every park and museum in their Jersey suburb. They'd gone into the city several times, and Kelli did her best to make sure Parker had plenty of opportunities for play dates. He had no siblings, and Kelli wasn't the best playmate for him, she knew that.

"This is Sanctuary Island," she told him as the ferry approached the dock. "We're not getting off here. This ferry will continue around the west end of the island and go on to Rocky Ridge."

"That's the last island on this side of the cove," Parker said. "Right?" He looked up at her.

"That's right," she said. "We flew into the middle

island. On the south side is Bell Island, and then Pearl Island."

"I heard they were going to build a highway to connect Bell and Pearl," someone said, and Kelli's anxiety spiked as she turned toward the woman standing there. She seemed familiar, but Kelli couldn't place her light green eyes and washed out brown hair.

"Really?" she asked, wishing talking to new people didn't freak her out so much. She was far too old to have a fight or flight response over making small talk on the ferry. "I didn't know that."

"Been some rumors among the locals," she said with a smile.

"Are you a local?" Kelli asked.

"Born and raised." The woman smiled, her eyes filling with pride. She was probably five years younger than Kelli, but the locals on Five Island Cove all knew each other.

"Do you know Robin Grover?" Kelli asked. "Her younger sister, Rosalee, still lives here too."

The woman's face lit up. "Sure," she said. "Rosalee and I were in the same class."

Surprise hit Kelli right between the eyes. "Really? What's your name?"

"Leslie Norman," she said. "Well, I was Otto, back in those days."

"Leslie Otto?" Kelli said, putting the name together with the girl she'd gone to high school with. "I'm Kelli

Watkins." She touched her chest, wondering if anyone from her younger days would remember her.

Kelli had the kind of face that was forgettable. She didn't speak up the way Alice did, and she hadn't been perky and popular like Robin. She didn't play sports and have boys fawning over her like AJ, and she didn't stick out academically like Eloise. Yes, Kelli was entirely able to disappear from memories as if she'd never existed.

"Kelli Watkins," the woman said, clearly trying to find the right memory with Kelli in it.

"I'm older than you," Kelli said. "I'm sure you don't remember me." She glanced back out over the railing of the ferry, the sunshine so bright today. No wonder so many people came to the cove in the summer. Everything about it soothed her soul, and again, Kelli was glad she'd decided to come.

"Did you have siblings?" Leslie asked, and Kelli nodded.

"Two sisters," she said, cutting a look at Leslie. "One older and one younger."

"Watkins..." Leslie made the connection, Kelli could tell, and she wanted to move away from the other woman.

"Heather?"

"Yes," Kelli said.

"I didn't know her very well," Leslie said, and at least her voice was kind.

Kelli nodded again, and thankfully, Leslie didn't try to strike up more conversation. Heather had not finished high school, so it wasn't surprising that someone like Leslie didn't know her. She'd left the cove when she was fifteen, and to Kelli's knowledge she'd never come back.

Everyone handled the demise of their family differently, and Kelli thought Heather had hung on for as long as she could.

Thankfully, the smudge of island on the horizon came into view, growing larger with every passing minute. "Here we are," Kelli said as the ferry pulled up to the dock. "One more car ride, and we're there."

She tugged her luggage along beside her, ready to be done with the travel already. Parker went in front of her, and Kelli edged her way off the boat and over to the line for a ride. She tapped on her phone and pulled up the address Alice had given her, and she read it to the driver while he loaded their suitcases in the trunk.

He peered at her phone, and then nodded. "I know where this is."

"Great." Kelli ushered Parker into the car, turning back to the line of people waiting for their car, her eyes catching on someone standing there.

Her feet stumbled as she realized that man had followed her to Rocky Ridge.

This couldn't be a coincidence.

Her breath froze in her lungs, but she managed to hurry into the car behind Parker and close the door. "Hurry, please," she said, and the driver pulled away from the curb. She turned around to see if he'd follow them, but he hadn't even been next in line. There was no way he could follow them.

Coincidence, she told herself, but her pulse would not settle down. Could it really be a coincidence? She'd never seen him in her neighborhood before yesterday, and she would've remembered those blazing eyes.

She felt like she had ants crawling all over her body, and she couldn't hold still for more than a few seconds. Alice owned a home clear up on the ridge, of course, as that was premium land, and nothing Alice did came in second.

"Thank you," Kelli said, passing the driver a tip. He unloaded their bags, and Kelli started up the front sidewalk to the mansion's front door.

"Wow, Mom," Parker said. "This place is huge."

"Isn't it?" Kelli said, peering up at the two-story giant in front of her. The exterior sported gray siding above a darker gray stone that looked very expensive. The front door probably weighed a thousand pounds, as it looked thick and sturdy.

She'd just made it to the top of the six steps to the porch when someone called her name. She turned, her heartbeat ricocheting around her chest.

That man stood there, trying to get his bag, pay the driver, and walk toward her at the same time.

"Parker," Kelli said, her voice quivering. "Hurry." She didn't bother to knock or ring the doorbell. She ran the few steps to the door and opened it, herding her son inside. She heaved his bag in after him, ignoring his question, and turned back to the man.

He'd left his bag on the sidewalk, and Kelli abandoned hers too. It was just a suitcase. She launched herself into the house and pushed the door closed with a deafening slam, twisting the lock immediately afterward.

"Kelli?" someone said behind her. A man.

A yelp came out of her mouth, because she didn't think there would be any men here. Honestly, anything would've made her cry out at this point. She could barely hear anything past her own heart beating in her ears.

Aaron Sherman stood there, concern on his face, and Kelli almost started crying in relief.

"What's going on?" he asked.

Kelli looked from Parker to Aaron, to Eloise, who came into the foyer too. "There's this guy following me," he said.

"What?" Eloise asked.

"I know it sounds crazy, but he's been everywhere I've been for the past two days."

As if to prove her point, the doorbell rang, and a fist pounded on the door several times.

Kelli once again cried out as she leapt away from the door. Eloise caught her arm and pulled her to her side with the word, "Aaron."

"You guys take the boy into the kitchen," Aaron said authoritatively. "Tell everyone to stay out of sight."

"What are you going to do?" Eloise asked.

Kelli reached for her son's hand, ready to hide in whatever closet, under whatever bed, she had to in order to keep him safe.

Aaron turned toward them, and somehow gave a smile that was both confident and curt at the same time. "I'm going to talk to him and find out who he is and what he wants." But as the doorbell rang again, and Eloise, Kelli, and Parker hurried into the kitchen, Aaron took his radio off his belt, and said, "I need backup to Upper Ridge Road, number 42357."

CHAPTER THREE

Eloise kept her hand on Kelli's lower back, who likewise followed Parker into the kitchen. "Mom," the boy said, "What's happening?"

"It's going to be okay," Eloise said. She pressed on Kelli's back to keep her moving past the long table in the dining room, and past the peninsula that jutted out from the wall. "Let's go into the bedroom, Kelli."

Kelli turned down the hall that led to Alice's master suite, and Eloise tried to calm her rapidly beating heart by taking a deep breath. She taught biology for a living, and that didn't include strangers following anyone and ringing the doorbell three times.

With Kelli and Parker safely in the bedroom, she turned back to the kitchen as the last chime of the bell faded into silence.

"What's going on?" Alice asked as she stepped through

the back door. She wore a bikini top and a flimsy piece of fabric that she'd called a skirt but that Eloise suspected was a scarf about her waist. "The doorbell has rung several times."

"Aaron's handling it," Eloise said, gesturing for Alice to come toward her. She needed to explain quickly, but she also wanted to listen to what was happening on the porch. "Get in, get in." She spoke in an urgent enough voice that Alice did what she said without asking why.

Robin and her two daughters followed, and Robin demanded to know what was going on. Eloise stepped over to the mouth of the hallway and said, "Shh. If you go in the bedroom, Kelli will explain."

She waited for the women and girls to file past her, and then she hurried to the edge of the wall, pressing her palm flat against the smooth texture and straining to hear. She couldn't, and she employed all the bravery she possessed to make herself step around the corner.

"What's happening, honey?" she asked as if she and Aaron owned this home. In reality, at least five of her brownstones would fit inside this mansion on the edge of the world. As if the views of the ocean and beaches and islands wasn't magnificent enough, Alice had a pool only steps out the back door.

"This man says he knows Kelli," Aaron said, lifting his arm and draping it around Eloise's shoulders. A warmth moved through her, and she looked up at him. He wasn't smiling, and he didn't seem impressed.

She looked back at the man standing on the porch. He sported short, sandy-blond hair, along with a pair of dark blue eyes that reminded her of the depths of the ocean. They sparked the way sunlight might glint off undulating water with an unyielding intensity—just like the sun.

Eloise shivered, and Aaron's hand on her shoulder tightened. "What's your name?" she asked. "I mean, I grew up with Kelli. Did you grow up here?"

"No," the man said.

"He won't give his name." Aaron shifted his feet, and that sent another round of nerves through Eloise. "I've advised him that I'm a police officer, and he's not coming inside this house."

"I just want to talk to her," the man said. "For a minute."

"I don't think that's happening," Aaron said, squaring his shoulders and glaring at the guy on the front porch. "She's scared, as she has a right to be. You've followed her all the way from New Jersey."

Eloise looked back at the man, trying to see more in his face. She considered herself a good judge of character, because she worked with a lot of young people who would just as easily lie to save themselves from getting a bad grade as they would breathe. She could tell this man didn't like Aaron's alpha attitude, and he emanated strength from his expression too.

"I can wait."

"I've already called for backup," Aaron said. "You can't wait on the property."

The man stood there, his jaw muscle working. "Fine," he bit out through clenched teeth. He backed up one step, then another, and Eloise thought he'd fall backward down the steps. But he spun on a dime and went down the steps, muttering something under his breath that Eloise couldn't hear.

He marched down the sidewalk to the road, where his suitcase still waited.

"Come on, Eloise," Aaron said quietly, drawing Eloise back into the house. She hadn't even realized she'd inched out onto the porch.

"Get her bag, Aaron," she said.

Aaron reached for Kelli's suitcase and brought it into the house, setting in in the foyer before closing the door. He twisted the deadbolt and looked at her. Eloise knew she was streaming her nerves from her eyes, but she didn't know how to turn it off.

"He can't come in," he assured her. But he didn't smile, and he glanced toward the cavernous back of the house. "Where are my girls?"

"They were out at the pool," Eloise said, her pulse leaping over itself. She started that way, because Robin had come in with her two girls, but Aaron's kids hadn't. "I'm sorry, Aaron." She still wasn't used to thinking about Billie and Grace, though she enjoyed it when Aaron brought his girls with him.

"I'm sure they're fine," Aaron said, following her. Eloise couldn't get to the back door fast enough, because Alice's house was so dang big. She finally made it, peering through the glass before she opened the door.

"They're out here." She got the door open and the squeals of one of the girls lifted into the air. Charlie, Alice's son, laughed with his sister, and everyone seemed to be having a great time. AJ lounged on a chaise a few feet away, a pair of sunglasses covering her eyes so Eloise couldn't tell if she was awake or asleep.

Probably asleep. AJ had arrived a day early, as had Eloise, and she'd shown up with one suitcase filled with only swimming suits and skimpy tank tops, and another with fruity wine coolers.

She claimed they just gave her a buzz, but Eloise wanted to know why AJ needed the buzz in the first place. She hadn't drunk much when she was here for Joel's funeral, so something had definitely changed in the past two months.

Kelli was the closest one to AJ, but she had her own set of problems right now. Eloise sat on the end of the chaise, hoping she wouldn't topple it, while Aaron called to his girls that it was time to come in.

"You too, guys," he said to the twins.

"AJ," Eloise said, reaching out and touching the woman's slim leg. She had an athlete's body, all these years later.

AJ moaned, but she shifted and raised her head.

"Eloise." The word barely left her mouth, so Eloise wasn't sure if it was slurred or not. "Time for dinner?"

"Almost," Eloise said, though she hadn't completed the order for pizza. She'd been right in the middle of tapping and adding extra cheese when Kelli had arrived. "But it's definitely time to come in. You're going to get fried out here."

AJ grinned and sat up. "Okay. Did you get the mushroom and spinach Alfredo?"

"Almost," Eloise said again, watching Aaron herd the children into the house. "Listen, are you okay?" She felt AJ's irritation, but as she tried to push herself up, her hand slipped and she fell back against the chaise.

"I'm fine," she said.

"I didn't know you were a drinker," Eloise said, trying to be as kind as possible. "Kelli just got here, and someone followed her, and she's pretty freaked out." They all were, and she couldn't imagine what Robin was doing in that bedroom. A natural worrier, Robin had probably run through a dozen scenarios by now. She'd have taken pictures of the man through the blinds, and she'd sit Kelli down and show them to her, asking her if she recognized him.

To Eloise, it was obvious that Kelli didn't recognize the man.

"Someone followed her?" AJ succeeded in getting herself all the way upright, and she reached up to run her hands through her hair.

"Yes," Eloise said. "You two are close, and I think we should go see what's going on with her."

AJ nodded, but she didn't move again. Eloise stood so she could put her legs over the side of the chaise.

"AJ," Eloise said again. "I'm invoking the summer sand pact."

"Already?"

"Well, you're not talking." Eloise cocked her head at the other woman. "So, according to the pact, you have to tell the truth, the whole truth, and nothing but the truth."

"What if I deny?" AJ said. "And pull out the safety card?"

Eloise started nodding. "Sure, you could do that." Part of the pact afforded everyone the gift of safety from the storms of their lives. They could shelter in the cove for two weeks and keep their secrets, avoid questions, and just absorb the support and sisterhood from their best friends.

"I'm going to," AJ said. "For right now." She pushed herself to her feet. "Let's go see what's happening with Kelli. I know she was having trouble even getting out the door to be here."

Eloise hadn't known that, but she pushed against the feeling that she'd been left out of something important among the friends. There were five of them, and while they all got along really well, it was natural to have closer relationships with certain people.

The problem was, Eloise felt like she was the fifth

wheel. Alice and Robin had a unique relationship, and so did Kelli and AJ. Eloise had always had a much harder time bonding with other women, even as a teenager. In all honesty, if she hadn't been in the Seafaring Girls with the other four women, she wouldn't have been friends with them.

Sometimes, she'd found herself spending time with Kristen and Joel, which was why she'd grown so close to them.

Foolishness raced through her, because Joel had betrayed something deep inside her that was still fractured. She'd returned to Boston, expecting to find her place there like she always had in the past.

But she'd been just as uncomfortable there as she had in the cove for the funeral. The only place she didn't feel like she didn't belong was with Aaron Sherman. At the same time, she knew their relationship was moving at a snail's pace. Familiar frustration moved through her as she followed AJ into the house, sticking a little too close to her to make she she didn't stumble backward.

Kelli and the others had left the bedroom, and everyone now sat at the dining room table.

"Did you order the pizza?" Robin asked, and Eloise shook her head.

"I got interrupted. I'll do it now." She pulled out her phone and continued her order, glad she wouldn't have to be in charge of a meal for another few days. They'd made a schedule last night, involving Kelli via a video chat.

Breakfast and lunch wouldn't be huge affairs, unless Robin wanted to make her chocolate chip pancakes. Everyone had brought their own groceries for those meals, and a lot of their days would be spent at the beach, where food trucks tended to gather during the busy summer months.

But dinner would be provided by one of the women staying at the house. They'd feed everyone, and they could order in or cook. Eloise had decided to do pizza and salad, but all she had to do for that was open a few bags, set out dressing bottles, and chop up a couple of cucumbers.

"I don't know," Kelli said. "I'd never seen him before."

The doorbell rang, and immediately following the initial chime, a heavy fist banged on the door. Kelli sucked in a breath, and everyone in the room looked toward the opening that led to the front door.

"It's my guy," Aaron said, striding toward the door. Eloise was one of the closest to the door, and she stepped back so she could see the front door as her boyfriend opened it. Sure enough, a tall man stood there in a police officer uniform, and he spoke to Aaron in a low voice. They both looked back toward the kitchen, and Aaron motioned for Eloise to join him.

"Eloise," Kelli said.

"It's okay," she said. "I'll be right back." She walked toward Aaron, her curiosity warring with her insecurity.

"Eloise," he said. "Dave says he talked to that guy out

there." He swallowed, and Eloise didn't like that. "Tell her, Dave."

"His name is Zach Watkins, and he says he's Kelli's brother."

Eloise's brain misfired, and her eyebrows drew down. "Kelli doesn't have any brothers." She was the middle child, with a sister older than her and one younger.

"He just wants to come in and explain," Dave said. "And if Aaron and I stay, maybe he can deliver his piece and then leave you alone."

Eloise was still trying to process what he'd said the first time. It took her a few seconds to realize both cops were looking at her, clearly waiting for her to give her permission.

"Okay," she said, numbness spreading through her. She turned and walked away on wooden legs, wondering how Kelli was going to weather this news.

CHAPTER FOUR

Robin didn't move very far from Kelli, her mother's heart skipping and jumping and stalling before then racing ahead. "What are they doing out there?" She pressed one palm to her heartbeat, which she could feel through her skin.

Alice shot her a dirty look, and she'd thankfully pulled on a tank top, though it was gold. Actually gold. It also didn't completely cover her midriff, and Alice looked like a million bucks.

Robin felt downright frumpy next to her, though she barely had any extra fat on her body. But her swimwear had been a one-piece for the past decade, and honestly, the day Duke had left for Alaska, he'd taken some of Robin's confidence with him.

"I just don't get it," Kelli said for the fourth time. "I'm nobody."

"You're not nobody," AJ said. "Stop saying that." Even she didn't seem as accommodating as she normally was. She looked over her shoulder as Eloise came into the kitchen.

"Kel," she said, but nothing else. Aaron appeared at her side, but Robin had seen that blank, shocked look on Eloise's face before.

The most recent time, she'd also been raging with anger, and she'd thrown papers into the air, asking, "Who am I now? Who am I now?"

Robin knew what she meant. She'd thought only men went through a mid-life crisis, but Robin felt in the thick of one herself. She wanted to buy everything she could find online, simply because she needed new things. She needed something to look forward to, and a package on the front porch made her whole day better.

Kelli stood up. "Who is he?"

"He wants to tell you himself," Aaron said. "And Dave and I are going to stay right here while he does, and then he'll leave."

Kelli looked at Alice, who wore a shrewd look on her face. "He's coming in here?"

"We're going to be here the whole time," Aaron said.

"Should we go into the living room?" Robin asked, already moving that way. She'd left Mandie and Jamie in the bedroom with Parker, as well as Aaron's girls and Alice's twins, and part of her wanted to go stand by the door and make sure no one came out.

In that moment, she also really wished Duke was there. Duke would know what to do. He'd take her into his arms or reach for her hand, and she'd have her anchor beside her. She hated that he was halfway around the world, but they'd talked about it and talked about it, and Robin wouldn't let her insecurities and weaknesses ruin this summer. Not for her, and not for her girls.

Not for her best friends who'd finally gathered for their summer sand pact.

Aaron started directing people around, and all the women moved into the living room with Robin. She sat on the couch, glad when Kelli sat right beside her. Robin reached for her hand and squeezed it, and once they all had a seat facing the dining room table, Aaron nodded at Dave, who went to get whoever had followed Kelli here.

"I'm not going to cry," Kelli said.

"It's okay to cry," AJ said, and Robin wanted to snap at her to take off her sunglasses while she was inside. But AJ probably had bloodshot eyes and was trying to hide them. Robin internally scoffed. Everyone knew why she was wearing the sunglasses, and she had to know she wasn't hiding anything.

"All right," Aaron said, nodding toward the front door. Robin felt like she stood on the edge of a precipice, about to jump off. She couldn't make herself do it.

The seconds ticked by, and finally Dave came into the kitchen first, followed by a tall, tanned, dark blond man. He seemed well-groomed, and he scanned the living room and stayed in the dining room, a huge couch between him and everyone else in the house.

Dave guarded the walkway past the couch and into the living room on the left, and Aaron did on the right. The only way this man could get to them was if he leapt the couch and came at them.

"Hello," he said, and his voice carried no accent. It was deep and rolling, and he'd fixed his gaze on Kelli and no one else. "There's no easy way to say this, and I just… didn't imagine this would be the way I'd get to talk to you." He cleared his throat, and Robin tensed.

"My name is Zach Watkins." He touched his chest with two fingers. "Kelli, I'm your brother. Technically, your half-brother."

Robin gasped, her head automatically swiveling to Kelli. Her mouth fell open, and she started at Zach with wide eyes.

"Do you have proof?" Alice asked, rising to her feet. She was utterly calm, and completely powerful, and Robin was glad she was here. Alice had always been tough, but she seemed a little more tightly wound now. And a tightly wound Alice could inspire fear in even the toughest man.

"My father was Guy Watkins," he said.

"Anyone can say that," Alice countered. "My father was Guy Watkins. See? Doesn't make it true."

"I have a birth certificate with his name on it. I've been looking for him for years."

"He's dead," Kelli said, her first words.

"I know." Zach's eyes moved back to hers, and a sense of urgency emanated from him. "I'm sorry."

Robin wasn't sure what he was apologizing for.

"We're still going to need proof," Alice said. "You can submit it to my lawyer, and we'll review it."

"Alice," Kelli said, standing up. She released Robin's hand and put hers on Alice's arm. Alice stepped sideways, and Kelli moved forward, her eyes glued to Zach's. "Who was your mother?"

"A woman named Sidney Tyler."

Robin's memory stirred, and she glanced at Eloise. They exchanged a glance, and she knew Eloise recognized that name too. But who was she? Robin didn't know any Tyler's in the cove, and she got to her feet too, trying to get a better look at Zach Watkins.

She paused when Alice sidled over to her. "Sidney Tyler?" she whispered.

"Who is she?" Robin searched Alice's face, because the woman obviously knew her.

"Sidney Tyler," Kelli repeated slowly. She reached the couch and couldn't get any closer to Zach. "How old are you?"

"Thirty-four," he said.

"My father had a secretary named Sidney Tyler."

"Yep," Alice said. "We met her once when we went to the glassworks for our community badges, remember?"

"My mother didn't tell me who my father was until

about five years ago," he said. "I didn't know she lived here. She wouldn't tell me." He glanced around at everyone in the room. "I just lost my job, and I figured it was a sign that I should find you and meet you." He tried to put a smile on his face, but it didn't quite fit right. As it slid away, he added, "I'm not dangerous. I just wanted to meet someone related to me."

"You don't have brothers or sisters?" Eloise asked.

"No, I don't. It's always just been me and my mom."

"Is she still alive?" Kelli asked.

Something flickered across his face. "Yes," he said, but Robin had teenagers, and she knew a lie when she heard one.

Kelli turned to Alice. "Is there room for him to stay here?"

"Kelli," Alice said, and Robin blurted out the name too.

"What?" She looked back and forth between Robin and Alice, who exchanged a look too. "He's my brother. He lost his job. He doesn't have anywhere to stay." She moved toward the end of the couch on Aaron's side. "Do you?"

"Not at the moment," he said. "But I can find—"

"This house is massive," Kelli said. She turned back to Alice. "Didn't your email say you had enough room for twenty-five or twenty-six people?"

"Kelli," Alice said again. "We don't even know him." She didn't bother to keep her voice down, and in fact, she shot a dirty look at Zach. "He hasn't produced any documents or any proof. He could be anyone."

"I have the birth certificate," he said. "It's a duplicate, because my mom didn't have the original." He was clearly holding something more back, and Robin folded her arms. For some reason, she didn't want Zach here either.

He wasn't part of the summer sand pact. The five of them had agreed to meet with their kids, and while technically, husbands had been invited, none of the women had brought their significant other with them.

Aaron wasn't staying at the house, because he still had to work, and his girls had routines he didn't want to take them from. Not only that, but Eloise had wanted the ability to talk about her relationship with Aaron, and she'd invoked the rights-of-first-refusal condition of the summer sand pact. That meant only she could bring up the topic of Aaron, and she got to say when the conversation ended too.

Robin was quite proud of herself that she hadn't asked Eloise anything yet. She and Aaron seemed so good together, and they obviously got along well. Robin wasn't even sure what Eloise would need to discuss, but she'd learned that she didn't truly know anyone once they disappeared behind a closed door.

Joel Shields had taught her that—after his death.

Her mind went to Kristen, and she couldn't wait to call her and tell her about Zach.

The conversation had continued around her, and she

realized that Zach had left and already returned. He handed a piece of paper to Alice, who read over it before giving it to Kelli.

"Quick discuss," she said, and AJ finally stood up from the couch to join the huddle of women. "Kelli, think about this. We're here with our kids. What are you going to tell Parker?"

She looked at the birth certificate and then up at Alice. Then Robin. She mentally pleaded with Kelli to see reason. "All right," she said. "You're right. Of course you're right." She broke the huddle and extended the paper toward Zach. He reached over the back of the couch and took it from her.

She didn't tell him he couldn't stay in the beach house.

"I'm sorry," Alice said. "But I simply don't have room at the house. But I'm sure we can help you find an affordable hotel."

"It's okay," Zach said, refolding his birth certificate and sliding it into an envelope. "I understand." He nodded, the defeat radiating from him. He looked around at everyone, his once-vibrant eyes filled with sadness now. "Thanks for letting me explain." He lifted the envelope and headed for the front door. Dave followed him, and Robin's heart pounded for some reason.

"Kel," AJ said, and that seemed to launch the petite strawberry blonde into action.

"Zach," she said, lunging around the couch. She hurried after him, and Robin moved over to Aaron so she could watch. "Maybe we could go to lunch. How long will you be in the cove?"

Zach turned back to her. "Lunch would be great." He searched her face, and Robin couldn't see Kelli's face. Awkwardly, and with stilted motions, he leaned toward Kelli and raised his arms, finally taking her in a loose embrace.

She patted his shoulder a couple of times, cleared her throat, and stepped back. Zach turned and left, and Kelli stayed facing the closed door. When she turned around, she was going to deflate, and Robin pushed past Aaron, saying, "Eloise, help me."

Thankfully, she reached Kelli just as she turned, and she was able to receive her into a tight hug as Kelli started crying. Eloise arrived, lending support on the left side and patting Kelli's back.

"What is happening in my life?" Kelli asked, her voice as high as if she'd inhaled helium.

"It's okay," Robin said, wishing she didn't need to be reassured of that fact too. The truth was, she felt only a breath or two away from a complete breakdown herself.

"Mom?"

Kelli pulled away from Robin and Eloise and turned her back on her son. "Just a minute, buddy," she said, her voice almost back to normal.

Robin turned toward the eight-year-old, who obviously came from part of Kelli. "Hey, Parker," she said, putting a bright smile on her face. "I'm pretty sure Eloise ordered pizza. Do you want to wait with me on the front porch for it?" She extended her hand toward the little boy, and he slipped his into hers. She tossed a look at Eloise as she left, and the brunette nodded. She'd take care of Kelli.

Now Robin just needed someone to take care of her, reassure her that everything would be okay this summer, and that Duke would be home before she knew it, and that their marriage and family would be okay.

CHAPTER FIVE

K elli wasn't sure when the sun had started to set. By the time she came back to her own mind, the scent of pizza hung in the air and the lights had come on around the pool. Parker had settled against her side, his game machine throwing blue and white lights on his face.

She blinked and looked up, the gold and navy in the sky absolutely gorgeous. A long breath later, Kelli finally felt like she was ready to make a plan.

Beside her, AJ texted someone, a playful, almost unknown, smile on her face. Kelli watched her best friend, wondering when she'd last felt like smiling at something someone had sent her.

In that moment, she realized how isolated she'd become. She had a few friends at the gym where she worked, but in reality, they should be classified as acquaintances. She didn't have a friend she went walking with in the morning, and she didn't have anyone she attended church with or put meal kits together with or that she chatted with while she went around the house, cleaning and sanitizing.

Her whole world had been narrowed to Julian and Parker, and if she were being honest, she clung to Parker so tightly because she barely knew her husband anymore. He worked so much, and even if he did manage to come home, he was glued to his phone the way AJ was—except with a heavy sigh coming out of his mouth and a frown pulling his eyebrows down.

Kelli looked away from AJ the moment AJ glanced up from her phone. "You okay?" she asked. Kelli nodded, drinking in the magnificence of the world around her. She had no idea what it would be like to own a home like this, with the beautiful pool, the trees that provided privacy and shaded the back yard. The gate in the back fence led across the street, and then it was a five-minute walk to the beach.

If Kelli listened closely, closing her eyes to block out the low voices of her friends, she could hear the waves greeting the shore. She looked at AJ, who stopped texting and met her eye. "Let's go down to the beach. Want to?"

AJ got up immediately, tucking her phone in a hidden pocket on the side of her leggings. She stood almost a foot taller than Kelli, and though they were opposite in every way, Kelli loved AJ like a sister.

Her own older sister had left the cove for college and never been back. Sabrina had married and had two teenagers in Maryland, where she lived with her husband. She hadn't come home for their father's funeral either. Kelli barely spoke to her, and a sharp tug of regret moved through her.

"Parker," she said, shifting so the boy would sit up by himself. "I'm going to go down to the beach with AJ." Her movement had drawn the attention of Alice and Eloise, who'd been talking about something. Robin, surprisingly, had sat way down on the other end of Kelli, but she'd gone inside at some point, because her chaise was empty now.

"Can you watch him?" she asked Alice, who nodded, her eyes wide open and all-seeing. In some ways, Alice scared Kelli. She couldn't imagine being as strong and as confident as Alice. What did that feel like? How did Kelli achieve it?

She once again reminded herself she didn't need to be Alice. She'd first been told that by Kristen after one of their Seafaring activities where Alice had literally won every challenge except for the physical ones that AJ had dominated.

Every person on this planet has their own strengths, Kristen had said. Kelli was still trying to figure out what hers were.

"The last step is loose," Alice said. "I'm going to have Charlie fix it tomorrow, but be careful."

Kelli nodded and leaned down to press a kiss to her son's forehead. AJ waited a couple of paces away, and Kelli trailed her fingers along the black iron patio furniture that probably cost more than she made in six months.

AJ linked her arm through Kelli's as she joined her, and they walked around the pool and onto the lawn. The temperature cooled, and Kelli gathered the jacket Eloise had given her until it was tight around her arms and shoulders.

"Who are you texting?" she asked AJ, thinking maybe they could ease into the harder conversation.

"Oh, just this guy."

Kelli heard the forced nonchalance, and she glanced at AJ. Away from the pool lights, darkness drenched everything, and it took a few moments for her eyes to adjust. "We don't lie to each other."

AJ looked at her, the last light of the day illuminating the surprise in her expression. Resignation quickly replaced it. "You're right. We don't." She looked out at the horizon too, and Kelli wondered what she felt when she did.

Kelli felt small and insignificant under such a wide, beautiful sky. With the swirls and tendrils of misty clouds stuck in the deepening navy, it looked like the work of a master painter.

"I broke up with Nathan," she said. AJ was a master at schooling her emotions. Kelli had seen her do it time and time again. She'd be crying on the sidelines of a basketball game, her coach in her face talking animatedly, and four seconds later, AJ had her game face on. She could flip a switch and be someone completely new. Go on to win the game. Run the fastest. Win the Gold.

"I'm sorry," Kelli said.

"I'm not," AJ said. "Not about the break-up." She glanced at Kelli as they reached the back gate. She opened it and went through first, and Kelli followed. Their conversation stalled as they focused on going down the several steps to the sidewalk beyond them. Kelli would've probably flown down them in her younger years, but halfway through her forties, and Kelli took more care and time with where she placed her feet.

"Are you lonely?" Kelli asked once they'd both navigated the loose bottom step and reached more solid ground.

"Even when I was with Nathan, I was lonely," AJ said.

Kelli laced her arm through AJ's again. "I know." Not only that, but AJ had always had someone. They hadn't kept up on a daily basis, but Kelli had known every man AJ had been with over the last thirty years, and there was a constant stream of them.

"We should get a tattoo," AJ said, and an instant smile sprang to Kelli's face.

She shook her head, her focus on the ground. "I'm not doing that."

"I can't believe you're still afraid of needles."

"I can't believe you haven't just gone to get the tattoo you want," Kelli said. "You don't need my permission."

"But I need your *support*," AJ said. "We said we'd do it together."

They fell into silence again, and Kelli's was because her memories were now flowing through her mind with such strength that she couldn't think and speak. She and AJ had said they'd do a lot of things together, not just the tattoo.

It was because of AJ that Kelli had jumped off the sailboat. It was because of AJ that Kelli had stayed in town after everything in her family had dissolved. It was because of AJ that Kelli had graduated and gone on to leave the cove. Without her showing up and packing her clothes, Kelli might still be trapped on Bell Island with her mother. Her very unhappy mother.

Fractures ran through Kelli, and she wondered how to fix them. How did people move on? How did they heal? How long would this night last before she got to see the burst of morning's rays and face the hope of a new day?

"Remember when we went to Friendship Inn?" AJ asked.

"I almost drowned," Kelli said, another smile painting across her face. "So yeah, I remember it."

"You did not almost drown." AJ pealed out a laugh. "You had a lifejacket on."

"I know I did Seafaring Girls for six years, but I really don't like boats."

AJ laughed again, the sound carefree and loud. "You have to ride a ferry everywhere here."

"Ferries are different than dinghies with too much weight in them and five girls who have no idea where they're going."

AJ finished chuckling and said, "I'll give you that. But we made it."

"It was a long forty-five minutes," Kelli said. And she had almost drowned, no matter what AJ said. Some days, she still felt like she was trapped beneath the unrelenting waves, staring up at the blurred, flickering sunlight through so much saltwater.

"Anyway, remember when we slept on the roof?"

"Yeah." The stars had been truly amazing that night. They'd gone in August, only a few days before the five of them had scattered across the globe. The summer sand pact was made at Friendship Inn, and Kelli wondered if the inn was still open.

"You said you wanted to explore the world."

Kelli had said that. She hadn't done it—the farthest west she'd been was Iowa, and she'd only gone there to visit Julian's aunt when his uncle had died. She hadn't gone around the world, because she'd been too scared— and she had no money.

She'd thought she'd been poor in the cove, and her family had been. But on her own, Kelli struggled to make enough money to pay for rent and groceries, and that battle between bills and the bank account balance continued to this day. Julian was smart and resourceful, but building a business from nothing took time and money, and Kelli still didn't live the life of luxury.

"Sometimes not all dreams come true," she said. When she'd said that she wanted to explore the world, all those many years ago at Friendship Inn, what she really meant was she had to get out of Five Island Cove to truly be free.

That had happened. After a few years in Connecticut and then New York, Kelli had felt reborn.

"What did I say?" AJ asked.

Kelli glanced at her. "Dream-wise?"

"Yeah."

"You said you wanted to compete in the Olympics."

AJ nodded, but she didn't say anything. They reached the beach, and Kelli paused at the edge of the sand. "I'm going to have to call my mother, aren't I?"

"I would," AJ said. "Find out if she knew about Sidney and the baby. Maybe she can confirm it for you."

"I should take Parker to see his grandmother anyway. She loves him, and he loves her."

"You've got two weeks," AJ said.

"Do you really think he's my brother?"

"Half-brother," AJ said. "And honestly, Kel? Yeah, I do." She stepped in front of her, blocking the view of the waves in front of Kelli. "What motivation would he have to lie about that?"

"I don't know," Kelli said. "Alice is right. We don't know him." She wasn't sure why she'd reacted the way she had when Zach had said he was her father's son. Maybe she simply felt a little less alone in the world in that moment. Maybe she could see the shape of her father's jaw, and hear some qualities of his voice, and feel the power of his charisma when she interacted with Zach.

Her father had been gone for a long time now, and while Kelli still held a lot of resentment and anger in her heart for what he'd done to their family, he was still her father. She missed him, plain and simple. She mourned the fact that she hadn't been able to fix the broken things between them before he'd died.

If she'd learned anything from coming to the cove for Joel Shields's funeral, it was that she didn't want to leave any bridges unfixed before she left this life. She wouldn't leave secrets in filing cabinets, and words unsaid.

"I'll call my mom tomorrow."

"We're going to Diamond tomorrow," AJ reminded her. "It's the annual boutique and car show."

"Right," Kelli said. She'd always looked forward to spending the day away from Bell for the boutique with her best friends. Tomorrow would be no different, and a new kind of hope began to shine within her. "But I'll have time for a phone call."

"Just don't let this devastate you," AJ said, taking Kelli

by the shoulders. "Promise me, Kel. This isn't going to be something that defines you. Your dad is gone, and nothing can be changed about what he did."

Kelli looked her best friend in the eyes and nodded. "You're right. This won't define me."

"It'll *add* to you," AJ said.

"Yes," Kelli said, seizing onto that, because she liked it so much. "It'll just add to who I am." She hugged AJ, and they looped arms again, turning away from the ocean. "All right, your turn."

"My turn?"

"Yep. Spill who you're texting if it's not Nathan. I saw that glow on your face, and I know it's a man, *and* that you like him."

"Oh, boy," AJ said with a light laugh. "I forgot how observant you are." She glanced at Kelli. "Any chance I could take the rights-of-first-refusal condition?"

"Nope," Kelli said. "Eloise already took that one."

"It can apply to more than one person."

"It's just you and me," Kelli said. "I won't tell the others."

AJ remained silent as they made the quick trip back to the luxury vacation home where they were staying. At the back gate, AJ paused. "I should tell everyone anyway. Isn't that why we're here? To get help with our lives? Provide support?"

"That's the spirit," Kelli said, smiling at AJ. "So we'll go up there, and you'll throw away all your wine coolers, and

Alice will make us mocktails, and you'll tell us." She opened the gate and stepped through it, expecting AJ to protest.

She didn't, and Kelli couldn't wait for AJ to start talking, because she always had something good to say. A little crazy, but always amazing.

CHAPTER SIX

Embarrassment accompanied AJ as she crossed the lawn toward the glistening turquoise pool. She'd lived in some fancy apartments and stayed in plenty of five-star hotels, so the pool didn't impress her that much. Everything Alice did, though. The woman had elevated herself above her roots, and she seemed to know the meaning of sophistication in a way AJ didn't.

AJ would classify her life as "extra," while Alice's was "rich." There was a difference, she knew.

Her stomach boiled when they arrived back at the chaises and found everyone exactly as they'd left them. Robin had returned too, and she glanced up from her reading device. "How's the beach?"

"Amazing," Kelli said.

AJ found her words blocked behind her tongue, even with Kelli looking at her. She could be strong for Kelli.

That was easy; that was something AJ had been doing for decades. But when it came to acknowledging the weaknesses within herself, AJ was less than confident.

"Alice, we're wondering if you'll make us mocktails," Kelli said. She dropped her arm from AJ's and reached for her son. "And Parker, it's time for bed." Her son went with her, and she called over her shoulder, "I'll be down in a few minutes."

AJ faced the other three women, her heart pounding in the back of her throat. Then Alice moved, and Eloise reached for her water bottle. Robin stood, closing the cover on her device and eliminating the steady glow coming from it.

"I can do mocktails," Alice said. "Eloise brought raspberries and oranges."

"I want that one with the limes," Robin said. "And I brought those." She grinned at AJ as they filed past.

She was going to lose her opportunity to get their help, and she didn't want to make the walk of shame herself. "I need some help," she blurted as Alice opened the back door.

The three of them turned back to her, and Robin's eyebrows went up.

"I need to throw away the alcohol I brought with me," AJ said, her hands automatically coming up to her hair. She pushed her fingers through it, her pulse racing while she waited for someone to say something.

"Thank God," Alice said, but not unkindly. She stepped around the others. "Just tell us where it is, AJ."

AJ swallowed, wondering how Alice knew she wasn't keeping it in the bedroom she'd been given for the next two weeks. She wondered what they would say when they found out she didn't have anywhere to stay after the two weeks was up, and she reminded herself that these were her friends. Real friends.

Not the kind that cut ties when things got hard. No, Robin stuck around. Alice dug her heels in. Eloise thought and contemplated and then asked the perfect questions so she could help. And Kelli...Kelli was the best friend AJ had ever had, and she hadn't known it until she'd come for the funeral.

"Over by the shed there," she said, the words tearing through her throat.

Alice nodded and started back the way she'd come. Eloise followed her, and then Robin, who paused next to AJ, the two of them facing opposite directions. "Thank you for not keeping it in the house, AJ," she said before she stepped away.

AJ spun to watch them file over to the shed, find her stash, and proceed to open all the bottles and empty them into the grass. Her fingers clenched and unclenched, but AJ made no move to stop them.

Drinking alone was terrible, and AJ couldn't believe she'd allowed herself to get to that point. But Nathan—

she cut the thought off, because it would be brutal enough to say it out loud to her friends.

"Maybe then you won't have to think about it anymore," she whispered as Alice started taking bottles to the recycling bin. When they finished, they rejoined her on the pool deck and engulfed her in a hug.

AJ's chest crackled with emotion, and she pressed her eyes closed so she wouldn't cry. "We love you, AJ," Alice said. "Now, come on. I know you like my raspberry lemonade virgin mojito."

"Can we make it limeade?" Robin asked.

"What's with you and limes?" Alice asked, glancing at Robin.

"Do you even have lemonade?" Robin asked, the two of them continuing to bicker as they went inside. AJ grinned at them and then Eloise. She didn't say as much as the other two, but AJ loved Eloise all the same.

"How are things with Aaron?" she asked.

"Oh, come on." Eloise smiled at her though. "I get to decide when we talk about him, and it's not right now." She gestured for AJ to enter the house ahead of her, and AJ did.

Kelli came down the steps a moment later, and she looked from Eloise and AJ near the door to Robin and Alice already in the kitchen. "All right. Is Alice taking requests?"

"As long as it's not lime," Robin said in a disgruntled

voice. She shot Alice a glare, but her face softened when she looked at the other three.

"Did you tell them?" Kelli asked.

"Tell us what?" Alice paused with a glass pitcher in her hand.

"AJ is going to tell us all about Nathan," Kelli said, and AJ wished the floor would open up and swallow her whole.

"Get the raspberries out," Alice said. "And hey, this one has lime juice." She glanced at Robin, who startled and then flew into motion. Alice flicked her eyes back to AJ, who gave her a silent *thank you* she hoped had made it across the distance between them.

"Kel, you can get the sparkling raspberry lemonade from the garage, okay?" Alice said. "Eloise, ice."

With all of them scurrying around, getting Alice the things she needed, AJ simply moved into the kitchen and took a barstool at the peninsula.

"The mint in these is so refreshing," Alice said as she tore fresh leaves off and dropped them into the bottom of a tall glass. At home, AJ would use the blunt end of a butter knife to bruise her mint, but Alice opened a drawer and pulled out a long, glass object.

"Only you would have an actual meddler," AJ said. "In your *vacation* home."

"What do you think we did here?" she asked, starting to meddle her mint. "I came here with Frank." Her left eyebrow rose as if to say *Drinking was necessary, thus, I have all the needed tools.*

AJ grinned, though a slip of sadness strummed through her. Alice wasn't a stranger to heartache, and AJ reminded herself of that as Alice went back to her preparation. Eloise set a bucket of ice on the counter and joined AJ on the barstools, and Kelli came in from the garage with a case of raspberry lemonade she set beside the ice bucket.

"Lime juice," Robin said, placing a measuring cup on the counter beside Alice. "Raspberries. And simple syrup."

They watched Alice expertly layer the mint, simple syrup, and ice in five glasses before she filled them with the raspberry lemonade. Fresh raspberries went right on top, where they stayed as the ice cubes held them up, and she added an unbruised mint leaf for garnish. "Drink up, ladies."

She raised a glass, and everyone reached for one too. With their glasses in the air, all of AJ's insecurities fled. If she couldn't tell these women the truth, who could she tell?

No one. She had no one else.

"To our summer sand pact," Alice said.

"To each other," Robin added.

"To an amazing couple of relaxing weeks." Eloise smiled around at the group.

"To friendship," AJ said, feeling more nostalgic in that moment than she ever had before.

"To a bright future," Kelli added.

They laughed as they clicked glasses and took their first sip of the raspberry lemonade virgin mojitos, and AJ could admit that the sweet, tart, fizzy drink hit the spot. It wouldn't give her a buzz, though, and she wasn't alone, standing in the shade beside the shed, guzzling down alcohol by herself.

"About Nathan," Alice said, leaning against the counter.

"Come sit," Robin said. "There's another stool here."

"I'm fine," Alice said, never removing her eyes from AJ's.

"I broke up with Nathan," AJ said. "Pretty much right after I got back to Atlanta after the funeral."

"Yeah, I think we all saw that coming," Eloise said.

"Yes." AJ drew her shoulders back, the slouching posture making her back hurt. "We'd been together for so long, but he didn't want to get married." She shrugged, but the pain and hurt and betrayal was already squirreling its way through her. "I thought he didn't want to get married, period. Like, at all. Ever. To anyone."

Robin breathed in sharply through her nose, but she didn't say anything.

"I had a co-worker send me an article while I was packing to come here," AJ said. Her insides seemed so hard, like someone had come in while she'd been sleeping and hollowed them out, replacing everything with wood. "It was about Nathan and this new girlfriend he had. Well, he was her new fiancée."

"No," Eloise said.

"That snake," Kelli added.

"Yeah." AJ lifted her drink to her lips again, and while it was delicious, she really wanted the buzz. She wanted the buzz to then burn, because then she could stop thinking about this. Stop the feelings of inadequacy and complete self-loathing from moving through her.

"It was then that I realized he just didn't want to marry *me*."

"I'm so sorry," Robin said, covering AJ's hand with hers. AJ looked at her, and while Robin was a suburban housewife who loved everything about Five Island Cove—basically the complete opposite of AJ—the connection to her streamed through AJ.

Robin was loyal and sincere, and when she said she was sorry, she was. She'd do anything to help AJ, and they both knew it.

"I almost didn't come," AJ admitted, her voice filled with pain. "I thought, how can I go there? How can I see Robin in her perfect marriage, and Alice in her perfect house with her perfect twins, and Kelli with her perfect son, and Eloise with her perfect boyfriend?" Tears burned in the back of her eyes, but she wouldn't cry. AJ never cried.

"My marriage is not perfect," Robin said quietly.

"You have one," AJ said, realizing just how much she wanted a lifelong partner for herself. She hadn't started out with that goal, and it had taken her years to even want it. "Even if it's not perfect."

Robin nodded and squeezed AJ's hand.

"I heard you in my head," AJ said, watching her. "And I knew she'd be so upset if I said I couldn't come. And she'd call me, and call me, and call me…"

Robin scoffed and shook her head. When she giggled, AJ did too. "You know you would've."

"I would've too," Alice said. "It was me who wanted us all here for this."

"Yeah, I thought of that too," AJ said. "Because you're the one who got me to come for the funeral, and once you found out…whew." AJ grinned at Alice. "I thought you might actually yell at me."

"Anything is possible," Alice said. "Though I'm trying to only get upset about things I can control. And this Nathan guy sounds like a real tool."

"I don't know if he is or not," AJ said.

"You loved him," Kelli said. "If he would've asked you to marry him, you would've."

"Yes," AJ said. "And it just…hurts. It hurts that he's with this other woman and she's already wearing his ring."

"He was probably seeing her at the same time as you," Eloise said, glancing up from her drink glass. "I mean —sorry AJ."

"No," AJ said, though a stinging sensation pulsed through her body now. Her phone vibrated in her back pocket, and she knew who it would be, but she didn't pull the device out. "Anyway, to get myself to come, I bought as much alcohol as would fit in my suitcase, and I got on the plane. I drank a lot so I wouldn't have to think about anything, and I've been hungover every morning since I've been here."

"Well, no more of that," Kelli said. "You don't need it here."

"Not when you have this," Robin said, sipping her drink.

AJ took a mouthful of her concoction too, and the vibrant mint and raspberry really was delicious. She went back and forth every half-second, trying to decide what to do. Eloise sighed as she finished her drink and said, "Alice, you're a genius."

"Are you going to talk about Aaron?" Alice asked.

"Nope."

"Come on," Robin said. "You know you want to, and some of us need some relationship talk."

"Who?" Eloise demanded. "Who needs relationship talk?"

Not a single one of them said anything, and AJ's pulse skipped around in her chest. None of them had perfect relationships, and she suddenly didn't feel so bad about the last four years with a man who didn't want her.

"I have some relationship talk," AJ said as her phone

vibrated again. She took it out of her pocket and set it on the counter way out in front of her, where everyone would be able to see it.

"Who's JD?" Alice asked, reaching for the phone. She swiped and looked up, surprise in her eyes. "AJ, he's texted you thirteen times."

"More than that," AJ said, a strangely warm glow starting in her stomach. "He's this guy I met on the plane here."

"While you were drunk?" Eloise asked, taking the phone from Alice.

"Before that," she said. "I fell asleep after the drinking."

"But somehow managed to get his number," Robin said, standing up and crowding Eloise to look over her shoulder. "He wants to meet up for dinner." She looked at AJ with wonder on her face.

"I worked hard for that invitation," AJ said. "I've been texting him for two days, and I didn't even know he'd asked me to dinner yet."

"Well, he did." Eloise handed the phone back to her. "And he's panicking a little that you haven't answered."

AJ didn't look at the phone. She could answer him in a few minutes. "So what do you think? Should I go out with him?"

"Uh, yes," Robin said.

"What does he look like?" Alice asked

"I would," Eloise said.

"Absolutely," Kelli said.

"What does he look like? Alice, really?" Robin said, shaking her head.

"What? It's a valid question."

"She should be attracted to him," Eloise added, and AJ was that. JD had a deep voice that had tickled her eardrums, and a bright smile, with a gorgeous black beard on his strong jaw.

"That's not the problem," AJ said.

"Then say yes," Kelli said.

So AJ pulled out her phone and started to reassure JD that of course she'd love to meet him for dinner, and that she'd just been too busy to respond for a few minutes. He didn't need to know that her friends had dumped out all her drinks and that her eyes had burned with tears.

She might not keep secrets from her sisterhood, but she had some to keep from him for a little while longer.

CHAPTER SEVEN

Alice slipped her feet into a pair of flat sandals that still gave her an additional two inches of height. The thick soles helped keep her loose, flowing, white pants from dragging on the ground, and she reached for the light blue sleeveless shirt she'd chosen for their day on Diamond Island.

She didn't mind walking around the boutique, though hand-painted wooden signs and aprons with geese on them weren't anything she was interested in buying. She'd loved it as a child, because the food vendors sold Mexican street corn, sweet potato fries with ice cream glaze, and seafood sliders with fresh cilantro slaw.

After her mother had died, most of Alice's diet came from a bottle or box, and she'd loved the food at the boutique. Today would be no different, because while

Alice wanted to maintain her figure post-divorce, she also wanted to enjoy the food she put in her mouth.

She didn't have Frank to appease anymore. Alice had thought she'd feel so free without Frank, but if she were being honest, with Frank, she knew the box she needed to operate inside.

Now, the whole world was wide open, without rules, and Alice didn't know what she should or shouldn't do.

She'd learn though, just like she'd learned how to take care of two babies at once. Then how to parent two completely different personalities that had arrived on the same day. Then how to be the wife of a man who had mistresses.

She could figure out how to be a divorcée too.

She smoothed her hands down her stomach to get the blouse to lie flat, and then she stepped across the hall. Knocking, she said, "Guys, we're leaving in an hour."

Neither Ginny nor Charlie answered, and Alice opened the door. She took in the room in one sweeping glance, and she noticed Charlie's bedclothes were rumpled, but he wasn't there. Ginny sat up in bed, her computer balanced on her knees.

"Hey," Alice said, and Ginny pulled out her earbuds. "What are you doing?"

"Talking to Sarah," Ginny said, turning the computer so Alice could see it. She waved to Ginny's best friend back in the Hamptons, and Ginny turned the laptop back to face her.

"Where's your brother?"

"No idea," Ginny said. "He wasn't in bed when I woke up."

Alice nodded, her muscles knotting. She left the room and closed the door, her eyes moving upward toward the ceiling. Charlie wouldn't be up there; Alice had given Robin and her girls a room to share that had a set of bunkbeds as well as a queen bed. It was in the corner of the house and had a balcony that overlooked the back yard and the ocean beyond.

If he'd snuck off with Mandie—which Alice suspected he had—she'd find them outside somewhere.

The front of the house faced east and took the brunt of the morning sun, which meant the back yard would be draped in shade. While it was mid-June, the morning in the shade was still a bit chilly, and Alice wrapped her arms around herself as she stepped outside. With the added breeze, she knew she wouldn't be going far to find her son.

She stayed in the doorway and did the next best thing: she called Charlie, almost expecting to hear his ringtone from very nearby.

She didn't, but Charlie said, "Hey, Mom," after only one ring.

"Where are you?" she asked, keeping the accusation out of her voice.

"Surfing," he said. "Remember, you said I could take the board in the shed?"

"Oh, right," she said, relief flooding her at the same time a new worry started. "I forgot. Did you go alone?" Going to the beach alone wasn't smart, as the waves and wind could be unpredictable, and she'd been taught and believed that the buddy system was best for boating, swimming, and surfing.

"Nope," he said. "Mandie's here with me."

Alice's stomach tightened. "And you're just surfing."

"Mom," Charlie said, plenty of warning in his voice.

"I'm just asking," Alice asked. "I'm allowed to ask."

"I didn't break the pact."

"Okay," Alice said, and she had to believe him.

"We'll be back in a few minutes," he said. "She's coming in from the waves right now. We're leaving soon, right?"

"Less than an hour."

"Yep, see you in a minute then." He hung up, and Alice gripped her phone in her fist, wondering why she was so worried about Charlie and Mandie.

At the same time, the answer to that was easy.

"Robin," she whispered. She didn't want her son to hurt Robin's daughter, and Charlie didn't know his own good looks or charm. She and Robin were close, but they weren't afraid to have honest conversations too, and Alice didn't want that jeopardized because of Charlie. Now that she lived here full-time, she needed the strength and stability of her friendship with Robin.

She stayed in the back yard until Charlie and Mandie

appeared, both of them carrying a surfboard and looking like they'd had a great morning in the waves. They carried the joy of youth, with smiles on their faces as they talked and laughed. Neither of them saw her standing in the doorway, and that gave Alice an opportunity to observe them and their relationship without them concealing anything.

Charlie didn't touch Mandie, but he did put the boards away, and then they walked toward the door. Mandie reached for his hand, and he glanced at her with a smile as their fingers intertwined.

If Alice had been watching a movie, she'd have sighed and reflected on an easier time of life when holding hands with a boy she liked had been life-changing.

"Hey," she said, taking a step out of the doorway as if she'd just come outside.

"Hey, Mom," Charlie said, dropping Mandie's hand instantly. "The waves were awesome this morning."

"Were they?"

"Big enough to get up," he said. "Not too big." He glanced at Mandie again, none of the shy smile in view. "Right?"

"Yeah," Mandie said. "I could only get up a couple of times, but Charlie did almost every time." She didn't look at him at all.

"I'm glad," Alice said. "You probably have time to shower, and I can make pancakes if you want."

"Sure," Charlie said, and he gave Alice a quick hug

before heading inside. Mandie gave her a tight smile and followed him, and Alice wondered what her face looked like. Was she sizing up the girl? Did she have a look of judgement on her face?

She felt her eyes narrow, and she worked to make them normal again. She went into the kitchen and got out the pancake mix. Parker, Jamie, and Ginny would probably eat pancakes too, and while Robin would whip up buttermilk masterpieces from scratch, Alice could only do what existed inside her skill set.

That was measuring water and whipping the dry mix with it while a griddle heated on the counter. Once she had ten circles baking, she got out a bottle of syrup and poured it into a measuring cup that would fit in the microwave.

People started coming down the stairs from the second floor, as well as up the stairs from the basement, and Alice put a stack of paper plates on the counter.

"I didn't think we were doing breakfast as a group," AJ said.

"We're not," Alice said. "I just felt like making pancakes. I'm not Robin, though, so don't get your hopes up."

"No one's Robin," AJ said with a knowing smile. "I love pancakes in all their varieties." She took two and slathered on butter before pouring the hot syrup over them.

Alice baked all the batter she'd made, and Charlie still

hadn't come down the hall. So she whipped up some more and kept churning out pancakes ten at a time until everyone had eaten what they wanted and the house from the kitchen to the living room was filled with people and chatter and laughter.

She paused for a moment and looked at everyone in this house. She'd hosted dinner parties here before, and she'd hated them, though she'd kept a smile on her face for hours. But this...this felt like family. She genuinely loved all of these people, and she was so glad they'd come to the house when she'd asked them to.

"Did you eat?" Robin asked, stepping next to her.

"No," Alice said. "I'm saving my calories for the corn and the sweet potato fries."

Robin laughed, and Alice tossed the spatula in the sink. "Come on," she called to everyone. "It's time to go."

"You're just going to leave all this?" Robin asked.

Alice unplugged the griddle and looked at the disaster in the kitchen. "Yes," she said, deciding on the spot. The old Alice would've never left the house without wiping down everything. That way, if Frank came home, he'd find the perfection he desired.

But life wasn't perfect. Families weren't perfect. Alice wasn't perfect.

"Who can I ride with?" Kelli asked, and from there, chaos ensued while they worked out the riding situation. In the end, Charlie had to cram into the back of Robin's minivan to be able to fit everyone in the vehicles they had, and they set off for the ferry station that would take them to Diamond Island.

"I JUST DON'T THINK YOU SHOULD GO ALONE," ALICE SAID later that day, her taste buds happy with the piece of Mexican corn she carried in her hand. She looked at Kelli, and then met Eloise's eye.

"Maybe your mother would go with you," Robin said.

"She's not going to go to lunch with her half-brother and her mother," Eloise said. "The man is a physical embodiment of Guy's cheating. What woman would want to face that?"

"Good point," Robin said. She took a bite of her corn too, and Alice thought about coming face-to-face with someone who'd come from Frank and not her. In the back of her mind, she knew that possibility existed. Ginny and Charlie could have half-siblings out there, and none of them would know it.

She agreed with Eloise, but she kept her thoughts to herself.

"I can go by myself," Kelli said.

"It's not smart," Alice said. "Just like we learned at the Seafaring Girls meetings. You shouldn't go out in a boat alone. Someone should be with you. You should always tell someone who you're with, and where you're going, and when you left."

Everyone glanced at her, and Alice wanted to squirm in her skin. There were a lot of people at the boutique today, and all the picnic tables had been full. So the lot of them walked slowly under the shade of some trees, enjoying their mid-afternoon snacks.

"I'll tell you all where I'm going," Kelli said. "And what time I expect to be done. We'll be in public. I don't believe he'll hurt me."

"But you don't *know*," Alice said.

"What is with you?" Robin asked, and Alice looked at the woman walking next to her.

"What do you mean?"

"I mean, you're so stuck on her not knowing him. Going to lunch is how she gets to know him."

"Yeah, I'm going out with JD tomorrow," AJ said. "And you're not freaking about that."

"I'm not *freaking* about this either," Alice said, frowning. "I just want Kelli to be safe."

"Hey," a man said, and Alice turned to her left to find Aaron approaching with his girls. He wore his police chief uniform, and Alice wasn't dead, so she admired the breadth of his shoulders and the sharp trim of his hair.

He grinned as he stepped over to Eloise and kissed her hello. She wore the same smile when he stepped back, and their hands pressed together as he joined the slowly walking group. Alice was so happy for Eloise and this new relationship for her. Aaron was absolutely perfect for Eloise, and she was glad the man had matured past his high school years and had finally realized what an amazing woman Eloise was.

They started talking about his day at work, and his girls exclaimed over the sprinkles shop, which advertised the most sprinkle-topped doughnuts right out front. They fell behind as Aaron started to buy his two dark-haired girls what they wanted.

Alice enjoyed the slow pace of the day, and she turned her face into the sunshine, a sense of bliss filling her. Maybe Robin had had the right idea all these years, staying in the cove and building her family here. The cove culture was vibrant, especially in the summer, with great food. The weather was pure perfection in the summer, and it was only the wind in the winter that made life hard.

Alice felt secure in her decision to come back to the cove now that she and Frank had split up, even if she wasn't interested in the small-town gossip. Being on Rocky Ridge would help, as it was an outlying island with a lot of people who'd lived on that particular island for generations.

She still planned to stick to her own personal summer sand pact and keep the news of her near-divorce to herself, as well as do something new any time she could.

She wanted to be the strong one in the group. The one everyone else looked to for their delicious mocktails, the safety of the roof over their heads, and the level-headedness she'd always had.

The problem was, Alice didn't feel like herself, so

when Charlie asked, "Mom, can we go over to the parade route now? We'll just save a spot if you guys want to stay here," she just shook her head.

"Why not?" he asked. "This is boring."

"Fine," she snapped. "Go."

Even Charlie blinked, and Alice regretted her flare of temper. Robin glanced at her and smoothed things over with Mandie and Charlie, and the group split at that point. Eloise and Aaron went with Kelli and all the kids to get a spot for the parade, leaving Robin, Alice, and AJ in the shade of the trees at the square where the boutique was held.

"Why does this thing with Zach scare me?" Alice asked.

"I don't know," AJ said.

"Because he's an unknown," Robin said. "It's fine. I just think you need to take it down a notch. Kelli gets rattled easily."

"She's not wrong," AJ said.

"Okay," Alice said. "I can take it down a notch."

"Everything okay with you?" Robin asked, her voice a touch too high.

"Yes," Alice said, finishing her corn though she probably had half a cob left. She slid the treat into the trashcan and took a deep breath. "What about you? How's Duke doing in Alaska?"

"Fine," Robin said, and they'd both just lied to each

other. Alice knew it, and she also knew Robin was smart enough to know it too.

"Okay," AJ said. "I'm calling you both on your crap." She shook her head with a laugh. "And JD is calling me, so I'm going to leave you here to hash this out."

"Nothing to hash out," Robin said, but most of the sentence was said to AJ's back. She sighed and looked at Alice. "New truth?"

Fear struck Alice right behind the heart, but she nodded.

"New truth," Robin said. "I'm scared. I don't like being separated from Duke, and I feel like every day I fall apart a little more. But I *can't* fall apart. I have Jamie and Mandie, and I know they miss their father too. And I feel like a jerk that this is my hard thing, and I'm determined that no one will know how I really feel about it."

She took a big breath, her bright blue eyes so wide. "So there you go. I know it's a first world problem. I know I have no right to complain, not when you think about what AJ is going through, or when I look at Eloise and how she's trying to make a long-distance relationship work with her boyfriend of two months. Duke and I have been together for twenty-two years. Of course we're going to be fine."

Alice nodded, because she knew what came next. "Except what if you're not?"

Robin's chin wobbled, and she looked away. "It's those

damn what if's that I hate." She threw her finished corncob into the next trashcan they passed. "Your turn."

They continued to walk past the booths, but neither of them went toward anything. Finally, Alice said, "New truth: I filed for divorce, and Frank's not contesting it. I'm not telling anyone but you, and if you make me, I'll never speak to you again."

Robin sucked in a breath, and her eyes got even wider. "Alice." She searched Alice's face, but Alice wouldn't meet her eyes.

"I wasn't happy," she said simply. "And he didn't love me. It was simply time."

"I'm...I don't know what to say, other than now I feel like an even bigger jerk for complaining about Duke being gone this summer." She sounded utterly miserable too, and Alice managed to put a smile on her face.

She slung her arm around Robin's shoulders, and said, "Don't feel bad about what's hard for you, Robin. Every situation is different, and I've had my husband live away from me. It *is* hard."

"You can't tell anyone what I told you."

"Your secret is safe with me, if mine is safe with you."

"Always," Robin said, putting her arm around Alice too. "Always, Alice."

"Thank you, Robin," she murmured.

"Are you going to look for someone new?"

"Not right now," Alice said. "For one, the divorce isn't

final yet. And number two, I think I need some time to figure out how to be myself, without Frank."

"If there's anything I can do, just say," Robin said.

"We're okay," Alice said, thinking of her children. "We're going to live in the house on Rocky Ridge."

"What?" Robin danced in front of her, joy filling her eyes now. "Do not joke with me about this, Alice. You're moving here?"

"We've *moved* here," she said, finally meeting Robin's gaze.

Robin blinked, and then she burst out laughing. She grabbed onto Alice, exclaiming how happy she was, and how much fun they'd have, and that Christmas in the Cove was so beautiful.

"All made up?" AJ asked, reappearing nearby. "Let's go. Eloise called to say the route is filling up, and she hates saving spots."

Alice stepped back, glad she'd unburdened herself, at least to one person. "Let's go see if we can't get Eloise to say something about Aaron."

"She won't," AJ said. "He's with her."

"Then tonight," Robin said. "We should've never let her invoke the rights-of-first-refusal condition. That was stupid of us."

"So stupid," Alice said.

"She obviously has something to say," AJ said. "So just give her space to say it. Sometimes we can be too pushy."

"Us?" Robin asked, in mock horror.

AJ laughed, and Robin did too, and even Alice enjoyed the humor in the conversation. Now she just had to figure out how to find the good in life again. How to laugh at herself again. How to find humor and happiness in a difficult situation or a difficult time.

And she still wanted someone to go along with Kelli when she met with Zach. She knew which battles to fight when it came to her twins. She just needed to figure out which ones to take a stand on with her friends.

CHAPTER EIGHT

Eloise looked down the road, her anxiety over the continued absence of AJ, Alice, and Robin beginning to seethe in her stomach. She wasn't sure why. After she'd turned away the last couple, no one else had come over to see if they could sit on the empty grass Eloise was saving for her friends.

No one else seemed to care about saying the space was taken. Aaron seemed cool as a cucumber, and when she glanced at him, he gave her a smile that made her relax slightly.

He reached for her hand and stroked his thumb over the back of it. "You okay?"

"Yes," she said. "It's just that it's about to start, and they're not here yet."

"They're coming," he said.

"Daddy?" Grace asked. "Do we have anything to drink?"

"No, Gracie," he said, pulling her onto his lap. "We'll get something after."

"I have some water," Eloise said, reaching for her over-sized purse. She never went anywhere without a bottle of water, and she pulled it out of her purse and offered it to the little girl.

Grace looked at her father, who nodded with a smile. "Thanks, Eloise," Grace said as she took the bottle.

Eloise smiled at her. Aaron had told her he'd sat his girls down and told them he and Eloise were dating. Eloise had no idea what ten and twelve-year-olds under-stood, though, and she wished she could've heard the exact words he'd said to them.

"I've got licorice too," Eloise said, pulling the bag of red twists out, then one of black. "I never go to a parade without licorice."

"Can I sit with you?" Grace asked, sliding off her dad's lap.

"Sure," Eloise said, surprise in the word. She helped the little girl up onto her lap and handed her the red licorice. "You just wanted this, didn't you?"

Grace grinned at her. "No, but I'll have some."

Eloise felt Aaron's gaze on the side of her face, but she didn't look at him. "Do you like black licorice?" she asked Grace.

"Ew, no," Grace said. "But Billie does."

The twelve-year-old turned at the sound of her name. "What do I do?"

"You like black licorice," Grace said, and Billie got up and came over to the side of Eloise's chair. She offered the older girl the package of licorice, and Billie took a couple of pieces.

"It's okay," she said. "Red licorice is better." She took a bite of the licorice and looked out into the street. "When is it going to start?"

"Soon," Eloise said. "Want me to braid your hair?" She'd been watching Internet videos to learn how to French braid and Dutch braid, but every time she offered to braid Billie's hair, the girl said no.

"All right," she said now, and Eloise's heart leapt in anticipation. She felt like she needed to get to know Aaron's girls as she got to know him, because if they ended up married, she'd be a step-mother to the two of them.

"Kneel in front of me," she said. "Grace, I can do yours too, if you want. You'll have to get down for a minute, though."

"Okay." She slid off Eloise's lap and went back to the blanket where she and Billie had been sitting. Billie knelt in front of Eloise, and her hands shook slightly while she smoothed back the girl's hair.

"You have a whole bunch of different colors of hair," Eloise said. Overall, she'd describe Billie as a medium brunette, with brown hair halfway between light and dark.

"Yeah," she said. "Dad says that comes from my mom. He even found a gray one once." She twisted and smiled at her father, and Aaron smiled back.

Eloise noticed it was a tighter smile than normal, and she met his eye. Something blazed there she hadn't seen before, and therefore couldn't decipher.

"Does your dad do your hair a lot?" she asked.

"Not really anymore," Billie said. "But he did for a long time. He's really good at pigtails and braids and high ponytails."

"Is he, now?" Eloise asked, adding a laugh afterward. "Well, let's see if I can get this right."

"I just usually leave it down now," Billie said. "Though I hate it when it's hot."

"Do you not know how to pull it up or anything?" Eloise asked.

"Every time I try, it looks bad," Billie said.

"I could probably help you," Eloise said, feeling like she'd just stepped out onto thin ice. "I have a *ton* of hair, and I always have." She sectioned Billie's hair and started with the French braid. She got a good rhythm going, and she was concentrating so hard that she didn't realize Billie hadn't answered her.

She picked up another section of hair and tucked it into the braid, pulling the next piece over the top and reaching for another piece to weave in. She worked around Billie's head, finally nudging her bag closer to the girl with her foot. "See if you can find an elastic in there."

Billie looked at her bag and then up to Eloise. "You want me to search through your purse?"

"Sure," Eloise said. "I always keep some hair bands in there. I'm sure I have one." Her fingers couldn't hold the braid for much longer, and she hoped Billie would hurry. Thankfully, she didn't have to look very hard, because Elise really did have a ton of elastics in her bag.

She secured the braid as a ponytail against Billie's head, just an inch or two below her ear and let the rest of the braid slip out. "There."

Billie reached back and lightly patted her hair. "Oh, you went around the back."

"It's so cute," Robin said, and Eloise glanced up as her friend arrived. Additional relief rushed through her. "So cute, Billie. Makes you look older, too." She smiled at the girl, who seemed to swell with the compliment. Eloise wondered how Robin knew exactly what to say to win the points Eloise had been working so hard to earn.

"My turn," Grace said. "Can you do pigtails, Eloise?"

"Sure," she said. "Kneel down." She used her fingernail to gently divide her hair down the middle, and she took the hair elastics Grace had found in her purse to make two symmetrical ponytails, one on each side of her head.

"How do I look, Robin?" Grace asked, skipping over to the blonde.

"Adorable," Robin said with a smile. "That Eloise knows what she's doing." She cut a look at Eloise, who gave her a smile back. Robin alone knew of Eloise's desire to make a bond with Aaron's kids, but Eloise almost regretted telling her now.

Grace returned to Eloise and climbed right up onto her lap. "Thanks, Eloise."

"Of course, sweetie," she said, feeling a maternal corner of her heart growing and expanding. She hadn't even known that section of her heart existed, and she found herself taking a deep breath of the little girl's skin. She smelled like licorice and sweat, and Eloise didn't entirely hate it.

Aaron reached over and slipped his fingers underneath Eloise's arm, and she looked at him again. This time, she could classify the fire burning in his eyes as desire. And happiness. He'd obviously wanted her to bond with his girls too, though they hadn't talked about it at all.

Eloise wanted to do a lot more talking with Aaron, about a lot of things. She hadn't, because she was still trying to figure out how to have a long-distance relationship. Not only that, she wasn't sure she even *wanted* a long-distance relationship.

An image of the Cliffside Inn flashed through her mind, and Eloise once again considered her options. She had to return to Boston for the fall semester, and she honestly didn't know what would happen with her and

Aaron then. If she quit at the university and returned to Five Island Cove, she could fix up the inn and reopen it. Plenty of people made their living running beds and breakfasts. Hotels. Inns. And the Cliffside Inn would fetch a high price for its location, especially if she could accomplish the vision for the inn she held in her head.

But Eloise wasn't what anyone would call a risk-taker, and she wasn't sure she could give up her tenure and pension at Boston University on a whim and a dream.

A police siren filled the sky, and Billie said, "Finally." She turned back to Grace and Eloise. "It's finally starting. Can we go down to the curb? They throw out popsicles form the cop cars."

Eloise looked from her to Aaron, expecting him to answer. Then she realized that Billie had asked her, not her father.

She had no idea what to say.

"Sure," Aaron said, rescuing her. "Try to get me a red one."

"Do you want one, Eloise?" Billie asked. "I can get you a blue one."

"Yellow," Eloise said. "I like the yellow ones."

The two girls went past the twins and Robin's girls and stepped off the curb as the motorcycle cops started roaring by in their formations and lines. A few minutes later, the cop car with popsicles spilling out of the trunk appeared, and Billie jumped up and down, calling, "Floyd! George! Daddy wants a red one!"

Eloise looked at Aaron. "How did you get out of this?"

"I've done it for years," he said. "And I'm the boss, that's how." He watched his grinning men pass out popsicles, and one of his officers brought over two entire bags of popsicles for the group.

"Thanks, Paul," Aaron said easily, and Eloise once again marveled that a man like Aaron would even remotely be interested in a woman like her. He was strong, and powerful, with a whole crew of men under him. He had to make decisions for the safety and well-being of five islands worth of people, as well as his two daughters, all by himself.

He handed her a banana popsicle, and Eloise took it with a, "Thanks."

After he passed out the popsicles to everyone who wanted one, he stood right behind her and leaned down, his lips practically brushing her earlobe. "Would you like to come back to my place tonight, after the parade?"

Eloise tilted her head, trying to hear what he was really asking. "I'm not staying overnight," she murmured.

"Of course not," he said. "I was thinking we can put the girls to bed, and then I'll get you all to myself for an hour or so."

Eloise's whole body tingled. "All right."

"Great." Aaron took his seat again as the first classic car drove by in front of them. He held her hand during the parade, and he was the perfect gentleman when he helped the group clean up. Men and boys were severely underrepresented among them, and a lot of work fell to Aaron. He didn't seem to mind at all, and Eloise wondered if he really didn't mind hanging out with her friends and their kids.

She'd ask him that night, once they were alone. Simple as that. She also wanted to know what he thought about their long-distance relationship. She'd left Five Island Cove two months ago, but she'd been back three times to see Aaron between then and this trip. Maybe he was fine with that. Maybe it was just her that hated the distance between them and that she couldn't see him every day.

"Kelli," she said as they walked back to the ride share line. "Will you take my car back to the house?"

She looked at Eloise, her eyebrows high. "Where are you going?"

"I'm going to Aaron's for a bit," she said easily. "I'll be home tonight, though."

"Do I need to give you a curfew?"

"Are you Robin?" Eloise asked with a smile.

"What?" Robin asked, turning around and walking backward.

"Nothing," Eloise said at the same time Kelli said, "She's going to Aaron's."

Robin's eyebrows went up too, her eyes filling with questions by the second.

"Just for an hour or two," Eloise said. She handed her

car keys to Kelli. "I'll get a ride back to Alice's tonight. You don't need to wait up."

"I'll wait up," Alice said, glancing to her left, where Aaron walked with his girls and the rest of the kids. They all adored him, and Eloise once again wondered how he got people to follow him like he was the Pied Piper.

"You don't need to wait up," Eloise insisted.

"But I want to hear how it goes," Alice said.

"How what goes?" Eloise asked, glancing at Robin and then Kelli. Even AJ was listening, and Eloise didn't like the squirming feeling in her stomach. "I'm not...doing that. We're not." She shook her head.

"Outline how this happened," Alice said, shooting another look over to her twins.

"He passed out the popsicles and then asked me to come back to his place tonight."

"He used the words 'come back to my place'?" Robin asked.

"Yes," Eloise said, confused. "So what?"

Alice exchanged a look with Robin and then AJ. Eloise felt like a moron, and she hated that. She never felt like this in her real life. In high school, she was the smart one. She'd earned scholarships at a half-dozen colleges.

Learning Joel had doctored her test scores had severely shaken her, because if Eloise wasn't smart, what was she?

At BU, she knew exactly who she was and what her day held. She knew she was right in her lectures, and she was hardly ever presented with a student or a situation she didn't know how to deal with.

But on Five Island Cove, she seemed to run into obstacles at every turn that left her second-guessing herself and what she did and said.

"Sweetie," AJ said, taking Kelli's spot on Eloise's right. "I think he probably wants to."

"I'm sure that's not true," Eloise said. "We've only been seeing each other for a couple of months, and if you put together all of the days we've seen one another, it's like fourteen days." She looked down the line of her friends. "That's soon, right?"

AJ shrugged, as she'd obviously been nominated to be the voice for the group. "I mean, I've done it with a guy on the first day we meet."

"Gross, AJ," Robin said. "That's not normal, Eloise."

Alice said nothing, and neither did Kelli. Eloise honestly didn't know what to say or do.

"I really don't think that's why he invited me to his place," she said. "His girls will be there." Eloise shook her head, the weight of her hair making her hot from head to toe. Or maybe that was the thought of being intimate with Aaron Sherman. "Besides, I'm not ready for that."

She couldn't even imagine letting Aaron see her at her most vulnerable. Not right now. Her heartbeat shot through her body, and she couldn't fathom ever getting to that point.

"So don't let him pressure you," Robin said.

"I can't believe we're talking about this," Eloise hissed. "I'm not fifteen."

"She's right," Kelli said. "Let's leave her alone. Eloise knows who she is and what she wants. She can handle Aaron."

"That's right," Eloise said, latching onto Kelli's words. "I can handle Aaron."

"I'd still like to stay up," Alice said. "You won't have to tell me anything if you don't want to. I just like to know you made it back safely."

A rush of love for the woman filled Eloise, and she nodded. "Thank you, Alice." Sometimes she felt on the outside of the friendship the five of them had, and then she was reminded how she completely fit with all of them. Even the sophisticated, rich, polished and poised Alice Kelton.

Alice squeezed her hand and drew Robin away from Eloise. Kelli gave her a shoulder squeeze, and AJ just smiled at her. "You'll miss the lobster rolls," she said. "And they're going to be amazing."

"Save me one," Eloise said. "Or two. Okay, three." She grinned at AJ. "I didn't know you cooked."

"Honey, I don't. I ordered them from Mort's."

"Okay, then I want six," Eloise said with a smile. "Sorry to miss out on dinner."

"You gotta do what you gotta do," AJ said. "Besides, I'm going to miss tomorrow night, and I think Robin is making her seafood pot pie from scratch." She glanced up to Robin and Alice. "And I haven't told them about the date with JD."

"So that's a go?" Kelli asked.

"He said he'll be back, whatever that means."

"Back?" Eloise asked. "Didn't he fly in with you a couple of days ago?"

"Yeah." AJ shook her head. "I'm pretty sure this is crazy. I'm going to cancel. I'm not ready for a new relationship right now." She looked miserable, and Eloise wished she could comfort her somehow.

"El," Aaron said. "I'm over here." He nodded toward a parking lot on his left.

"See you guys later," she said, making the detour toward Aaron. He took her hand with a smile, and they wove through the parking lot to his cruiser.

"Little girls in the back," he said, and his kids climbed in the back. He walked her around to the front passenger side and asked, "What do you want for dinner?"

"Oh, I'm easy," Eloise said, immediately regretting the words. "I mean, maybe..." She drew a blank, and Aaron narrowed his eyes at her.

"Pasta?" he asked. "As soon as I ask them, you're going to get pasta, pasta, pasta." He rolled his eyes. "I'm sick of pasta."

Eloise giggled and slid her hand down one side of his face. "So what should I say? What do you want?"

"I want something with meat," he said. "Pizza or a meatball sub. Seafood. Something with some protein."

"You can get a beef bolognese or something," she said, smiling at him.

"It's going to be three against one, isn't it?" He grinned back at her.

"Not at all," she said, sobering. "They used to have a great roast beef sandwich at Freshly Caught. Is that still a thing?"

"Yes, it is," he said. "And my mouth is watering now."

"And Freshly Caught is on the west side," she said. "No ferry traffic."

"Let's go," Aaron said, removing his hand from her hip and opening her door.

"We're hot, Daddy," Billie complained as Eloise got in.

"Okay, sorry," Aaron said, hurrying around the front of the car and getting in quickly. "So, what are we having for dinner?" he asked, throwing a flirtatious look at Eloise.

"Pasta," Billie shouted.

"Yeah, pasta."

Eloise suddenly wanted to side with the girls. She'd definitely win some brownie points with them if she did. She cast a look at Aaron. "I love the sandwiches at Freshly Caught," she said. "And girls, they have spaghetti and meatballs."

"No, they don't," Grace said. "It's spaghetti in clam sauce, and it's gross."

"Then you can get the fried PB&J," Aaron said without missing a beat.

"Maybe we can go two places," Billie said.

"Billie," Aaron started, but Eloise thought that was a great idea.

"What pasta place do you guys like?" she asked, twisting to look at the girls through the barrier between the front seat and the back. "Wait. Let me guess." She smiled at them, and Grace especially liked guessing games.

Billie just looked out the window. Eloise's heartbeat pulsed out a couple of extra beats. "The Palace? You guys like The Palace, don't you?"

"Yes!" Grace said, and even Billie seemed impressed, though she was trying very hard not to look like it. Eloise saw the glint in her eyes though.

"I'll call them right now," she said. "They'll have it ready by the time your daddy and I have our sandwiches, and I'll run in to get your pasta."

"Eloise," Aaron said. "You don't have to do that."

"It's easy," she said. "The Palace is on the way back to your house." She met his eye, hoping he'd understand why she wanted to do this. They didn't have to make a habit of it. She lifted her phone to her ear when he didn't protest again.

"I want the spaghetti and meatballs," Grace said. "Billie wants the vegetable lasagna."

Vegetable lasagna? Eloise mouthed to Aaron, surprised by that order. "Yes," she said when a woman answered the phone. "I'd like to put in a pick-up order...yes, thirty minutes should be fine..."

Forty-five minutes later, Aaron turned a corner and said, "That's us on the right. Third one." He pulled into the driveway, the scent of roast beef mingling with marinara in a way that made Eloise's stomach roll. Or maybe that was because she'd never been to Aaron's house before, and this felt like a giant step forward in their relationship.

That's what you wanted, she told herself as she got out and assessed the house. "You must have a gardener," she said, noting the pristine lawn, the weedless flowerbeds, and the brand new bark around the trees.

"I pay a boy down the street," Aaron said. "You should see the back yard. It's not pretty."

"That's because Prince tears it up," Billie said, passing Eloise with her bag of pasta. "He's already barking, Daddy."

"Go let 'im out," Aaron said, ducking back into the cruiser to get his soda.

They didn't use the front door, but Billie punched in a code for the garage door opener, and they waited for it to lift. Another vehicle filled one half of the garage, and Eloise noted the black truck she'd never seen before. "When do you drive that?"

"Oh, I don't," he said. "It doesn't run. I tinker with the engine when I have time."

"You're kidding," Eloise said, completely shocked by that. Number one, the man didn't have free time. Number two, she'd never thought of him as someone who liked to take things apart and put them back together.

"Nope," he said. "I haven't worked on it in a while, though." He followed the girls up the few steps in the garage to a door that led into the house. Eloise took up the rear, trying to take in everything at once. The house was normal, and it was relatively clean inside. A couple of bowls in the sink from breakfast, and plenty of drawings, schoolwork, and reminders on the fridge.

Eloise smiled, because this place felt like a home.

"We're eating at the table," he said as Billie opened a drawer and took out a single fork.

"I wanted to watch H2O."

"You can after," he said. "One episode before bed."

"It's summer," Billie said. "I shouldn't have to go to bed before the sun goes down."

"Do not start with me, Billie," Aaron said. "Or I'll take your tablet and you'll get no episodes of H2O." He quirked his eyebrows at her, challenging her to say something or argue with him again.

"Sorry, Dad," she mumbled, and Aaron nodded to the table.

"We're eating as a family tonight," he said. "And then Gracie-Lou needs a bath and Bills can have her tablet."

"What's Eloise going to do?" Billie asked, and Eloise remained silent as he pulled out the sandwiches they'd gotten at Freshly Caught.

"She's gonna watch a movie with me," Aaron said

lightly. "Or we'll take Prince for a walk. Or sit in the swing in the back yard." He put a stack of plates on the counter and picked up his sandwich. "Now, tell me the car in the parade that was your favorite."

A couple of hours later, Eloise had thoroughly enjoyed dinner with Aaron and his girls, and walking Prince, though the dog seemed more like a menace than a pet, and the movie Aaron had put on in the living room while his girls watched their episodes and took their baths.

"Okay, they're down," he said, sighing as he rejoined her on the couch, easily lifting his arm around her shoulders.

She leaned into him, comfortable but also a little nervous too. "They're great," she said. "I promise I won't make you go to two places every time we go out to eat just to appease them."

He chuckled and pressed his lips to her temple. "It's okay. I know why you did it."

"Do you think they like me?"

"Absolutely I do," he said. His fingers moved up and down her arm, and Eloise knew all she had to do was turn toward him, and he'd kiss her.

So she did, pulling in a breath through her nose as Aaron kissed her.

"It's good to have you here," he whispered, placing a kiss on her chin and then her neck.

"Let's talk about that for a second," Eloise said, pulling back. "How's this long-distance thing working for you?"

"It's not bad," he said, his dark eyes meeting hers. "What about you?"

"I don't really like it," she said.

"You've said that." He touched his mouth to her forehead. "But I don't know what to do about it." He kneaded her closer, kissed her again, deeper this time. "I like you, Eloise."

"I like you too, Aaron," she said, her voice mostly made of air. She pulled away again. "Maybe I should just quit at the university. I have that inn."

"Did you look into your retirement benefit?"

"No."

Aaron frowned. "Didn't you say you were going to do that?"

Eloise had said that. "I just need to make an appointment with HR." She pulled away. "I'm tired, Aaron."

"I can get you a ride to the ferry."

"No." She looked at him. "I'm tired of thinking about what I should do."

He trailed his fingers up her forearm and back down. He simply gazed at her.

"This is hard for me, Aaron. I always know what to do, and with this, I don't know what to do."

"I hate that I'm causing this," he said. "Maybe a relationship between us is a little too complicated."

"Don't say that," Eloise said, suddenly afraid she'd lose him. "Please, don't say that unless you really mean it."

"It's not too complicated for me," he said. "But I'm the one who's making it complicated for you."

"How?"

"Because I'm not willing to relocate. My life is here. My job is here. My girls are here. So I feel like a giant jerk, because I *really* like you Eloise, and I'm making your life hard by insisting you fly here to see me." Frustration came with his words, and Eloise didn't like it.

"You're not a jerk," she said. "If I were in your shoes, I'd feel the same way. I wouldn't be willing to leave. I don't want you to come to Boston. That's not what I'm asking."

"What are you asking, Eloise?"

"I'm asking...I'm asking—I'm asking if we're serious enough for me to quit my job and move back here to fix up the Cliffside Inn." She studied him, trying to see every little blink, every movement, every breath.

Aaron leaned toward her, those dark eyes burning with fire. "Yes," he said, his voice throaty and low. "For me, Eloise, this is serious enough for that." He took her face in his hands, and Eloise had never felt so cherished. "Okay?"

She nodded, her eyes drifting closed, and Aaron kissed her again.

CHAPTER NINE

Robin snuck away from the dining room table, most of her food gone. AJ had ordered from Mort's, and even though they'd had to carry the food with them on the ferry for forty-five minutes before they could eat it, it had still been delicious.

Alice had made coffee and brought out all the flavored creamers while AJ had laid out all the delicious seafood, and they'd enjoyed the feast. The teens were planning a movie in the back yard once the sun went down, and Robin was looking forward to nursing a cup of coffee with her friends until Eloise returned.

She wanted to hear the latest news too, though Alice had told her to give Eloise some space. Eloise didn't really want space, Robin knew that. She wanted someone to tell her what to do; Robin knew, because she felt exactly the same way.

She ducked out the back door and tapped the phone icon to connect Duke's call. "Hey," she said, her breath coming out in a long sigh.

"Hey, baby," Duke said, his voice hearty and full of happiness. "How's the cove? The girls? Did you go to the parade tonight?"

Robin smiled and leaned into the bricks of Alice's house. Duke loved to ask a bunch of questions up front. "It's only three o'clock there," she said. "What are you doing calling me so early?"

She'd been staying up until midnight or later to take his calls, and she'd never complained once. Robin didn't seem to need as much sleep as other people, but she was feeling all of her forty-six years lately.

"We came in early because of a storm," he said. "Don't worry," he added quickly. "We're fine. That's why we came in." He always spoke in the plural "we" as he'd gone to Alaska with Bryan, a fellow fisherman from the cove. They lived in a tiny shack on the coast of Alaska, and Duke had shown Robin and the girls his living conditions via video chat the day he'd arrived up north.

Robin missed him so much, and she closed her eyes and bit back her emotions while he told her about the last couple of days. "But enough about fish," he said. "You're at Alice's place, right?"

"Yes," Robin said, glad she'd managed to get her emotions in check. She didn't want Duke to know how difficult this situation was for her, though if he didn't know, he wasn't as smart as she thought he was. He knew him being gone was hard for her. He knew she worried about him while he was out on the waters around the cove. And him being in unfamiliar waters, in a completely new part of the world...Robin worried every single second of every single day.

"We've been having fun," she said. "Pizza and pool party last night. Boutique and classic car parade tonight. AJ ordered dinner from Mort's. We're in the middle of that now. The kids are going to watch a movie in the back yard later."

"How are the girls?"

"Good," Robin said, summing up complicated things with simple words. She worried about Mandie, but Robin could earn a Gold medal in worrying if it was a sport in the Olympics.

"Mandie behaving?" Duke asked.

"She's about the same as when you left," Robin said, sighing. "I'm trying to be patient with her, but she's—and I feel bad saying this—but she's annoying. Always smiling and laughing at her phone, and when I ask to see it, she throws a little attitude fit."

"She lets you see it, though, right?" Duke asked.

"Yes," Robin said. "In the end, she does."

"And?"

"And I can't find any evidence of anything bad or scandalous." Robin was grateful for that. No one had prepared her for raising teenagers in the digital age, that was for sure. She hadn't grown up with cell phones and the Internet, and she hadn't known about sexting and cyberbullying until a friend of hers had a son getting inappropriate pictures from girls.

Then, Robin had freaked out and instituted a nine p.m. curfew on the girls' phones, and she made them plug them in out in the kitchen. That way, she could look at them while they were asleep. She'd combed through Mandie's phone countless times, and either the girl was very good at hiding her activity, or she really wasn't doing anything wrong.

"It's good to hear your voice," Duke said. "Tell me something else that's happened since the last time we talked."

"Anything?"

"Yeah, just talk. I got up at two a.m. this morning, and the sound of your voice soothes me."

Warmth filled Robin from top to bottom, because it sure did seem like Duke missed her as much as she missed him. "Okay, so AJ showed up a couple of days ago, and she was obviously drunk. We had to have an intervention—well, kind of. Kelli got her to admit why she'd brought wine coolers and we dumped them all out last night."

She continued the story, only pausing to ask Duke if he was still awake once.

"Right here, baby," he said, and his voice did seem sleepy.

"I'll let you go," she finally said. "Thanks for talking to me, Duke."

"I love you, Robin."

"I love you, too." The call ended, and Robin pressed her phone over her pulse. She took several long breaths and went back inside. Charlie and Ginny had taken up spots in the kitchen, and she watched as they made a cake. Actually made a cake.

"Don't ask," Alice said, stepping to her side. "I have no idea where they got it from either." She lifted her coffee mug to her lips and sipped while she watched her twins. "But they claim to be able to make a banana cake with brown butter maple cream cheese frosting, and it appears they can."

"That'll go well with coffee," Robin said. "Is there any of that left?"

"Plenty," Alice said.

"Where is everyone?" She really meant her girls, but she didn't see Kelli or AJ either.

"Your girls went upstairs to find a movie," she said. "Kelli put Parker in the tub. AJ got a phone call and disappeared." She looked at Robin over the top of her mug. "How's Duke?"

"He's good," she said, because Alice didn't need details. Besides, she'd already confessed to Alice about her fears and worries, and she didn't need to go to that place again. "Is AJ talking to that guy?"

"Yep."

"Think she's going to go out with him?"

"I wouldn't be surprised at all."

Robin nodded as footsteps came down from the second floor. Mandie carried a stack of five or six DVDs in her hand, and she walked past Robin and Alice as if they were ghosts. Not even there.

"Okay," she said, approaching Charlie and Ginny. "We've got Ferris Bueller's Day Off..."

"At least Kelli hasn't said anything else about Zach," Robin said while Mandie continued to read off the titles of the movies she and Jamie had found.

"That's just a bomb with a timer," Alice said.

"Can I really not wait up with you for Eloise?"

"Nope."

"Fine." Robin sighed. "Then I'm going to go take a hot bath and go to bed. I'll be up at five to run along the beach."

"If there's something major with her," Alice said. "I'll text you and you'll see it before dawn."

"Deal." She turned toward Alice and hugged her, holding her tight for several long moments. "Thank you, Alice. This is exactly what I needed this summer."

"You can stay all summer if you'd like," Alice whispered.

Robin pulled back, her eyes widening. "I—I'll think about it." She didn't want to admit that she hated going to her house when she knew Duke wouldn't be there. She thought she'd be able to handle Duke's absence better than she was. He went out on his boat here for days at a time, and Robin weathered that just fine.

But she always knew when he was coming home, and when he was home, everything was better. Robin didn't like being alone, and she didn't want to be a single mom. Her heart bled for Alice and the countless other single parents in the world in a way she'd never understood before.

She knew she still didn't understand it now, because Duke was making money. Robin did have her event-planning, and she'd have to get back to it before long, as she had an anniversary party in August that still needed a lot of details worked out. She'd also booked an October wedding, and she needed to carve out some time this summer for that.

How would Alice pay her bills? Buy the gold-laced tank tops and the beautiful shoes and keep the pool clean with the right amount of chlorine?

Robin needed to ask her, because Alice had not mentioned getting a job here in the cove. Maybe Frank would be paying for everything.

Robin soaked in a hot bath, like she said she would, but she couldn't go to sleep. After trying for about an hour, she padded back downstairs to the living room, where AJ, Kelli, and Alice had gathered and were chatting.

"I thought you were going to bed," Alice said.

"I'm not terribly tired," Robin said, noticing the flickering blue lights in the back yard. "The girls are okay out there?"

"As long as Mandie and Charlie aren't up to no good," Alice said, shooting a look at the back door.

Robin's heartbeat clashed against itself. "I talked to her before we came."

"I know you did." Alice gave her a smile. "They like each other. They both have equal responsibility for what happens." She sighed and ran her fingers through her hair. "I talked to Charlie too."

"I won't blame you if something happens," Robin said, glancing into the kitchen. "Is there any cake left?"

"I saved some for you and Eloise," Kelli said, getting off the couch. "I'll get it out for you." She went into the kitchen and opened a high cupboard, stretching up on her tiptoes to reach the plate she'd stashed there. She got a fork and brought it to Robin.

She smiled at Kelli, her heart full of love for the woman. "Thank you."

Kelli just gave her a closed-mouth smile, and Robin sat down in one of the wingback chairs. "What were you guys talking about?"

"Trying to make a plan for tomorrow," AJ said. "I suggested sailing. Kelli thinks we need a lazy day on the beach."

"I voted for the beach," Alice said. "It's your turn for dinner, and that gets you back here in time to start on whatever elaborate menu you've concocted."

"The beach sounds nice," Robin said. "Here? Or are we going over to the black sand?"

"Just here," Alice said. "My dad and Della want to meet us at the black sand beach one day, and they can't tomorrow. Maybe this weekend."

Robin nodded and took a bite of her banana cake. The taste of sugar and banana, maple and caramel, tickled her taste buds. "Wow, this is amazing." She instantly scooped up another bite, though she wasn't a huge cake-eater.

"Ginny claims she learned something in her foods class." Alice grinned, an action that softened her face. "I'm just glad she won't starve when she goes to college."

Robin giggled too. "Please, Alice. You didn't starve when you went to college."

"Yeah, I just went into even more debt by ordering take-out." A moment of silence filled the room, and then the four of them laughed together. Robin's spirits lifted, and she smiled around at everyone.

"Remember when Kristen tried to have each of us make dinner for a meeting?" Alice said. "And she ended up with food poisoning from the undercooked chicken I made?" She continued to laugh as she shook her head.

"We should get Kristen out here," Kelli said, glancing around at everyone. "Did anyone invite her?"

"I did," Alice said, a bit of defensiveness in her voice. "She said she didn't want to crash our party, but she'd come for a day or two."

"I'll call her in the morning," Robin said. "It'll give me something to do."

"I thought you were going to go running."

"Well, besides that." Robin smiled and took another bite of cake. "Hey, I have to do something to combat the lobster rolls and banana cake."

"Yeah, I just think you need it to clear your head." Alice gave her a knowing smile, and Robin simply took it.

"I have to call my mom tomorrow," Kelli said, her gaze dropping to her hands. "I don't want to ask her if my dad cheated on her." She looked up and met every woman's eye. "I mean, how does one bring that up?"

"I have no idea," Alice said, her voice on the haunted side.

The back door opened, and the teens filled the house with chatter and the scent of dampness and popcorn.

"That's my cue," Alice said, getting up with a groan. "Come on, guys." She put her arm around her son's shoulders. "Time for bed. We're going to the beach in the morning, and we have to go to the store first."

"Can we get Mountain Dew Zero Sugar?" he asked.

"You think the one grocery store on Rocky Ridge is going to have Mountain Dew Zero Sugar?" Alice trilled out a laugh as they rounded the corner and went back to the bedrooms behind the kitchen.

"I'm going to bed too," Robin said, getting up. She hugged AJ and then Kelli, holding her tight. "You'll figure it out." She smiled at her, and she followed her girls upstairs. She'd just reached the top of the steps when she heard Kelli coming up behind her.

AJ and Eloise were staying in rooms in the basement, and there were still empty bedrooms in the house. Robin felt absolutely no jealousy when it came to Alice and her money, and she was glad about that.

"Phones," she said to her girls as they went into the bedroom they were sharing. Robin could've had her own room, but she didn't mind sleeping with the girls. When she'd asked them what they preferred, they'd both said they wanted her in the room with them.

Mandie didn't roll her eyes, but she did slap her phone into Robin's hand a bit too hard. Robin chose to ignore it and took Jamie's phone from her too. "I need help with dinner tomorrow night," she said as she plugged in all of their devices on the nightstand next to her desk. "We're in charge, and I'll have jobs for both of you."

"Okay, Mom," Jamie said.

Robin pulled back her covers, waiting for her oldest to confirm. "Mandie?"

"Okay," she bit out, and Robin turned to look at her. She'd already climbed onto the top bunk, and she lay with her back to Robin. Jamie shot her a look, and Robin shook her head.

She had to choose her battles carefully, and this wasn't a good one. She was too tired anyway, and she simply got in bed and snapped off the light.

———

SOMETIME LATER, ROBIN BECAME AWARE OF SOMETHING happening in the room. Someone was up. One of the girls could've possibly needed to use the bathroom. Robin blinked, her eyes already accustomed to the darkness.

Not that she needed to be able to see well in the dark to see Mandie sitting up in the top bunk. Her phone illuminated her face, and Robin's irritation sparked. She had no idea what time it was, but it was either too early or too late, and Mandie shouldn't have anyone to text at this hour. Not to mention that she wasn't allowed her phone in the middle of the night for this very reason.

Slowly, so as to not alert her daughter that she'd been caught—yet—Robin reached for her phone and rolled over once she had it in her hands. She quickly texted Mandie.

Send one more text and that phone is mine for a week.

She sent it, and she rolled over and sat up.

Mandie's alarmed expression turned toward Robin, and she slid off the top bunk and brought the phone back. "Sorry."

"Who are you texting?"

"No one."

"Did you erase them? Because that makes the phone mine too."

"I didn't erase them." She stood there in front of Robin.

Robin held her daughter's gaze for a few moments, hoping she could convey her annoyance and her disappointment with a simple look. Then she swiped on Mandie's phone and saw she'd been texting a lot more than no one.

"Charlie," she said, though that conversation had stopped a few minutes ago. "Brady. I thought we were just friends with him." She tapped on that thread, and they'd been sharing memes back and forth, and Mandie had started the night's conversation with *I'm boooored* at just after midnight.

"You're supposed to be asleep at twelve-oh-seven," Robin muttered. She went back to the main screen. "And Sam." She looked up at Robin. "What's going on with him?"

"Nothing," Mandie said.

Robin opened the text string and there was definitely something. Nothing she couldn't un-see though, so that was nice. No pictures or memes in this thread. He'd started it with a compliment, and he'd been telling Mandie that they needed to get together that summer. Over and over.

"He's asking you out." Robin looked up. "You haven't confirmed."

"Yeah, well, I'm still trying to decide how I feel about Sam." Mandie came over to Robin's bed and sat down beside her. "He's nice, and he's cute, but Jenna told me he kissed Pam while he was dating Dani, and well, that turned me off."

"Do you know if he kissed Pam while he was dating Dani?"

"No."

"Why would Jenna say that?"

"I don't know."

"So you're just talking to him, because he is nice, and you like him, but you're not sure you want to be the one he cheats on."

"Yeah, something like that."

"And you like Charlie?"

"Mom." Mandie ducked her head.

"It's a yes or no question." Robin started tapping again to see what she and Charlie had been talking about. Again, she was surprised to see basically nothing. Talk about going surfing again in a couple of mornings. He'd check the tide. She'd show him she could get up on the board. Lots of smiley faces and sentences without capitals or punctuation.

"Yes," Mandie said.

"You hate volleyball," she said, finally getting to the end of the thread where Mandie had said she'd play volleyball with Charlie at the beach tomorrow. She felt for the cord on the nightstand and plugged Mandie's phone back in. She'd had it for over thirty minutes, which really annoyed Robin.

"You don't have to change who you are for a boy," she said.

Mandie said nothing, and Robin felt an invisible wall go up between them. Now was not the time for this lesson. "All right," she said. "Back to bed. And I don't want you to be cranky tomorrow and treat the rest of us like trash. You do that even *one* time, and I'll bring you home and put you down for a nap like a toddler." When Mandie didn't say anything, Robin barked, "Confirm."

"Confirmed," Mandie said, climbing the ladder to get back into the top bunk.

Robin glared at her though the darkness, but Mandie didn't even acknowledge her. *She apologized*, Robin told herself as she lay back down.

"Duke, I wish you were here," she whispered to her pillow, allowing herself one moment of self-pity. Then she took a deep breath and strengthened her resolve to make it through this summer one day, one hour, and one minute at a time.

CHAPTER TEN

Kelli took off her sandals and left them at the edge of the sidewalk. Even if someone came by this early in the morning, they wouldn't steal her shoes. A couple of people dotted the waves in front of her, but they were far enough away to be very large ants.

She breathed in the tranquility of the morning, appreciating the pale blue sky above her as the sun brought life and light to a new day. She felt stronger than she had in a while, but not the physical kind of strength she'd built from doing aerobics in the morning.

Kelli rarely slept past five-thirty, and last night, she'd hardly been able to rest at all. Thoughts of her mother plagued her, and Kelli couldn't go another day without calling her.

She'd taken a whole day to not think about Zach and

his claim to be her half-brother. Twenty-four hours to just breathe and try to figure out how she felt. The truth was, she didn't know how to feel about the blond man who'd followed her to Rocky Ridge from New Jersey. Short of a paternity test—which Kelli wasn't going to ask for—she had no way to verify what he'd said.

He'd shown her the birth certificate, and it had her father's name on it. As she strolled through the dry, loose sand far from where the water met the land, she heard Alice's voice in her head.

Guy Watkins isn't that unique of a name.

Alice could be right, and a hint of nervousness made Kelli's stomach flip. She told herself to breathe, and she took a big lung full of oxygen in, held it, and then pushed it out.

She had a lot of decisions to make, and she needed to listen to her own intuition.

"Call your mom," she told herself, her voice barely louder than the breeze rustling the tall reeds growing out of the sand. "Then call Julian."

Of the two phone calls, she couldn't say which one she wanted to make, and that said something very bad about where her relationship with Julian was at the moment.

When she'd rounded the island enough to see the lighthouse in the distance, two islands away on Diamond, Kelli paused. The sun had steadily risen, and the time wouldn't prevent her from making the required calls.

With a well opening in her soul, she tapped on her phone and got the line ringing.

"Kelli," her mother said, always with a note of surprise in her voice.

"Hey, Mom." She automatically lifted her hand to chew on her fingernails.

"What's going on?"

Kelli hated how there had to be something going on for Kelli to call her mother, but she wasn't wrong. Kelli didn't have the type of relationship where she just called to shoot the breeze. She had girlfriends who called their mothers while they cleaned the house each week, just to "catch up."

Kelli and her mother were so far behind, a conversation would need to happen every day—a very hard conversation—in order for them to get all caught up.

"Remember, Parker and I are in the cove."

"Oh, that's right." Her mother's voice brightened considerably. "Out at Rocky Ridge, right? Alice's place?"

"Yes," Kelli said, starting to relax. "I'm sure you'll want to see him."

"Of course. What's your schedule like?"

"Oh, let's see." Kelli sighed. "We don't really have one. We sort of sit down at night and make a plan for the next day. So let's just do what we want, and I'll tell the girls if I can do it or not."

"Okay." A page flipped on her end of the line, and Kelli

smiled. Her mother had to be the only woman left on the planet who still used a paper planner for her work schedule. "I'm working tomorrow and Friday, but I have the weekend off."

"Wow, that's lucky," Kelli said.

"I picked up another shift for this woman who has a sick baby," her mom said. "So I got scheduled off on Saturday so they don't have to pay me overtime."

"Oh, I see." Kelli's heart pinched. Her mother had lost everything too, and she'd been making ends meet by working at the grocery store. She'd been there for a long time now, and she managed the customer service counter, but apparently, she couldn't work more than forty hours each week.

"So maybe Saturday," Kelli said. "We could go to the beach, or isn't there that hot air balloon festival this weekend?"

"Yes," her mother said. "It'll be really crowded though."

"Still might be fun," Kelli said, hoping her mother would agree. Going to her house and just sitting there was torture. She didn't have anything to occupy Parker, and though they got along great, and he loved doing the video chats with her, eight-year-olds very rarely carried conversations. They sometimes cooked together, while Kelli tried to keep the mood light and carefree.

It was so much work to visit her mother. It they had an

event to attend or somewhere to go, they could see each other, talk, and have something else entertain them.

"There's a miniature golf tournament too," her mom said. "Maybe Parker would like to do that."

"He does like mini golf," Kelli said. "Where's that?"

"There's a new one here on Bell," her mom said, without a hitch of emotion in her voice. But Kelli couldn't think of Bell Island without her chest automatically constricting in a painful way. "That's quite the ferry ride from Rocky Ridge. You two will have to get up early."

"I'll ask him," she said. "And find out more about it."

"Okay."

Silence came through the line, and Kelli wished she had better small talk skills. "Great," she said, trying to take some of the bright sunlight and infuse it into her voice. "I'll call you again soon and let you know what we decide."

Something screamed in her head, and she realized she hadn't called her mom to make plans with her. "Wait, Mom?"

"Yeah," her mom said. "I haven't hung up. I was actually...I have something to tell you."

Kelli's heart started drumming in her chest. "Okay," she said, swallowing because her ears suddenly felt like they'd popped and everything was echoing. "I have to ask you something too. But you go first."

"Okay." A long pause came through the line. "I've

started to, uh, put myself out there a little bit. I met a man, and we've started to see each other."

Kelli blinked, her feet slowing to a stop. She couldn't think of her mother dating and walk at the same time. "I'm sorry. What?"

"His name is Devon Gregory. He's lived on the island for about five years. He's a retired real estate agent."

With every word she spoke, Kelli understood more and more. "That's great, Mom."

"It is?" Her mom sighed and laughed a little. "Yeah, I guess it is."

"Are you happy?"

"So far," her mom said. "It's only been about a month."

Kelli's throat stung, but she couldn't very well ask her mom why she hadn't told Kelli about Devon until now. There was plenty they didn't talk about. "I'm glad," she managed to say.

"Okay, your turn," her mom said. "And if you want to meet Devon, we can go to lunch or dinner with him on Saturday. He won't hang out with us all day or anything."

"All right," Kelli said, her words getting stuck in her throat.

"All right." Her mother did sound happy, and that made a dose of joy move through Kelli. She deserved someone to love her and take care of her, something Kelli's dad hadn't done for the last several years he'd been alive.

She reminded herself that Joel had tricked her father out of his glassworks shop. And that Kristen had given it back to Kelli. Perhaps her father had simply been... human. He'd handled the loss of something very dear to him poorly. Honestly, he was probably allowed to do that.

"Are you still there?" her mother asked.

"Yes," Kelli said, pressing her eyes closed. She felt completely alone in the world, on a stretch of beach that would likely be filled with people in a few hours. She honestly didn't know how many people chose the small island of Rocky Ridge for their summer vacations. They definitely didn't have as many people as Diamond Island, but travel between the islands was so easy, most of the beaches definitely filled up when the tourists came to the cove.

"Mom, I just...I met a man the other day, who—" She cleared her throat, wishing she'd written down what she needed to say. Then she could just read it. "He said he was my half-brother. He said his mom was Sidney Tyler and Dad, and I just wondered, do you think...wasn't she Dad's secretary? Could that be true?"

Nothing came from her mother's end of the phone. Kelli simply waited, because she knew the call hadn't been disconnected.

"Yes," her mother said, and that was all. Kelli had asked two questions, but that single word answered them both.

"Okay," Kelli said.

"I'm sorry," her mother said.

"Why are you sorry?" Kelli tilted her head, trying to figure out what her mom meant by that.

"I tried to protect you girls from the worst of him," her mother whispered. "Sidney wasn't the only woman he slept around with."

The earth seemed to sway beneath her feet. "Are you saying I could have more half-siblings?"

"I honestly don't know," her mom said. "But I know he slept around with Sidney, and then she quit one day, and that was that."

Kelli remembered that Zach had said it was always just him and his mom. That she wouldn't even tell him who his father was. "Do you remember when?"

"Oh, let's see." Her mother exhaled heavily. "She was one of the last secretaries at the glassworks. You were probably twelve when she was there, because she arranged with Kristen for the Seafaring Girls to come to the warehouse. She left very soon after that."

"Left?"

"Yeah, your dad went to work one day, and she was there, and the next, she was gone. He was angry she hadn't even given two weeks' notice."

Kelli marveled at how her mother could talk about her husband and these sensitive things without even a tiny quiver in her voice. "Okay," she said. "Thanks, Mom. I'll call you again soon."

"Kelli," her mom said, and once again a stretch of silence moved between them. Her mom finally said, "This doesn't change anything for you. You know that, right?"

"Yeah," Kelli said. "I do know that. He just seemed desperate for some sort of familial connection, and I wanted to make sure his story was plausible."

"You don't owe him anything."

"I know," Kelli said, but she could sense when another soul was suffering, and Zach had been suffering. "Thanks, Mom. I love you."

"Love you too, sweetheart." Her mother's voice did pinch then, and Kelli's whole heart warmed. "Talk soon."

The call ended, and Kelli let her arm drop to her side. That was actually one of the better conversations she'd ever had with her mother, and she needed a moment to just think.

When she lifted her phone again, she didn't dial Julian. She texted Zach instead.

HOURS LATER, KELLI SAT UNDER A MULTI-COLORED umbrella, the breeze barely ruffling the flaps hanging off the frame. Beside her, Robin was on the phone with her husband in Alaska, and on the other side of her, Alice sat in the middle of everyone, the queen on her throne.

Kelli did love Alice, but she was a special woman that required a special kind of affection.

When she'd returned to the house, breakfast was in full swing, and she'd searched for and found Parker eating a piece of toast. She'd learned that Charlie had made it for him, and she'd thanked the teenager.

Now, that same teenager played out in the water, settled in a blow-up ring that Alice had bought on the way to the beach that morning. She'd bought whatever her twins wanted, and they'd all stocked up on sub sandwiches and potato chips before hitting the sand.

Her stomach growled, as it was almost lunchtime, but she'd wait until Robin or Alice suggested feeding everyone. Robin finished her phone call and sighed.

"How's Duke?" Kelli asked, watching the blonde woman who seemed to have everything figured out. Robin had always been confident, and she'd taken that trait into adulthood. Her kids were well-mannered and put together, and Robin ran her own event planning business. She had a great husband and a great house, and Kelli was happy for her.

"He's good," Robin said, her voice only slightly too high. She flashed a smile at Kelli. "Have you talked to Julian?"

"Not today," Kelli said. She didn't want to admit that they hadn't communicated since his texts only an hour after she'd left two days ago. She put a smile on her face too. "But I talked to my mother, and she thinks Zach's story is probably true."

Alice perked up, and Kelli looked in the opposite direction of Robin.

"Are you going to meet him?" Robin asked.

Kelli kept her face toward the ocean. Parker bobbed in the waves, clearing enjoying himself. She smiled at him, beyond glad he was getting along with the other children in their group. Aaron hadn't arrived yet, but when he was with them, he had two girls closer to Parker's age. He was still the youngest by a couple of years, but Kelli hadn't noticed him being left out or ignored.

"I don't know," Kelli said, not wanting to admit that she'd already texted Zach and made some lunch plans for Friday. "What are we doing tomorrow?"

"No idea," Robin said.

"Eloise wanted to talk to us today," Alice said, inserting herself into the conversation. Kelli worked to tamp down her annoyance, and she nodded.

"I'm what?" Eloise said.

"You wanted to talk to us about something," Alice said. "I assumed it was Aaron, but Kelli is apparently trying to make plans with Zach."

Kelli bristled at her dismissive tone, but no one called her on it.

"Yes," Eloise said, and Kelli turned to look down the row of women. "But it shouldn't impact that."

"Great," Kelli said.

"Well, it might," Alice said, swinging her head from

Eloise to Kelli and back. "Maybe we'll need to go to lunch, and we've all been assigned dinner already."

"Mine is tomorrow," Kelli said. "I won't miss it." She also didn't mean to speak with so much bite. She wasn't sure why Alice was bothering her so much right now, only that she was.

AJ got up from the chair down on the end and joined the rest of them in the middle of the shade. "I just got a date with JD." She wore a grin the size of the Atlantic Ocean, and she obviously hadn't heard any of the conversation they'd been having.

"When?" Alice demanded.

Even Robin looked at her, and Kelli glared at her too. "That's great, AJ," she said, finally turning her attention to the leggy woman who had been at Kelli's side for so long. Even when they'd grown apart, Kelli knew she could rely on AJ. One phone call, and AJ would've been there.

Now that they were renewing their friendship, it was like she and AJ had never stopped talking.

"Today," AJ said, still smiling. "I figured we're just sitting on the beach, and he said he'd take the ferry here to meet me."

"Where are you going to go here?" Alice asked, as if Rocky Ridge didn't have a single decent restaurant.

"I don't know." AJ tossed her hair over her shoulder and glanced at Kelli. They had an entire conversation in that one moment, and Kelli smiled and looked away.

"You're going to wear your bathing suit?" Alice folded her arms, and Kelli wondered what her problem was.

"Tons of people in the cove wear their bathing suits to lunch," Kelli said, causing everyone to look at her. Alice glared, and Eloise and Robin looked utterly surprised. A wind blew through Kelli, and she shook her head. "Let her do what she wants. You're not in charge of us just because we're staying at your house."

Her lungs shook. Kelli couldn't believe she'd stood up to Alice.

"I never said that," Alice said.

"You're acting like it." Kelli met Alice's eyes again, and she would definitely lose this argument. Alice had gone to school to be a lawyer, and she wore a look of fierceness that Kelli had never felt inside her before.

"I am not," Alice said. "I simply asked when she was going to lunch with this new man, mere days after she broke up with her long-time boyfriend."

"Hey," AJ said, and Kelli stood up. she wasn't sure where this fire had come from, but it warmed her, and she liked it.

"Alice, you're being rude," Kelli said. "If she wants to go out with him, she can go out with him. She's forty-five years old. And I'm going to breakfast with Zach on Friday, even if you don't agree. You're not the queen."

"Kelli," Robin said, reaching over and putting her hand on Kelli's arm. "It's okay. Sit down, sweetie. Alice isn't saying you guys can't go to breakfast with people."

She looked at Alice, and Kelli wished she could see Robin's face. She and Alice had a whole conversation silently too, and Eloise looked between all of them.

"I'd like tomorrow," Eloise said.

"For what?" Robin asked.

"Better ask Alice," Kelli mumbled as she dropped back into her beach chair.

"Kelli," Alice said, her voice full of warning.

"I don't need to ask Alice," Eloise said, looking at her phone in her lap. "I'll tell you guys after dinner tonight, okay?" She got up. "Aaron just got here." She looked at the four of them. "Tonight?"

"Tonight," Robin said. "And we'll reserve tomorrow for you." She looked at AJ and Kelli. "Right, guys?"

"Fine with me," Kelli said, folding her arms. "But you really better check with Alice. She seems to be the one who wants to micromanage us."

"I am *not* micromanaging everyone," Alice said. She stood up too, her swimming suit cover-up billowing in the breeze as Eloise walked way.

AJ got to her feet too. "I won't go if you don't want me to, Alice."

A stab of betrayal moved through Kelli. What kind of game was AJ playing? Kelli would not be saying the same words to Alice. She did not get to decide what Kelli did with her time in the cove.

"It's okay," Alice said. "You don't have to ask me."

"I don't want you to be upset."

Kelli didn't either, and she should've bitten her tongue the way she had many times in the past.

"I just..." Alice exhaled. "I just wanted this to be an amazing two weeks, and I feel like I'm failing at giving you guys that." She slumped back into her chair. "Robin hosted us so well for Joel's funeral, and I wanted to do the same."

"Alice, you're doing fine," Robin said.

"Fine?" Alice asked, shaking her head.

"I'm sorry, Alice," Kelli said, looking over to the powerful woman. "Really."

"I am too," Alice said. "I just...I love you guys, and of course I know you can make good decisions. I guess I just wasn't anticipating everyone running off on their own over the next two weeks."

"So maybe we need to revisit the summer sand pact," Robin said. "Make some ground rules we can all live with?"

Kelli nodded, because she needed freedom to go visit her mother too. AJ nodded, and Robin said, "Great. We'll talk about that tonight too." The mood lightened as the tension drained away.

Aaron arrived with his girls, who immediately ran down the sand toward the water.

"Alice?" AJ asked. "Can I borrow one of your cover-up dresses for my lunch?"

"Of course," Alice said, bending to get it out of her bag.

"Time for lunch," Robin said, standing and yelling at

everyone to come get something to eat. Kelli let the activity happen around her, and she fed Parker and herself, feeling a new kind of energy inside her she hadn't had before.

She really liked it, and she hoped this new confidence would stick around for a while.

CHAPTER ELEVEN

AJ pulled Alice's cover-up over her head, surprised it actually fit. The woman was a wraith, made of only bone and sinew. She meant well, though, and AJ knew she had a good heart. She wanted the best for all of them, and that shouldn't be ignored.

While she walked up the hot sand to the sidewalk, she sent a quick text to Kelli. *Thanks for standing up for me. Look at you taking on the queen!*

I feel like a jerk, Kelli messaged back.

You apologized.

She means well.

She does. AJ looked up as a text came in from JD. He'd arrived, and she spotted the car he was in a moment later. She lifted her hand, and the white sedan continued toward her. She kept her shoes in her fingers and gathered the long skirt up so she could step into the car with the man she'd met a few days ago.

The car came to a stop, and AJ reached to open the door. "Hey," she said, sliding into the back seat. JD's presence filled the car from top to bottom, front to back. He grinned at her, and the salt-and-pepper beard on his strong jaw called to her. She smiled back, thrilled when he leaned toward her and placed a kiss on her cheek.

"Good to see you again, AJ," he said, and she'd forgotten the deep tone of his voice. Maybe she'd been too drunk to remember.

A hint of embarrassment squirreled through her, and she ducked her head. "Good to see you, too."

"All right." He settled on his side of the seat and looked up to the driver. "Where are we going?"

"Uh, let's see," she said. "I haven't been here long, and I've been gone from the cove for a while..."

"There's a great bistro on the wharf," the RideShare driver said. "Pretty new, so they're not super busy right now."

AJ looked at DJ, who raised his eyebrows. She could get lost in blue eyes like that, and she shrugged one shoulder. "Sounds good."

"Let's give that a try," DJ said, and the driver eased the car away from the curb.

"So where were you?" AJ asked.

"Where was I?"

"Yeah, you said you'd *be back* in time for lunch today."
She watched him, because she was determined to do everything different in this relationship. Everything. Maybe then
it would end in her walking down the aisle with a handsome
man waiting for her at the other end. Before, she'd have
looked out the window and given him a chance to come up
with whatever excuse he needed in order to explain himself.

He blinked, clearly confused. "I flew to Atlanta and
back."

"Why?" AJ narrowed her eyes at him.

His expression softened, and he started to laugh.
"Okay, I can see I didn't explain properly on the plane."

"Explain what, exactly?" she asked. She was eternally
grateful that she'd put the cover up on. She had one, of
course, but it barely covered her, and if she'd worn that,
she'd be showing the entire length of her leg.

"I'm a pilot, AJ," he said, still smiling at her. "I fly to
Atlanta and back oh, five or six times a week."

"You do?"

"Yeah."

"But you weren't flying when I came here."

"No, but I needed a ride home. I got a seat. Didn't you
hear the announcement that said not to be alarmed if you
saw a pilot in the cabin?"

Heat filled AJ's face. "I guess I missed that." Maybe
when she was ordering a glass of wine.

He reached over and took her hand in his. "I live here,

but I'm honestly on the plane as much as I am in my house, especially in the summer."

"What about the off-season?" she asked.

"We still fly twice a week."

"Do you go to other cities?"

"Sometimes Halifax," he said.

"Nothing further west?"

"No, we only fly from the East Coast. Small jets."

"How long have you been a pilot?"

"Twenty years." He squeezed her hand. "And you're a news broadcaster."

"Kind of," AJ hedged.

Something flickered in his expression. "That's what you said on the plane."

"That's what I've been doing the last several years," she said, clearing her throat. "I actually left my job just before coming here." She hadn't told anyone that, not even Kelli. For some reason, it was more humiliating to tell her friends that she'd quit than it was to say she'd broken up with Nathan because he didn't want to get married, only to have him get engaged less than two months later.

"Oh," JD said. "So what are you going to do now?"

"I have no idea." AJ tacked a laugh onto her sentence, and JD smiled too.

They continued their small talk about the superficial details of their lives until the driver pulled up to a trendy-looking building that overlooked the water. JD paid while AJ surveyed the place, and it didn't look big or busy.

JD took her hand again with, "Ready?"

"Yes," she said, her stomach cramping for something to eat.

He led the way inside, and AJ basked in the good energy of this place. It smelled like lemons and saltwater inside, and a woman in a pencil skirt and a white blouse met them with a smile. "Two?" she asked, already gathering menus.

"Yes, please," DJ said, and he followed the woman to a booth with a large window that had a beautiful view of the ocean.

"Wow," AJ said as she slid into one side of it.

"Our special today is wild salmon stuffed with blue crab," the woman said. "Are we drinking today?"

"I'm not," JD said, glancing at AJ.

She shook her head no, and the hostess swept away the drink menu. "We have a great selection of mocktails, right on the menu." She smiled. "Your waiter will be Adam, and here he comes." She eased away and Adam arrived.

"Celebrating anything?" he asked, setting down some cardboard drink coasters.

"It's our first date," JD said, smiling at him.

Adam looked back and forth between JD and AJ. "Wow. Well, welcome. I'll give you a couple of minutes to look at the menu."

AJ didn't pick hers up. She already knew she wanted the special. She watched DJ as he looked at the menu, and he didn't even look up as he asked, "You're not going to look?"

"I'm going to get the special," she said. "I love blue crab."

DJ nodded, and several seconds later, he set down his menu. "Which island did you grow up on?"

"Pearl," she said. "My dad is still there. You?"

"Oh, I didn't grow up here," he said. "I'm from the Lowcountry, in South Carolina."

"No wonder you have that sexy, Southern twang," she said, falling easily into flirting with him. She pulled back on that, reminding herself that she wouldn't be going home with him that night.

He gave her that sexy, Southern smile she'd liked on the plane. "I actually live on Pearl now."

"Really?" AJ straightened and shook her hair over her shoulders. "Where?"

"They put in these new townhomes," he said. "With businesses on the bottom level, house on the upper two levels. I live in one of those, and I rent out the business space to my neighbor. She has a salon, and her business exploded when the only other salon on the island went out of business."

"I know exactly what you're talking about," AJ said. "I heard there were a lot of people who were devastated when Gigi retired."

"Gigi, yes." He snapped his fingers. "Anyway, my neighbor is Indy, and she needed the space. She hired more girls, and they're *busy* there." He reached for the glass of water Adam set on the table and took a drink. "Where's your mother if your dad is the one on Pearl?"

AJ blinked, because she hadn't had to tell anyone about her mother in years. Decades. Everyone in the cove knew the story of Diane Proctor, and how she'd simply left her family behind one day.

"I don't—," AJ started, but the waiter appeared and knocked his knuckles on the table.

"Are you ready to order?" Adam asked, and AJ looked up at him, never more relieved to be interrupted.

"I'll have the special," she said. "And I want a mocktail with orange, lime, and strawberry."

He didn't write anything down but simply looked at DJ.

"I'll have the braised short ribs," he said. "Extra bleu cheese, please."

"You got it." He picked up the menus. "Anything to drink?"

"Just water for me," he said, and Adam walked away.

"You're one of those men who runs on the beach and doesn't drink anything with carbonation, aren't you?" she asked, reaching for her own water. She didn't trust it though, because the water in the cove had a metallic taste, no matter which island she was on.

JD laughed, and AJ enjoyed the sound of it. "Kind of,"

he said. "I do like to run on the beach. I don't drink much soda or carbonation."

"But red meat is okay," she said.

"Well, my oncologist hasn't specifically banned red meat from my diet yet."

AJ blinked and leaned back in the booth as if his words had punched her in the chest. "Your oncologist," she said.

"Yeah," he said, looking down at the table where his menu had once been. "I once had this little brain tumor. They got it out."

AJ wanted to say something. Her mouth even opened. But nothing came out.

"There's no good way to tell anyone this," he said. "But I like to get it out of the way real early in a relationship."

"Why's that?" she asked, her throat so dry.

"Imagine if we started dating. I'm not saying we're going to, though just based on the last twenty minutes with you, I'd call and ask you out again." His dark blue eyes sparkled at her, and he smiled with all those straight, white teeth. "But let's say we start dating. And it's going well, and weeks turn into months, and then one day, I have to go in for my body scan, and you're like, 'wait. Body scan? For what?' and that's when you find out."

AJ searched his face. "This happened to you, didn't it?"

"Emma was pretty upset," he said. "And ultimately, she said she'd lost her faith in me because I didn't tell her I had cancer." He drained nearly half his glass of water. "So now I try to tell women right up front about the..." He pointed to his head. "You know, the tumor."

AJ didn't know what to say next. People needed time to absorb words like *cancer* and *tumor*, didn't they?

"The Sunrise," Adam said, setting an enormous glass filled with a bright orange liquid in front of AJ. "Your food should be up in a minute."

"Thank you." AJ reached for the paper straw Adam had left on the table, hoping the icy fruity drink would help her brain to start operating again.

"Tell me something shocking about yourself," DJ said. "Like what the A and the J stand for in your name."

"If I tell you mine, you have to tell me yours."

"Oh, I think I can handle that." He leaned into his elbows, his smile made entirely of flirtatiousness.

"AvaJane," she said.

"And you came up with AJ?"

"Yes," she said. "I insisted on using it when I went into middle school and got serious about sports."

"AJ was more conducive to sports." DJ wasn't asking. "Interesting."

"Your turn." She swirled her straw in her drink, finally putting her lips on it and taking a sip.

"Daniel Joseph," he said. "See, my mother and father couldn't agree on a name for me, so I got two."

"I hate to break it to you, Daniel Joseph, but I have two names too. Most people do."

He smiled and leaned back as Adam arrived with his

braised short ribs. AJ got distracted by her plate too, as it looked like a work of art. Alice would love this place, and AJ determined to bring the group of them here the next time it was her turn to provide dinner.

Her bank account groaned just thinking about it, because she had terminated her employment and paid a moving company to come pack up what she owned. She'd already bought dinner at Mort's for everyone, and seafood wasn't cheap.

The other option was to buy groceries and cook, and AJ knew her strengths and weaknesses. Cooking definitely went in the weakness category and using a credit card if necessary was one of her strengths.

"Yes, well," he said, picking up his fork. "I have a lot of names."

"Let's hear them." AJ took a bite of her rice pilaf as she watched him.

"Daniel Joseph Reynolds Jenkins," he said. "The third."

AJ burst out laughing, not caring that the sound was too loud. "That's not true," she said. "I don't believe you."

"It's entirely true," he said, chuckling too.

"Yet you just said your mother and father couldn't decide on a first name for you, so you got two." AJ cocked her eyebrows in challenge.

"Yes, that's true." He scooped up a bite of beef and swiped that through his mashed potatoes, no further explanation given.

"That's it?" She wanted a taste of everything in one bite, so she got salmon, the blue crab, a bit of rice, and made sure to dab it in her cream sauce before putting it in her mouth. A low groan came from her stomach as the salty and sweet, creamy and crispy all joined together.

"In my family," he said. "The first born is named Daniel Joseph, unless the parents can agree to a different name. My mother and father could not agree, so I got the traditional Daniel Joseph."

"How very...odd," she said.

"Right? And my mother wonders why I've never been married." He flashed her a grin, and AJ thought he was about as close to perfection as she'd ever seen. Of course, she'd felt like that about several men over the years, and she once again pulled back on her instincts to plow full steam ahead into a relationship with him.

"What about you?" he asked. "Have you ever been married?"

The blue crab lodged in her throat, and AJ had to cough to get it out. "No," she said, her muscles all tight now. "No, I haven't." She reached for her fruity drink and sucked at it, trying to get everything inside her to cool.

They finished eating, the conversation light and easy. AJ liked him a whole lot, and she'd definitely gone home with men she knew less about than DJ Jenkins. He held her hand in the car, and he said, "I need a minute," to the driver when they got back to the beach.

He got out of the car too and came around to embrace

her. "So, what did you think? Do you want to go out with me again?"

She liked that he was straight-forward. That he just asked what he was thinking. There were no games with DJ.

"Yes," she said. "I think I'd like that."

"Great," he said, his lips landing on her neck just below her ear. Part of AJ wanted to melt into him, and the other part tensed with every muscle in her body.

"DJ," she said, her voice once again a bit breathless. "I think I'm going to...I don't think..." The problem was, she couldn't think, not with his hands on her waist, burning through that flimsy cover-up, and his lips against her skin.

"I'll call you later," he said, stepping back. He turned and got in the car, closed the door, and lifted his hand in a wave.

AJ watched the car drive away, and she dang near collapsed in the sand. "Oh, boy," she whispered to herself. "You're in trouble with him. Big trouble."

She turned to go back to the row of chairs and coolers and kids, her feet sort of stumbling in the soft sand. Commanding herself to get ahold of her emotions, she made her steps sure as she continued on.

When she reached the shade, she found the women she'd left a couple of hours ago. It seemed none of them had moved at all, though AJ knew that couldn't be true. Robin wasn't wearing her swimming suit cover-up any longer, so she must've gotten in the water at some point.

Eloise had her hair up in a ponytail now, and a bag of trash hung from the arm of her beach chair.

There had definitely been activity in the sand, as it now housed a castle with a partially drenched wall around the moat.

AJ sighed as she sat down, and she let it linger as it came out of her mouth so as to draw all of their attention.

"That bad?" Eloise asked.

"That good?" Robin countered. "I think that was a happy sigh."

"It was," AJ said, her mind running through all the things she could tell them.

"So lunch must've gone well," Kelli said. "Did you kiss him?"

"No," AJ said, her thoughts circling. "I'm trying to do things a little differently." She thought about how he'd just laid out the word *oncologist* as a way to tell her he'd had a brain tumor. "So I need to tell you guys something."

"There's more?" Alice asked.

AJ looked at her and smiled. "I sold my apartment and hired a company to pack everything I left behind. I currently have nowhere to call home, and no idea when anything I own will arrive."

She laughed, though the idea of being homeless and living in only swimming suits and flip flops actually made her physically sick.

CHAPTER TWELVE

Alice let the others around her exclaim over what AJ had just said. Her first thought was to offer AJ a room in the beach house.

Her real house now. Alice really needed to start thinking in a different way. A singular way. Her chest tightened at the reminder, because it was proving to be much harder than she'd anticipated.

She'd never thought much about how much money her bank account held. There was always what she needed and wanted. But after buying food and beach toys at the store that morning, she'd gotten a text from her bank for a low balance alert.

She'd never received one before, and it had put her in a foul mood. Not even the sunshine, laughter, or the roar of the waves had cheered her. She needed to speak to Frank, but she hadn't been able to formulate an excuse to step away from her friends and make the call. Not only that, but she didn't want anything to disrupt her tranquil time on the beach. Or for the two weeks when everyone would be here.

But Kelli's outburst earlier had disrupted the tranquility, and Alice knew it was her fault. She'd snapped at her and AJ, and she knew it was because she was stressed. She'd kept her eyes on Charlie as he and Mandie played in the water, the thought of money never leaving her mind.

AJ met Alice's eyes, and she quickly put a smile on her face. "You should stay with me," Alice said.

"With you?" AJ asked, and Alice sucked in a breath. She'd forgotten she hadn't told anyone except Robin about her move to Rocky Ridge being a permanent one. She threw a panicked look at Robin, who seemed to be able to interpret it easily.

"Yes, of course," Robin said, swooping to the rescue. "Alice doesn't have renters in the house for weeks after we leave. You could definitely stay there, AJ."

AJ looked at Alice, a glint of hope in her eyes. "That might work," she said.

"Of course it will," Alice said. She was ready to leave the beach and shower the sunscreen off her skin.

"We should get going," Robin said. "Dinner will take a couple of hours, and that should give everyone enough time to clean up." She stood up and reached for a towel that had been discarded on the sand nearby.

"Okay," Alice said, and she didn't waste any time getting to her feet and starting to pick up her kids' towels. Kelli went down to the water and started getting all the children to come out of the waves.

Thankfully, Alice's twins were old enough not to argue. Aaron had a near-mutiny on his hands, and it wasn't until Eloise said, "Girls, we can come back any day we want," that Grace and Billie calmed down.

"But Dad has to work," Billie said.

"Then you should stay at the house with me," Eloise said. "I'll bring you with us first thing next time we come."

"Can we?" Billie turned to Aaron. "Dad, can we stay with Eloise?"

Their eyes met, and Alice watched them communicate without speaking. She mourned for the time when she and Frank had been able to do that. Unbidden and quite suddenly, Alice's eyes filled with tears. Tears that made no sense.

She did not miss Frank. They hadn't gotten along for quite some time now, and he'd been stepping out on her for years. There was definitely no love between them.

But she *had* loved him once, and those tender feelings seemed to prick at her until she found herself sniffling as she tucked an errant sandwich bag into the trash bag she carried.

Charlie, dripping wet, started to take down the umbrellas, and chairs got folded up and tossed into the sand. Everyone helped, even Parker, and relief filled Alice when she finally got behind the wheel of her SUV.

At the house, she yelled over the chaos that the house had two water heaters, and they quickly made a list for showering.

Alice shuttered herself in the master suite at last, relishing the silence and sighing as she undressed and stepped into a hot shower. Afterward, rejuvenated, she dressed in a pair of comfortable pants made of a stretchy black fabric that flowed when she walked. She paired that with a lavender top that stretched over her curves. She didn't bother with drying her hair, because it was thin enough that it would dry on its own in only a few minutes.

Out in the kitchen, she found Robin and Jamie already working to bring dinner to everyone on time. "What are you making?" she asked.

"Seafood pot pie," Robin said, her voice filled with tension.

Alice watched her for a moment, then glanced at her youngest daughter. "Can I help?"

"No," Robin said, shooting her a daggered look that Alice didn't understand. "It's our night for dinner, and we'll handle it. Take a drink out to the pool or something."

"I can't sit in the sun for another minute," Alice said. "But I know when to get out of the kitchen." Away from Robin, too, when she was in a mood like this one.

She practically slammed a pot on the stove and said, "The stock goes in here, Jamie."

Her daughter did what she said, and Alice left the kitchen as Robin picked up a chef's knife. No, Alice did not want to be around when an angry Robin had a sharp object in her hand.

She didn't want to go outside again, and everyone else seemed to be in various stages of cleaning up from the beach. The twins had put their bags on the table, and Alice cleared them away, brushing sand to the floor. The entire house would be covered with it before long, and Alice would have to call the housecleaners.

Immediately, she recalled the thought. She didn't have the money to pay a maid service. Perhaps now would be a good time to call Frank, and Alice glanced into the kitchen to see what time it was.

Wednesday, almost three-thirty. Nowhere near quitting time for Frank, but Alice was going to go mad if she didn't at least speak with him briefly. She could even text him to find out what the problem with the bank account was.

Her phone rang, and a sigh of relief pulled through Alice. "It's Kristen," she said to no one in particular, and she strode back into the bedroom to answer the call. "Kristen, hello," she said.

"Alice, dear, how are you?" Comfort came with the older woman's voice, and Alice practically sagged against the door behind her.

"Well enough," Alice said. "When are you coming to Rocky Ridge?"

"Oh, Robin asked the same thing," Kristen said with a light laugh. "But I don't want to crash the party."

"You won't be crashing anything," Alice said, complete sincerity in her voice. "We want you here. We all want you here."

"You're so kind, Alice," Kristen said, her voice breaking on Alice's name.

Alice crossed to the bed and sank onto it. "Come tomorrow," she said, though Eloise still hadn't disclosed what she wanted to talk about or why she needed a whole day to do it.

"I can't come tomorrow," Kristen said. "Rueben's wife has a doctor's appointment, and I'm to be at the lighthouse while they're gone."

"Friday then," Alice said, though Kelli would be upset if she missed Kristen. But she could make her choice—the woman who'd been present for a lot of years of her life, or the half-brother she'd met once.

"Perhaps the five of you would come to the lighthouse for a clam bake on Sunday," Kristen said. "Rueben has dug a fantastic pit, and we've had it twice this summer already."

"I'll talk to the girls," Alice said.

"I just need you to come," Kristen said, and Alice paused for a moment.

"So is everyone else not invited?"

"No, they can come," she said. "I just know your father

is in the cove, and Kelli's mother, and Eloise's, and I wasn't sure if you had plans."

"We're making them day-by-day," Alice said. "I can talk to everyone tonight."

"Okay," Kristen said. "But I really just need you to come. I have—I found something that concerns you."

Alice's pulse pounded, and she was grateful she was already sitting down. "Found something?" They'd found so much two months ago, and Alice could not go through that again.

"It's a good thing," Kristen said. "I should've led with that."

"You sounded nervous."

"I'm not," Kristen said. "It'll just be a little shocking."

"Kristen, just tell me now."

"I can't do that."

"Then I'll come tomorrow."

"Alice, it's okay," she said. "Don't worry about this, okay? Talk to the girls about coming on Sunday. I'll cook for you all."

Alice tried one more time to get Kristen to tell her what she'd found, but Kristen wouldn't. The call ended, and no one seemed to need Alice, so she quickly called Frank before she lost her nerve.

"Alice," he said instead of hello. "What can I do for you?" So business-like, as if she were one of his clients and not his wife.

Surely he knew why she was calling. Yesterday, they'd

had thousands of dollars in their joint checking and savings accounts. Today, nothing.

Frank did not like emotional conversations. He appreciated facts and an even voice.

She lifted her head, refusing to let him beat her down from across the water. "I went to the store this morning, and I got a low balance alert," she said. "When I checked the account, there was hardly anything there."

"Yes, I'm restructuring the accounts over the next couple of days."

"What does that mean?"

"It means I'm removing myself from the joint account and setting up a personal account that you won't have access to."

Alice paused, her mind working quickly. "Oh," Alice said. "Perhaps I should get my own account too."

"Not necessary, dear," he said, but it was a completely different kind of *dear* than the one Kristen had used. "You can keep the account we have now. Once I'm off of it, you'll be the only one with access to it."

"Okay," she said, knowing there was more and not liking his initiative with this. He shouldn't be touching their money until things were settled with a judge. "And then...?"

"And then I'll split our assets according to the decree of the judge."

"I'm out of town and need money for food and activities," she said.

"Our hearing is on Tuesday next week," he said. "Am I to assume you won't be there?"

The wheels in Alice's head started to whir. Something loud told her she better be there, or Frank could say anything he wanted to the judge. It was probably someone he knew, and Alice could see her future disappear before her eyes.

"I'll be there," she said, her voice unemotional and strong. "You should know it's illegal to move money during a divorce proceeding."

Frank laughed, but it wasn't a happy sound. "I know the divorce laws, Alice."

"Then you should know I'll have statements in my possession when I walk into that hearing on Tuesday. You can't take money from our joint account, effectively cutting me off financially, before the judge makes his decision."

"I'm just restructuring."

"You'll put that money back into all the appropriate accounts by five o'clock tonight, or I'll file a motion with the judge that you're trying to hide assets so you don't have to pay child support or alimony." She would too, and she'd win. She knew the divorce laws too, better than him, as she'd worked in family law while he finished his degree.

"Alice," he said, his tone placating now.

"Frank," she said. "I thought we agreed to everything. You signed the papers."

Silence came through the line, and she knew exactly what had happened. He'd told someone at work about the divorce, and they'd said he didn't have to agree to her demands. Which, legally, he didn't. But he'd signed the agreement, and they both knew it would hold up in court. Alice simply didn't want to have to go to court. Not over this.

"Fine," he said.

"Thank you," Alice said. "I have to go." She hung up without saying goodbye, her hands trembling the littlest bit. Before she went out into the kitchen, she took a few minutes to take some deep breaths and find her center.

She wanted to be here with her friends. With the twins. With Aaron and his girls.

So Alice did what Alice Kelton had been doing for years: She smoothed away the cares, buried the emotion, straightened her clothes, and went out into the kitchen.

Robin was currently breaking down a lobster, and the ferocity with which she did it made Alice think she'd like it to be Mandie's neck she was wringing. Alice hadn't seen the girl in a while, and that meant she wasn't helping with dinner.

"Are you sure I can't help?" Alice asked. "The twins don't need me."

Robin looked up, her eyes filled with so much she was trying to hold back. "You can get the dishes out. We'll put this in the oven and be ready in a half-hour."

Alice nodded and turned to get plates out of the

credenza. A few minutes later, the door opened that led into the garage, and laughter came inside with AJ and Mandie. They carried grocery bags, and the fifteen-year-old didn't seem to have a clue that her mother had turned into a tropical storm.

"They didn't have any Oreo pie crusts," AJ said. "So we just got ice cream and toppings."

"Wonderful," Robin said, her voice holding a deadly undercurrent of sarcasm. She shot a look at her daughter, and that got the girl to abandon the frozen treats on the counter and get to work in the kitchen.

Alice muted her smile and kept her head down. She knew how difficult it was to deal with teenagers, and she wouldn't want someone watching her too closely. Her heart filled with love for Robin, because they seemed to be on the same path at the moment, and none of it was easy.

Everything had come together, and Robin had just called for everyone to come gather round the huge dining room table for seafood pot pie, salad, hot rolls, and ice cream when Alice's phone chimed.

She discreetly pulled it from her pocket as Robin spoke, and first noted the time. Almost five. Her pulse squeezed in her chest, but she opened the text from the six-digit code.

Relief poured through her, and she was aware of the sigh that escaped her lips. Frank had put all the money back in the account.

ALICE SIPPED HER COFFEE, THANKING WHOEVER HAD invented decaf. She loved a hot drink in the evening to unwind, and while she'd consumed wine in her younger years, she found coffee had the same effect at soothing her and didn't leave her inhibited in the least. Not to mention the headaches she'd woken with the next morning were gone.

AJ finished her story, and everyone laughed. A lull in the conversation had Alice looking around at the group, so grateful they'd all come. It had been much easier to get them to the cove this time, and a smile slipped through her soul at the bond they all had.

"What do you think Eloise will do about the inn?" Robin asked, lifting her mocktail to her lips as if she hadn't thought about it at all. But Robin thought more about everything than anyone else, and Alice shot her a look that Robin ignored.

"I don't know," Kelli said with a sigh. "I suppose it'll depend on how things go tonight, won't it?" She looked around at everyone, and AJ nodded. Robin wouldn't say what was on her mind, that was for sure, and Alice didn't care what Eloise did.

Eloise was smart, and she'd make her choice. After that, Alice would help her any way she could. Simple as that.

She'd sent a group text earlier to say she wanted the

five of them to go to the Cliffside Inn tomorrow, together. She'd offered to buy lunch—and talk about Aaron, effectively using her rights of first refusal. Alice could admit she was excited about hearing what Eloise had inside her mind.

"Mom," Charlie said as he came down the steps. "What's going on tomorrow?" He looked around the room at the other ladies, his gaze quickly skating back to Alice's.

"We're going to the Cliffside Inn," Alice said.

Charlie made a face as Ginny and Mandie giggled on the stairs behind him. They arrived in the living room too, and Alice felt like she might have a war on her hands. "You guys don't need to come," she said. "But we need to go. Can you stay here and keep an eye on Parker?" She glanced at Kelli, who met her eye and then looked at the teens.

"Sure," Charlie said. "So can we set up the volleyball net in the back yard?"

"Yep," Alice said. "In the morning. It's getting late." That was code for *it's time to go to bed*, and she lifted her mug to her lips again.

"Can we order pizza for lunch?" Ginny asked.

"Yes." Alice didn't need to do anything special to take care of the kids. They had her credit card numbers, and they'd sometimes ordered in when she had to go out for meetings or auctions or any of the other things she did as Frank's Wife.

With a jolt, she realized she didn't wear that skin

anymore, and she wasn't quite sure if she felt naked without it, or suddenly freer and lighter.

"Thanks, Mom." Ginny grinned at Mandie and added, "I think I left my shoes by the pool." The two girls went that way, and Charlie wore a look on his face that Alice had seen many times. He was half-annoyed that his sister had created an excuse that didn't allow him to leave the room with her, and he was half-panicking about what he could come up with to get himself out of whatever situation he was in.

"You probably left something out there too," Alice said. "Go check."

"Right." Charlie didn't waste a second following the girls, and Alice smiled around at her friends.

"It's so awkward being fifteen."

"I still feel like that," Kelli said, and that set off another round of laughter.

An hour later, everyone had gone to bed except for Alice, and she sat on the front porch, her hands tucked into the pockets of a sweatshirt she'd pulled on as she'd come outside. The massive, black sky stretched in every direction above her head, and she kept returning to it, trying to find order among all the pinpricks of light in the heavens.

Sitting there, waiting for Eloise to come home, Alice let herself feel all of the emotions she needed to feel. Everything she couldn't let anyone see.

The desperation pulled at her, and the hopelessness

gnawed. She managed to chase those away by reminding herself that Frank was not a cruel person. He'd always provided for her and the children, and he'd do what was right.

A moment of calm passed, after which a storm raged in her soul, breathing out threats with the wind and raining fears through her mind.

Then she'd look up into that sky, and everything would turn still again.

The hum of a car's engine met her ears, and Alice looked down the road, the emergence of headlights following the noise. A car pulled up to the house, and Eloise got out of the back seat. She handed something through the driver's window and started walking down the sidewalk.

"I really wish you wouldn't have waited up."

"I'm not tired," Alice said, and she wasn't lying. She scooted over, and Eloise took the spot of concrete next to her.

She didn't say anything for a moment, and then she looked at Alice. "How do you sit here? It's so hard."

Alice laughed lightly, and that chased away some of the thunderclouds inside her. "Keeps me awake."

"You just said you weren't tired."

Alice linked her arm through Eloise's. "I know. How's Chief Sherman?"

"He's good," Eloise said, her voice light and guarded at the same time.

Alice didn't need to know all the details. She wasn't Robin, and she wouldn't ask any embarrassing questions. She did remember the first time Eloise had tried to get Aaron Sherman's attention though, and true concern tugged at her heartstrings.

"Good," she said, because Eloise had first-rights to begin a conversation about Aaron.

"He said he's really serious about me," Eloise said, ducking her head and letting her hair fall between them.

"I'm glad." Alice squeezed her arm against her body. "Are you really serious about him?"

Eloise looked up and tucked her hair. She met Alice's eyes in the moonlight, and the hope and desire was laid bare for the whole world to see. Alice had felt like Eloise at some point in her life. Hopeful, optimistic, smitten.

"We're all going to the Cliffside Inn tomorrow, right?" Eloise asked.

"Yes," Alice said. "Good call texting us. Robin interrupted Kelli and took center stage to read the messages out loud." She smiled and shook her head; they'd all gotten the group text. Robin didn't need to read it to anyone.

"Oh, dear," Eloise said. She giggled, and before Alice knew it, the two of them were cackling like wolves howling at the moon.

Alice stood up and extended her hand to Eloise, who took it and got to her feet with a groan. "I really can't sit on cement like that." She preceded Alice into the house and turned to take her into a hug at the top of the stairs that led into the basement. "Thank you, Alice."

She wondered what Eloise's gratitude was specifically for, but she just clung tightly to her friend and said, "Anytime."

Eloise went downstairs, and Alice waited until she couldn't hear her anymore. She hoped their visit to the inn tomorrow would provide Eloise with the answers she needed to be able to move forward, and she tossed up those good thoughts as she went into the master suite.

CHAPTER THIRTEEN

E loise found chaos in the kitchen when she emerged from the basement the following morning. Mandie and Charlie had attempted to make red velvet pancakes, but the sink and surrounding wall and countertops looked like they'd been splashed with blood.

Eloise paused and took in the scene, not quite sure what to do. Robin stepped into the house from the back patio, and she came to Eloise's side. Her pause only lasted one second before she flew into the kitchen with, "What in the world is wrong with you guys?" She glared at them as she wiped up the carnage. "If Alice sees this..." She shook her head and glared some more.

"Sorry, Mom," Mandie said. "Things got a little out of hand."

"I'll say." She tossed the rag into the sink and practically yanked the spatula from her daughter's hands.

Eloise's eyebrows went up, because while she'd seen Robin upset before, this was a new level of irritation she hadn't witnessed in a while.

This was an angry-upset, not a sad-upset.

Mandie, wisely, left the kitchen, while Charlie attempted to wash the red dye out of the rag and wipe the counter again.

"Come get some coffee, Eloise," Robin said, her voice completely pleasant now. Eloise jolted into action, and she'd just spooned in some sugar when Alice came out of the bedroom.

"Ah, Charlie's famous red velvet pancakes." She beamed at her son like he'd cured cancer and poured her own cup of coffee.

Robin rolled her eyes, flipped the pancakes, and called, "Breakfast."

Parker and Jamie got up from the couch, where she'd been playing a game and he'd been watching. Kelli came in off the patio with AJ, and Eloise suddenly wanted to go.

The sooner they could get to the inn, the sooner she could explain everything and make a decision. Things moved quickly after that, and Eloise made the wise move to get out of the house and into her car.

She could nurse her coffee there as easily as in the kitchen. The other women spilled out of the house a few minutes later, and they piled into her car, Kelli in the front seat.

"Let's do this," Robin said, as if she'd been designated

to pump everyone up. She *had* been a cheerleader, but Eloise thought she'd outgrown that stage of her life quite well.

Eloise backed out of the driveway and headed toward the ferry station. "First," she said. "I want to thank everyone for coming with me today." She looked in the rear-view mirror and then at Kelli, feeling open and exposed. "I took Aaron to the inn when we first started dating. It needs a lot of work."

"What are you hoping for us to help you with?" Robin asked.

"I don't know." Eloise sighed. "I'm thinking maybe we'll just get there, and you guys will have the right thing to say to help me." They had in the past. Those conversations and epiphanies had usually happened at the lighthouse, though, and Eloise wasn't sure the magic of Kristen and the Seafaring Girls would reach all the way to Sanctuary Island.

"You seem to be getting along with Grace and Billie," Robin said.

Eloise should've been annoyed at the lead-in, but she wasn't. "Yes," she said. "I'm glad too. I have no idea what to do with little girls."

"You were great with them," AJ said from the back seat. "How was dinner with Aaron?"

"Good," Eloise said, her fingers tightening on the wheel. "I sent an email to my HR department this morning." She cleared her throat, because the idea of leaving

Boston and returning to the cove permanently made breathing hard. "I asked them about retirement and if I could get out of my fall classes if I did so before August."

A beat of silence hit the car, and Eloise basked in it. She knew it wouldn't last long. Sure enough, she'd barely taken another breath before all four of them said something.

"Wow, Eloise," Alice said.

"Good for you," Kelli said. "If you want to move here and be with Aaron, you should.'

"You're going to quit?" AJ asked.

"I'm so excited you might be back in the cove permanently," Robin said.

Eloise just shook her head. She wasn't sure if she was surprised, glad in her thoughts, scared of quitting, or excited. So many things ran through her head, it was honestly a jumble.

She managed to park and get on the ferry. They five of them got an oversized RideShare from the ferry station to the inn, the vehicle going up and up and up until it reached Cliffside Drive.

The landslide that Eloise had worried about last time hadn't closed the road or done any damage to the inn. The building came into view, and Eloise's heartbeat started leaping around inside her chest as if it had morphed into a frog.

The building was tall and beautiful, with pinkish-red brick on the bottom half that was the original structure.

Her father had built an addition on the second floor, and it was covered with white siding. Well, siding that had been white at some point in the past.

The circular drive out front needed to be sealed and lines repainted, but she could see guests pulling up to the inn and taking in their first glimpse of it. She wanted them to smile and mention to one another that it certainly looked like an amazing place to spend a few nights while they vacationed in the cove.

Sanctuary Island wasn't as busy as Diamond, but the ferry ride was short between them, and this island had plenty to offer that Eloise could put online. The way her mind moved, she thought she probably already had her answer about what she *wanted* to do.

She just didn't know if it was the *right* thing to do.

"Here we are," the driver said, and Eloise hastened to pay him before anyone else could. The five of them piled out of the car and stood in front of the inn, a sense of reverence among them.

"Remember when we came here for your birthday party?" Alice asked.

The whole night played out in Eloise's head in just a breath of time. "Of course," she said. "The pool is still back there too. It needs some work, but..." She let her voice trail off, because she could say that about literally everything on this property. It had been abandoned years ago, and Mother Nature had done her best to try to reclaim the land, the cement pads, and the house itself.

"There's a bit of algae that grows on the siding," she said, catching sight of the greenish tint on the white. "But Aaron said it would come off with a power sprayer."

"It will," Robin said. "That's what Duke uses on our house." She pointed to something on her right. "And that hard water stain comes off too. Even on the brick."

Eloise nodded, her memories still flowing fast. "Let's go look around, shall we?" She led the way, and she realized then that everyone had been waiting for her to move. "The doors here are still good." She arrived at the double front doors. "Original, too." She ran her hand down the pane of one before fitting the key in the lock and opening the door.

Just inside, a staircase when up to the second floor, easily twenty steps. Twenty-three to be exact, as Eloise had traipsed up and down them more times than she could count. She and Garrett, her only sibling, would often come to the inn with their father to clean it up after the winter months and get it ready to open.

Her dad talked about the inn like she was a ship, always using a female pronoun and smiling fondly when he said things like, "We've got to get her shiny and new," or "She deserves to have the best pool in the cove."

Eloise had once locked her memories of her childhood far away, but since returning to the cove for Joel's funeral, she'd flung the doors wide open. She had a decent relationship with her mother now, and she'd left both of her cats here the last time she'd been in the cove.

That alone had probably solidified her decision to retire from BU and return to the cove to fix up and open the Cliffside Inn. She just hadn't realized that. She'd thought allowing her mom to take the felines had been related to ease in seeing Aaron, but maybe it was more.

Maybe she really had already subconsciously decided to abandon her life in Boston and build a new one here, on top of this cliff.

The very thought felt insane, but as she led her friends around to each of the thirteen rooms at the inn, she grew more and more excited.

The living quarters where she'd stayed with her father and Garrett sat behind the garage. There'd only been one bedroom, and she and her brother had often slept in sleeping bags overlooking the ocean, the waves far below lulling her to sleep. If it rained, or the wind got too bad, they'd sleep in the living room of the tiny caretaker's apartment.

When she opened that door, a musty smell hit her in the face. "Oh." She hadn't gone in here last time, unable to face some of the most painful things she'd kept hidden behind locked doors.

"Something's gone wrong in there," Alice said. She'd hardly said a word during the tour, and Eloise found herself wanting to know what Alice really thought. "It's moldy, Eloise." She covered her nose and mouth with her hand and shook her head.

Eloise frowned, because now that Alice had said that,

she could definitely smell the rotted, wet scent of mold. Being a professor of biology, she knew mold was bad.

And expensive, she thought, some of her hopes and dreams crashing back to Earth. Eloise was nothing if not pragmatic and sensible, and she didn't go inside. "Right," she said, reaching to pull the door closed and re-locking it.

Her friends had retreated from the back door and gathered pool-side. As she joined them, she wondered what they were thinking, each of them looking down into the barren basin, which held more dirt, leaves, and debris than ever.

"I used to clean this thing four times a day," she said, her voice starting out soft and hollow, filled with the past. "I hated it back then, but I think I'm excited to do it now." She looked at AJ, who stood right next to her.

"This place suits you," AJ said with a smile. She turned and gazed at the house and threw her arms wide. "I can see you here. I can see what the inn used to be, and listening to you talk, I can see what you want it to be again."

"I want it be a place of good memories," she said, facing the back of the inn too. "This place was always where things went right." So much had gone wrong elsewhere, but never here. Her father never drank here. He was a completely different person at the Cliffside Inn than he'd been at home, and it had taken Eloise a decade to realize he'd done the very best he could.

He and her mother never should've married, and they'd both been unhappy every single day. When he wasn't around her, he truly came to life, and while Eloise didn't know that then, she knew it now.

She could accept it now.

"Where did your dad go after everything?" Robin asked, sliding her arm along Eloise's waist and leaning into her. Eloise pressed her cheek to Robin's, a hitch of emotion sticking in her chest. Robin may be nosy, and she may annoy Eloise from time to time, but there was no one as loyal. No one as kind. No one as concerned about Eloise at all.

Aaron is, Eloise thought, because he'd texted her that morning to say he hoped she had a good day at the inn. The one time she'd brought him had not conjured up quite so many good memories of her father, and she couldn't wait to tell him that this trip had been different.

"He's...last I heard, he was in Florida," she said. "Some retirement community down there that doesn't enforce wearing a shirt." She looked at Robin, at the shock in her blue eyes. It melted away, and the two of them laughed.

"He never did like wearing a shirt," Robin said.

"No, he didn't."

"Eloise," Alice said.

Eloise turned toward her, and Alice pointed at something in the sky. She shaded her eyes and looked up, finding several birds flying there. A song sounded in her soul. "Shearwaters," she said.

"Must be good luck," Alice said, smiling at her.

Eloise met her eye, the memories from Friendship Inn filling her mind. It was the one and only time Eloise had seen Alice cry, and the woman looked dangerously close to doing it again. She shook her head as if Eloise had already asked her what was wrong and turned back to the sky to observe the shearwaters.

The mini-albatross had indeed been good luck for Eloise in the past, and she wasn't above taking the sighting as a good omen.

"I think we should talk about our plans for the next few days," Alice said, her back turned to everyone.

"Alice, it's not even lunchtime yet," AJ said. "We don't need to fight already."

"It's not a fight," Alice said, facing the group. "Kristen invited us to the lighthouse on Sunday for a clambake. She said she had something for me." A moment passed where Eloise felt the oxygen leave the air. "It's not bad," Alice added. "At least she said it wasn't."

"What is it?" Robin asked.

"She wouldn't say. Only that she'd found something for me."

"We found enough at that lighthouse," Kelli said, folding her arms as if cold. The wind on top of the cliff could be chilly sometimes, but Eloise knew that wasn't the reason her skin was crawling.

"I'd like to go," Alice said. "She said only I need to come, but I think we should all go." She glanced at Robin.

"I know Robin makes it a point to go see her often, but the rest of us...we should go."

"I'll go," AJ said. "She's the best cook in the cove when it comes to clams."

"I'll go," Robin said. "The girls love going to the lighthouse."

"Can I invite Aaron?" Eloise asked. She hated how she had to constantly battle between deciding to spend time with her friends or with him, but somewhere deep in her gut whispered about how serious they'd become in a such a short time, and she wanted to have bonding experiences with him and this girls while she was in the cove.

"Of course," Alice said. "Kelli?"

"Fine," Kelli said. "I'll go." She lifted her chin and surveyed the group. Eloise had never detected any fire inside Kelli until the past few days, and she didn't know what to make of it. "I'm going to breakfast with Zach tomorrow morning, but then I'm free. What's the plan for tomorrow?"

"I need to see my mother at some point," Eloise said. If she walked a dozen steps to her left and looked down over the island, she could find the road where she'd grown up. Only three miles away, and yet, everything here at the inn had been so different.

"So do I," Kelli said.

"And I need to take the twins to see my father and Della," Alice said. "Let's do a split day on Saturday? There's a hot air balloon festival on Bell this weekend, and some of us could go to that. Robin could just relax in her quiet house." She smiled at Robin, who hadn't said much about the plans for someone who usually had a loud opinion.

"Sunday is the clam bake day. Tomorrow...tomorrow, let's go to Pearl and shop at all the expensive places." Alice wore a glint in her eye. "My treat."

"Alice," Robin said, a touch of condescension in her voice. "You don't need to do that."

"I don't even like those shops," AJ said.

"They're not the same," Kelli said. "The Navy Pearl closed, and that took most of the business. It's just cheap jewelry shops now."

Alice's face fell. "Okay," she said, rebounding quickly. "There's always the beach and the pool."

"And seafood," Robin said with a smile.

"So a lazy day together tomorrow," Alice said. "We can decide if we want to go to the beach once Kelli gets back from breakfast." She looked at her. "How does that sound to everyone?"

Choruses of "Good," and "Great," went around.

"And then," Robin said. "On Monday, we go to the black sand beach." She grinned around at everyone. "For the summer sand pact." She whooped and put her hand out, as if she were still a cheerleader and expected everyone to put their hands in and send up a yell to the sky.

To her surprise, Eloise did just that. She put her hand

on top of Robin's and looked at the others. AJ smiled and did the same, and Alice and Kelli put their hands in simultaneously.

"To the Seafaring Girls," Robin said.

Everyone repeated it, and a slip of foolishness moved through Eloise. The cheer continued, and by the end, she felt the uncertainty and doubts she'd harbored fly right out of her and into the sky as she cheered.

Laughter followed, and Eloise linked arms with Alice and Kelli. "Okay," she said. "Talk to me in terms I under-stand." She looked at Alice. "It's going to cost a fortune to fix this place up, isn't it?"

"Yes," Alice said simply.

Eloise looked at Kelli. "And a lot of hard work and hours and hours of my life. Days and weeks and months."

"Yes," Kelli said with a smile.

Eloise gazed out into the clear, blue sky, a smile forming on her face too. "I still want to do it."

"Then do it," Robin said. "Do it, and you'll be in the cove, and you can see Aaron every day."

That caused a pinch of worry to rain on some of Eloise's dreams. He'd kissed her last night like he was seri-ous, though, and she never doubted him or his intentions when they were together.

"You just want us all back in the cove," Alice said.

"So what if I do?" Robin asked, the two of them walking away as they continued to bicker. Eloise loved listening to them, because neither was truly upset, and neither would back down either.

Eloise took a deep breath and turned back to the Cliffside Inn. Yes, her future was here, and she could almost see it, hear it, and taste it.

Almost.

"Guys," Kelli said, looking up from her phone with eyes as round as dishes. "Zach just texted to say he got something really exciting to show me in the morning."

"What is it?" AJ asked like such a thing was no big deal.

Eloise watched the color drain from Kelli's face, and she put her hand on her forearm. "Not everything someone gets or finds is bad news, Kel," she said.

"It is in my life," Kelli said. Her phone rang, and Eloise looked at it, expecting to see Zach's name there. Instead it was Julian's, Kelli's husband.

"Excuse me," Kelli said, marching away. She'd taken five or six steps before she lifted the phone to her ear to speak to her husband.

"There's something going on there," AJ mused, her eyebrows set in a frown.

"What?" Eloise asked. "Do you know?"

"No," AJ said, drawing the word out. "But I'm going to find out." She made to follow Alice and Robin around the side of the inn toward the front yard, and Eloise took out her phone to call them a ride.

She had no doubt they'd all find out what was going

on with Kelli and Julian sooner or later. They always seemed to. Even when Eloise wanted to keep a secret from these four, she couldn't. The bond between them called to her, inviting her to share her deepest worries and fears with them.

"Yes," she said to the driver who answered. "We're up at the Cliffside Inn, and we need a transport for five to Coddington's Crab Shack."

Seafood couldn't fix everything, but in Five Island Cove, sometimes it felt like it could.

CHAPTER FOURTEEN

K elli wasn't even sure what Julian was saying. "Start over at the beginning," she said, probably a little harsher than she meant to. Everything with her had been harsher and bolder than before. Since arriving in Five Island Cove, Kelli had some sort of lightning inside her she hadn't known existed.

She peeked around the corner of the inn to make sure the RideShare hadn't arrived yet. The other four women stood there in a huddle, chatting and giggling. Kelli felt as she often did around them—like she didn't belong.

At the same time, she knew the moment she walked up to the group, they'd part like the Red Sea to make room for her.

Julian sighed like she was being dense on purpose. "There's another courier service," he said. "They're failing. I want to buy them out."

"But if they're failing, why would you want them?"

"That's how business works, Kel," he said.

Oh, she hated that dismissive tone. Just because he'd been to college and she hadn't didn't mean she was stupid. It also didn't mean he knew more than her, but he often acted like it did. "But why do *you* want to buy this particular business?"

Money was already tight. The thought of buckling down even more made her stomach clench.

"They deliver for Zurinck," he said.

"The technology firm?"

"Yes," Julian said simply. "It's a huge contract, Kel, and I've been after it for three years."

"So why don't you just let this place go out of business, and then secure the Zurinck contract?" That made so much more sense to her—and it wouldn't cost over a million dollars. For a failing courier service.

"That's not how it works."

Kelli sighed long and loud this time. She had so much she wanted to say to him, but none of it was nice. Kelli bit it all back, wondering why she'd been operating on annoyed with him since this trip had begun.

She normally loved her husband. She loved being home during the day to make sure everything was in its proper place, and she enjoyed making dinner for her and her boys. Sure, sometimes Julian worked late and forgot to call, but she always had dinner ready for him when he walked through the door.

She managed the household finances, so he could focus on the business. She took care of Parker, so he could take care of the business. He was a good father, an exceptional lover, and a hard worker.

She loved him, and everything inside her urging her to fight calmed down. "If you think this is the right thing to do," she said. "I'll support you."

"Yes," Julian said, clearly not to her. "Right there, Tiff. Thanks."

Kelli was very used to him having multiple conversations while he was on the phone with her. This wasn't the first time, nor would it be the last that her husband's attention was divided. "Sorry, hon. What did you say?"

"I said I'd support you in buying the courier," she said. "If you feel it's right."

"I really do. It feels like I need to strike while the iron is hot, and I don't need you to do anything but sign a few docs. The bank will send them to you via email. You sign digitally."

"Okay," Kelli said. "I can do that."

"It'll all be marked," he said. "Tiff, grab that bag too, okay? I'm right behind you."

Kelli didn't know who Tiff was. Probably one of his bikers, as Julian owned and operated one of the largest bike courier companies in Newark. They went across the bridges to New York City too, and he'd been expanding and expanding the last few years.

He'd promised her the money would come after the

NBC contract. Then after the Simon & Schuster contract. But Julian took all the money and put the majority of it back into the business.

That's how businesses grow, Kel, he'd said. He'd hired more people, and she'd worked as a secretary for him for a while. But she had a hard time leaving when Parker got home from school, and they'd decided having her as his employee wasn't good for their marriage.

So now she saw him when he finally arrived home from the huge warehouse-like office space he rented along the river's edge. He stored all the bikes there, employed three bike mechanics, four people to sort the deliveries as they came in, and then assign them to couriers, and a full-time secretary.

But her name wasn't Tiff.

A car pulled up to the inn, and Eloise turned to find Kelli. "I have to go, babe," she said. "I'll look for the docs."

"Sure," Julian said. "I'm on my way out too."

Kelli stepped around the side of the inn and waved to Eloise. "Okay, love you."

"Bye," Julian said, and Kelli painted over the sting of him not saying he loved her too. She told herself he was simply busy and stressed, being pulled in a dozen different directions. Whenever she'd start to feel this distance between them, she'd text him during the day that she'd made his favorite dessert and to hurry home as quickly as he could.

He never did make it home at a normal time, but that

was okay, because "his favorite dessert" was simply code for something else. Parker needed to be in bed for him to unwrap his dessert, and Kelli wished she was back in Newark so she could make love to her husband that night.

They needed to find the same path to be on, because she didn't know how to navigate these rough seas by herself. She climbed in the front seat again, glad she'd have a little privacy for the text she was about to send.

I miss you, she typed out. *Call me later, and maybe we can share our favorite dessert over the phone.*

She hit send before this new boldness she'd found in the past couple of days faded back to the mousy version of Kelli and stuck her phone under her leg. "I didn't hear the final verdict," she said, turning to face Eloise in one of the bucket seats in the middle of the minivan. "You're definitely retiring to move here and marry Aaron?"

Eloise made a choking noise, and Robin gasped. Alice simply blinked, but AJ burst out laughing. Kelli smiled too, something new and wonderful bubbling inside her.

"Funny," Eloise said darkly, reaching inside her bag for a bottle of water.

"Come on, El," Kelli said. "When are you going to talk about Aaron?"

"First-rights," she said.

"No," Kelli said. "No more. I'm calling for a Tell-All at lunchtime."

"No *way*," Eloise said, her face actually turning a shade lighter.

"Called," Kelli said, though she'd been on the other end of a Tell-All, and she'd been petrified and furious. So about how Eloise looked right now.

"Seconded," AJ said.

"Third," Alice piped up.

"Fourth," Robin said. Everyone looked at Eloise, and she glared back at all of them.

She finally slumped against the door and folded her arms. "Fine. But I was going to buy lunch for everyone, and now I'm not."

"I will," Kelli said, though the very thought of even buying her own lunch made her lungs seize. She had a credit card, though, and she didn't want any of the women in this car to know she couldn't afford to buy lunch. "Because you'll be busy talking." She grinned and faced the front again. "There's a crab shack—"

"Yes," the driver said. "Coddington's. Whoever arranged the ride put it in already."

"Oh, well, perfect," Kelli said, settling in for the winding drive down the cliffs to the seashore. She loved being on an island and thinking about how it was a tiny nub of land poking up out of the water. She wondered what would happen to it during a massive storm, or a tsunami, or just if sea level continued to rise.

She couldn't imagine not having all five islands in Five Island Cove, though she knew there used to be a sixth, many years ago. She'd known kids in high school who'd chartered a boat out to the lost sixth island and done a dive, and the stories they told had made her head spin.

Whole houses underwater, with cars just sitting there on the street. Sometimes, in a really dry summer, the tip of the lost island could be seen off the coast of Rocky Ridge, though Kelli had never seen it for herself.

She hadn't done very many brave things in high school, unless surviving counted. And for her, it did. It had. That was all she was capable of doing. Again, her thoughts wandered to Heather, who hadn't coped quite as well as Kelli, who'd basically fallen apart.

She'd call her tomorrow, after she breakfasted with Zach and saw the exciting thing he'd gotten that day and couldn't wait to show her.

She picked up her phone again and sent him a quick text, realizing she hadn't yet responded to him. *Can't wait to see.* She added a smiley face, and sent the message zipping across the space between them.

Before she looked away from her phone, a text came in from Julian. It was simple and direct, much like Julian was. *11:30?*

Done, she sent back, suddenly hot from head to toe.

"Coddington's," the driver announced, and Kelli looked up as if she'd been caught doing something she shouldn't be.

She spilled from the van and followed everyone inside, ready to hear Eloise's tales. They had drinks and had ordered before Eloise tossed away her straw wrapper, which she'd been tying into a series of knots.

"I'm scared to commit to moving back here," she said. "Because it feels like if I do, then it's because of Aaron and not because fixing up the inn is what I want to do." She met Alice's eye, pure, unadulterated fear in hers. "What if it's not that serious? What if Aaron and I break up? Then what?"

Alice covered Eloise's hand with hers, a sympathetic smile on her face. Kelli watched them for a moment, sensing something between them she didn't know about. With five of them, some of the girls had had stronger friendships than others, and that was definitely true for her and AJ. She just hadn't put Alice and Eloise together. It was always Robin and Alice, and Robin and Eloise. Sometimes the three of them.

"What's happening here?" AJ asked, usually the more bold one. Her journalism background helped with that.

Alice slid her hand back and said nothing. Eloise glanced around. "In high school, I went to a party once. Alice went with me. It was out on Pearl Island, and I went solely to..." She cleared her throat. "Well, to talk to Aaron Sherman."

Robin reached for her drink in a seemingly calm manner, but Kelli saw the twitchiness in her fingers.

"I danced with him, and he held me close and he held my hand as we danced around the fire." Eloise sighed. "It was awesome. I thought for sure he liked me the way I liked him. I left for a few minutes to get a drink and go to the bathroom, and when I came back, he was dancing with someone else. Holding her close. Holding her hand in the bonfire ritual." She shook her head. "It meant nothing to him. He doesn't even remember it."

Kelli had no idea what to say. Eloise had never gone to school dances, though she was beautiful and smart. It was the smart that had thrown the boys for a loop. Decades ago, when they were in high school, boys hadn't known what to do with a girl that was smarter than them.

"Have you asked him?" Robin asked gently.

"No," Eloise said. "I know he doesn't remember it. We've talked about that party, and he hasn't said anything."

"The fact is," Alice said. "Aaron Sherman is simply a nice guy. So he danced with everyone that night. He held them all close. He did the bonfire line dance a hundred times."

Eloise nodded, her eyes glued to the tabletop. "It was special for me. Meant nothing to him, and I'm just worried this relationship is like that too."

"Oh, I don't think so," Robin said with a mild laugh. She shook her head and met Eloise's eyes with intensity in hers. "Eloise, no. Come on. You don't really think that."

"Don't I?"

"Of course not," Robin said, looking around the table for backup. "We've seen the way Aaron looks at you. He's not fifteen anymore, and there's no way he'd bring you around his kids if he wasn't serious."

"I think he's serious," Eloise said. "But I don't want to throw my life away until there's a reason to do so."

"Sometimes you need to take a leap of faith," Alice said, her voice catching on itself on the last couple of words. Kelli switched her attention there, because Alice had just said so much more than a simple sentence.

She exchanged a glance with AJ, and she tried to catch Robin's eye. But Robin was suddenly engrossed in the dessert menu, of all things.

Kelli snatched it from her. "What's going on here?"

"What?" Robin asked innocently.

"What?" Kelli asked, looking around. "This is a Tell-All. That means everyone tells all." She narrowed her eyes at everyone at the table. No one said anything, and that fire that had been licking her insides since she'd run into Alice's house afraid for her life came roaring back. Now it blazed into an inferno, swirling and smoking inside her.

"Fine," she said, leaning back. "I'll go first. My husband just called, and he wants to buy a failing courier business for one-point-one million dollars. Which we don't have. In fact, I had to use my credit card to buy gas and groceries last month. I'm pretty much broke." She looked around the table, her gaze feeling sharper and sharper as it left her eyes.

Everyone looked back at her now, and for maybe the first time in her life, Kelli didn't hate the spotlight. She reached for her glass of diet cola with a perfectly steady hand.

"Who's next?"

"I got an email from a sports studio in New York City this morning," AJ said. "They want to do a phone interview on Monday."

Kelli looked at her best friend in the whole world. "Wow, AJ. That's awesome, but...are you looking for another job?"

AJ visibly flinched, her eyes widening. "Oh, uh, didn't I tell you guys?"

"Tell us what?"

"As part of the packing up what I own and moving it, I quit my job. So I'm currently looking for another one." She downed half of her huckleberry lemonade in a couple of swallows.

"You quit, quit?" Eloise asked.

"What did you guys think I'd done when I said I'd sold my apartment and had nowhere to stay?"

"I thought you were taking a leave of absence," Robin said.

Kelli hadn't thought about it at all.

"I quit," AJ said. "And that's two for me, so I get a pass on the next Tell-All." She looked at Eloise.

"I've already said mine," she said. "I'm falling in love with Aaron—"

"Whoa, whoa, *whoa*," Alice said. "You did *not* say that."

"Oh, was that not obvious by the way I'm *seriously*

considering quitting my prestigious, high-paying job at a major university to come back to Five Island Cove and open a dilapidated inn?" Eloise looked around at everyone, landing on Alice again at last. "Huh, I thought that was obvious."

Alice burst out laughing, and that broke the tension at the table. They all joined in, and that was one of two ways a Tell-All ended. With all of them laughing, or all of them crying.

When the last of the giggles died down, Alice took a deep breath. "I'm really worried about what Kristen has for me." She looked around at the others. "I feel like I want to go to the lighthouse right now, and I never want to go again."

That summed up the lighthouse for Kelli, and she mourned that fact. The lighthouse had once been a place of safe harbor for her. The *only* safe place in the cove where she could go and be loved and accepted, no matter what.

"It'll turn out okay," Robin said, giving Alice a side squeeze. She was all that was left, and she looked at the placemat in front of her, which was crawling with red, cartoon crabs. "I miss my husband terribly. I'm trying to hold it all together, but I'm honestly not made to be alone." She looked around at all of them, her eyes brimming with tears. "I've never been good on my own, and I'm so glad you're all here."

She reached across the table and took Kelli's hand in hers, giving it a healthy squeeze.

"We've got the crab cakes," the waitress said, appearing with plates of food that would hopefully swing this Tell-All back to the positive side. At the same time, Kelli wondered what was different about Robin and Duke's relationship that she and Julian were missing.

The truth was, she'd barely missed her husband since leaving town a couple of days ago. He'd barely communicated with her. The only reason he'd called today was because he needed her signature on the business loan documents so he could get the money he needed to buy the competitive courier.

Sure, she might sneak out of the bedroom she was sharing with Parker that night and talk dirty to her husband, but that didn't mean they had the kind of relationship Robin and Duke did.

In fact, as Kelli indicated that the lobster rolls with avocado were hers, she had the very real feeling that her marriage was in very real trouble.

CHAPTER FIFTEEN

R obin woke early the following morning, ready to run off some of the bread and butter she'd eaten yesterday. After a delicious lunch on Sanctuary Island, and an all-around amazing day, Mandie had made brownies.

She'd stayed up too late again, chatting with her friends and drinking too much coffee, even if Alice insisted decaf wouldn't keep her up at night.

It seemed like everything these days was keeping Robin up at night. Coffee was the least of her worries.

She sat up and immediately glanced to the bunk beds where her girls were sleeping. Or were supposed to be sleeping.

A vein of absolute exhaustion pulled through her at the sight of the empty top bunk. Mandie was going to be the death of her.

In that moment, a rush of affection for her own mother filled her. She was sure she was responsible for some of her mother's earliest gray hairs. They still didn't see eye-to-eye on a lot of things, and Robin couldn't remember the last time she'd called her mom and hadn't been frustrated during the conversation as well as after.

She normally vented to Duke about her mother and the girls when it got to the point that Robin was going from fine to furious in less time than it took to breathe. She hadn't been doing that since he'd gone to Alaska, and she honestly felt like a lobster trap—tense and ready to explode.

She dressed in her running clothes, as she'd planned to jog on the beach that morning. She'd probably see Mandie and Charlie there, as Alice had mentioned that the pair had gone surfing in the morning a couple of days ago.

Neither of them had seen any harm in that, and even when Alice had told Robin that Mandie and Charlie were holding hands, Robin hadn't been alarmed.

Mandie was almost sixteen years old. It was okay to hold hands with a boy. They'd talked about sex and the price of it at such a young age, and to Robin's knowledge, Mandie hadn't even kissed a boy yet.

She tied her shoes and settled her visor in just the right position before grabbing her sunglasses from her purse and heading downstairs. She took her time stretching and warming up her muscles, and when she left the house, she did so at a jog.

The sun's rays had barely started to kiss the sky good morning, and Robin had never experienced a more tranquil time of day. She loved the wispy clouds in the sky, trapping the purples and pinks from the midnight color and holding onto them until the sun finally forced them to turn orange and gold.

She felt good that morning, and she was determined to outrun her feelings. She hadn't said anything else about Duke or Alaska during the Tell-All, and no one had asked. Alice had tried, but Robin had shut her down. She was fine. Women lived apart from their husbands all the time, and as she found her stride and the rhythm of her breath, she reminded herself that her and Duke's situation was temporary.

He wasn't overseas, fighting a war. He wasn't dead. They weren't divorced.

He'd come home, and he'd realize how much he loved Five Island Cove, and everything would go back to normal.

Robin had always been optimistic, and today was no different. She ran down the beach until the huge cliffs that gave Rocky Ridge its name started to tower over her. She slowed for a moment, turned around, and started back to the house.

She hadn't seen Charlie or Mandie yet, and her worry grew teeth and sunk them deep into her mind. She stayed on the beach even after she could've turned to go up to the house, and she still didn't see them.

She slowed to a walk and kept moving. When she reached the sidewalk, she started her cool down procedure, and that included stretching her arms and side and back to make sure she wouldn't have any aches and pains later that day.

After casting one more look at the beach and finding it barren of anyone she knew, she went back to the house. Maybe Mandie had gone out to a couch somewhere and was sleeping. If she wasn't, Robin had no idea where she was.

Her irritation with her teenage daughter increased with every step she took, as did her panic. Had Mandie gone missing? Why hadn't she made sure she knew where her daughter was before taking a morning run?

She pushed through the back gate, her heartbeat sprinting as quickly as if she was still running. In a lot of ways, she was. Running from the idea of dealing with a near-grown daughter. Running from her own fears. Running from telling her friends everything she felt and then relying on them for support.

The truth was, Robin wanted to be that support for others. Taking it for herself was much, much harder.

So focused on getting inside to start looking for Mandie, Robin didn't realize what she was looking at for several seconds.

She'd found her daughter, and she was currently kissing Charlie Kelton with everything she had.

"Mandie," Robin barked, something sparking in her head. Her vision flashed as if with lightning, and she strode over to the chaise where the two of them had just jumped apart from one another. "Up," she commanded. "In the house. Now." She glared at Charlie. "Both of you."

"Mom," Mandie started, actually having to pull her tank top over to get herself covered properly. True, she wore less while on the beach, but they weren't on the beach right now, were they?

"What are you doing out here?" she asked.

"We just got back from surfing," Mandie said, standing up. "It didn't seem like anyone was up."

"So you thought you'd just make out next to the pool." Robin folded her arms, still trying to work through the shock of finding the two of them like that. She'd fully expected her daughter to share her first kiss with her, but she hadn't expected to actually witness it.

"Mom," Mandie said under her breath. Her dark eyes sparked with anger too, and Robin had half a mind to go off on her right then. Only the memory of her own mother embarrassing her in front of her boyfriend stopped Robin from doing it.

As well as the man who called, "Hello?" over the side fence. All three of them looked that way, and Robin automatically moved in front of the teens. "I need an Alice Kelton."

"Why didn't you knock on the front door?" Robin asked, glaring at the stranger. "This is private property."

He didn't seem worried about anything she'd just asked. "Are you Alice Kelton?"

"No."

"Will you sign for this?" He held out a legal-sized envelope that had no markings on the outside of it.

"No," Robin said again. "Go around to the front door, and I'll get Alice for you."

He made a face but turned to do what she said. She faced the teens again, and to Charlie's credit, he hadn't slunk away while her attention was elsewhere.

"Let's go," she said. "I want you guys at the kitchen table." They went inside, and there was no one else around. Robin didn't think it was that early—it was obviously late enough for deliveries—but when she knocked lightly on Alice's bedroom door and then entered, she found her friend asleep.

A sigh passed through her lips, and she turned to go sign for the blasted envelope. Anything to get that guy to leave.

At the front door, she said, "She's still asleep. I'll sign."

He handed over his tablet, and Robin put in a terrible signature with her forefinger. "It's really early to be delivering packages."

"Yeah, he wanted it delivered early so he wouldn't miss her."

"He? Who's he?" Robin took the envelope, which

seemed to hold a thick sheaf of papers.

"Have a great day," the man said, and he turned and walked away.

Robin frowned at his retreating back and then looked down at the envelope. Papers. Who would want to make sure Alice saw whatever was inside this package before the day's activities began?

She turned the envelope over and pulled up the prongs. The papers came out easily then, and she saw the official letterhead from a law firm. A prestigious one, no doubt.

To Alice Kelton:

Frank will not be abiding by the claims and requests heretofore contained in the document he signed on May twenty-first.

Robin didn't need to read any further. This was not good news for Alice, and finding a couple of teenagers kissing suddenly didn't seem like that big of a deal.

She hurried back inside, closing the door behind her, and continued into the kitchen. Robin always had something to say, but facing Charlie and Mandie, both of whom looked at her with wide eyes and plenty of fear in their expressions.

Good, she thought. *They should be afraid.* Robin felt almost on the edge of her sanity, and a crazed Robin was not someone they wanted to deal with.

"So we're seeing each other now, is that it?"

"It's not called 'seeing each other,' Mom."

"What's it called then?" She looked between Charlie and Mandie. "It better not be hooking up. Or casual. So you're dating?" She zeroed in on Charlie, as it seemed like Mandie had deferred to him.

"I don't know," he said, not looking at anyone else.

"You don't know?" Mandie asked, her voice almost breaking on the last word. Robin instantly wanted to comfort her and tell her that sometimes boys said some really stupid things. That was why she had to be careful on dates. She needed to keep both eyes open when it came to relationships, and Robin knew she was ill-equipped to deal with them.

"You said I wasn't a substitute for your stupid friend in the Hamptons," Mandie said. "You said you didn't kiss her."

"I don't," Charlie said, his dark eyes blazing now too. "And you're not a substitute for her." He glanced at Robin. "I don't kiss her. I don't."

"But you were kissing my daughter."

"Mom."

"Yeah," Charlie said. "So yes, I guess we're dating." He stood up. "Can I go now?"

Robin wanted to go too, and she wished her life was as easy now as it had been at fifteen. "As long as we can eliminate 'hanging out' and 'hooking up,'" she said. "Then yes, both of you can go."

Mandie scattered so fast that Robin wondered if she'd always been able to take the stairs three at a time. Charlie stayed for a moment and said, "We're not hooking up, Mrs. Glover."

"Great," Robin said, her mind so full in that moment. She just wanted to go back to bed and sleep for as long as possible.

Charlie nodded and passed through the kitchen to the doorway that led to his room.

Alone in the kitchen now, Robin sighed and reached up to rub her hand along the back of her neck. Her sweat had dried there, and she felt grimy and gross.

Footsteps sounded somewhere, and she scooped up the envelope and headed for the master suite again. She'd have to wake Alice now; there was no way around it.

"Alice?" she said into the semi-darkness, noticing that Ginny slept in the huge king-sized bed with her mother. Robin had a very still moment seeing the two of them sleeping. Alice was a very good mother, and she'd do anything for her kids. In so many ways, she was exactly like Robin, and Robin felt an extreme connection to her.

Alice had put up blackout curtains, but they hadn't been closed all the way, so shadows chased across the floor. "Alice." She sat on the edge of the bed as her best friend opened her eyes.

"What?" Alice asked, sitting straight up in bed. "What's wrong?"

Robin wanted to assure her that nothing was wrong. Absolutely nothing. Instead, she lifted the envelope. "This came for you this morning."

"What time is it?" She reached for her phone, a frown marring that lovely face a moment later. Realizing the hour was yet early, she sank against the headboard. "You scared me, Robin."

"Sorry." She handed the envelope to Alice. "I'll let you go through that in private."

Alice took it and lifted the flap, but she didn't take anything out. "Wait," she said just as Robin was about to twist the doorknob. "Stay, would you?" She gave a nervous laugh. "I might need the support."

"Of course." Robin knew Alice needed support from time to time. Everyone did, but Alice had held herself a cut above everyone else for a long time now.

She nodded and pulled out the pile of papers. She only read for a few seconds before she swore under her breath. "He signed the document," she argued with the cover letter. "That's a binding legal contract."

She threw the papers back into the envelope in disgust. "He's going to fight me for everything."

"You don't know that," Robin said. "You read one letter."

"Gut feeling," Alice said, staring at nothing across the room. "I have to go to the Hamptons for a hearing on Tuesday." She looked at Robin. "Would you watch my kids?"

"Of course." She met Alice's eyes with plenty of unknowns in her eyes too. "What are you going to tell the others?"

"The truth," Alice said, tossing away what had just been delivered. "But not today. Okay, Robin? Not today."

Robin wondered if today might be a good day for her to find out that Charlie and Mandie were kissing. Charlie was an extremely good-looking teenager, and Robin could see why Mandie had fallen for him.

"Okay," she said. "I think you should know I just caught Mandie and Charlie making out in one of the chaises by the pool."

Alice looked up to meet Robin's eyes. She looked like Robin had just dumped ice water down the front of her expensive-looking silk pajamas. "You're not kidding."

"No, I am not," Robin said, sinking onto the bed again. "What are we going to do?"

"There's nothing to do," Alice said. "Keep them talking to us and trust them that they'll make the right choices."

"Trust them?" Robin gave what could only be described as a cackle. "Mandie can barely find her phone most of the time. She lost her brain two years ago, and I think it's under the bed, collecting dust. She's completely driven by what's popular on social media and her hormones."

And that was a very, very dangerous combination.

"Let's talk to them together," Alice said.

"Do you have an outline for what this talk might entail?"

Alice sighed and ran her hands over her face. "Not a clue. Why is there no manual on this type of thing?"

"How to talk to your teen about hooking up and hanging out," Robin said. "It'll be an instant bestseller." She grinned, because sometimes it was easier to do that than to allow herself to break down.

She hated crying in general, but especially in front of other people. She pulled back on the emotions as Alice said, "If they're hooking up, I'm going to kill him."

"He said they weren't," Robin said. "I was actually quite impressed with him."

"With Charlie?" Alice's eyes were as round as saucers. "No."

"Yes," she said. "He didn't give me any attitude, for one. With Mandie, I can be one-hundred percent right about something, and she'd roll her eyes."

"She's *your* daughter. Charlie will give me that attitude," Alice said. "Besides, teenage girls are a special breed."

"Can you imagine our poor mothers?" Robin shook her head, the memories of what she'd done growing up to her family and specifically to her mother could make up her nightmares now, as a mother herself.

Perhaps it was time to get everything out in the open and start to let it heal. She'd have to call her mom to do that and be willing to have an honest conversation about everything. If only her mother would recognize that Robin wasn't the sixteen-year-old she'd once been, calling and talking would be so much easier.

"Remember when I told my mom I was sleeping at

your house, but really I went over to Dwayne's?" Alice laughed quietly, shaking her head. "I'd be mortified if I found out Ginny had done that."

"You said you didn't sleep with Dwayne," Robin said.

"I didn't," Alice said. "But I was still in his bedroom in the middle of the night." She shuddered. "The thought of my kids doing what I did...horrifying."

Robin could agree to that, and she stood with a big sigh. "I'll see what we have for breakfast."

"Let's talk to them sometime today," Alice said

Robin agreed and left Alice alone in her bedroom. She may have wanted Robin to stay in the beginning, but she needed to go through every paper in that file and find a way to bend it to fit her purposes. The Alice Robin knew would want to do that in private.

Robin found Eloise in the kitchen making coffee, and she said, "Good morning," to her. Eloise turned, and she looked well-rested and beautiful in the morning light. She didn't have a single gray hair and she'd already dressed for the day in a pair of shorts and a blue shirt with pink flowers on it.

"Morning," she said.

She didn't have teenagers, so she didn't have the stress-related gray hair or the pinched worry around her eyes.

"I'm going to go shower," Robin said. "I'll be back in a few minutes." She went up the steps, praying for a miracle that Mandie had calmed and that she'd shelve her arguments and her attitude and just listen to Robin—for once.

CHAPTER SIXTEEN

Kelli hugged her son tightly and said, "Mommy will be back in a couple of hours, okay?" She bent down and looked into his face. He was an equal mix of her and Julian, and she loved him so much. Sometimes he struggled when Kelli left him behind, and today looked like it might be one of those days.

"You can go have one of those breakfast sandwiches Robin made," Kelli said, putting a sunny smile on her face. "Mandie said they were going to take the sports stuff to the beach. You like football."

"Yeah," Parker said, hanging his head. Kelli was never sure if he really didn't want her to go or if he was putting on a show. She'd left him with her mother-in-law a few times recently where he'd acted just like this, and Ivy had said he'd completely transformed the moment Kelli was gone.

He'd talk and laugh and be perfectly happy without her.

"Okay." Kelli straightened and pressed a kiss to the top of his head. "Go on, then. Be sure to say please and thank you, and stay with AJ." She'd asked her to keep an eye on Parker than morning, and AJ had looked up from her phone long enough to agree. She lived life so differently than Kelli, and she couldn't imagine the casual way AJ existed on a day-to-day basis.

Last night, AJ had said not to worry about breakfast that morning, but the doubts had literally been consuming her stomach for a full day now. She worried she was going to upset Alice. She worried she was getting into a situation she wouldn't be able to predict or control. She worried about what might happen then.

She swallowed, trying to tame the feelings and rid herself of them. The physical lump in the back of her throat went down, but Kelli had barely made it to the curb and the RideShare car she'd called before it returned.

"Benedict and Bacon, please," she said as she closed the door, and the driver didn't say anything before simply easing back onto the road. Kelli watched the island scenery go by, noting that the beach houses on the north side of Rocky Ridge had returned to the bright colors of the fifties.

Alice's father had a lot of pictures showing what the island had looked like previously, and he didn't understand houses like the one Alice had. Too much brick and glass, he'd said, but Kelli liked it.

The wooden houses and stacked apartments had charm too, though, and she allowed some of her nerves to seep out. The sky was bright blue this morning, without a single cloud anywhere, and when she got out of the car in front of the breakfast joint, the salt air blew off the water lapping against the shore only a hundred yards away.

Kelli did love the cove, and she would never see anything like this in Newark. In fact, the water there wasn't even safe to swim in, and she couldn't remember the last time she'd taken a deep breath of the air in the city.

As the car drove away, leaving her at Benedict's, she closed her eyes and tried to reach down inside herself to find her focus. This was something she taught others to do in her beginning yoga classes, but today, she failed.

She couldn't focus.

Armed with her cell phone and the last of her bravery, Kelli entered the restaurant. Chatter and the clattering of silverware and dishes met her ears, and she instantly wanted to leave. Benedict's had been operating on Rocky Ridge for decades, and they were the hipster joint for breakfast year-round.

A lot of restaurants and businesses closed in the off-season, but enough locals liked Benedict's that they could stay open. At least that was what Alice had told Kelli yesterday afternoon when she'd asked where Kelli was meeting Zach for breakfast. Alice had suggested Benedict's, so perhaps she wasn't upset Kelli would be gone for a couple of hours this morning.

When she'd left, Robin had been manning the kitchen for breakfast, offering cold cereal to everyone, coffee for the adults, and a tray of breakfast sandwiches she'd "whipped up."

Kelli didn't normally eat breakfast anyway, and she'd skipped everything but the coffee. Now, her veins vibrated as she looked around to find Zach.

He wasn't in the waiting area, though several other people were, so she stepped over to a woman wearing an apron and a name tag. "Welcome to Benedict and Bacon," the woman said. "How many?"

"Two," Kelli said, her voice cracking on the number.

"About ten, fifteen minutes," she said.

Kelli nodded, gave her name, and retreated, easily slipping into the background, behind everyone else. She was comfortable there, as she'd always existed in that space. It wasn't until she'd left the cove that she'd even wanted to be in the spotlight, and the only reason she'd met and caught Julian's eye was because she'd put her art in a show which he'd attended.

She'd never done anything since, and she'd never told her friends about that singular show in the Bronx that she'd done. No one knew—except for Julian.

Kelli thought of the man she'd left in Newark, and how worried she'd been about her relationship with him.

She still felt some distance between them, but she thought it could just be the actual physical distance causing the doubts. He'd called at eleven-thirty as they'd planned, and Kelli could admit she'd enjoyed the interlude. She wasn't very experienced when it came to lovers or love-making, but Julian had called once when he'd been out of town for a convention, and one thing had led to another...and Kelli really liked this new part of their love life. She could say things to him she wouldn't otherwise, and as they made love miles apart, she found everything about him more exciting.

She fanned herself as she glanced toward the door as it opened, hoping it would be Zach. She didn't like waiting by herself.

Zach did walk in, and relief rushed through Kelli. He hadn't changed at all in the few days since she'd met him and learned he was her half-brother. Today, he brightened when he saw her, and Kelli stepped away from the wall where she'd been waiting to give him a hug hello.

He held a shoebox in one hand that he moved out of the way as they embraced. "Sorry I'm late. Have you been waiting long?"

"Maybe five minutes," Kelli said. "I put our names on the list."

"Perfect." He beamed down at her and held up the box slightly. "Guess what this is?"

The box was old, the red color looking like it had been rubbed off in some places. The lid was the only thing keeping it square, and when he lifted it, one of the corners had been ripped.

"Letters." He sounded one step away from pure joy, and Kelli looked into the box. There were letters inside, dozens of them. Maybe fifty. Maybe one hundred. "They're from our father."

Kelli's gaze snapped back to his, her heart pounding instantly. "What? They are?"

"Yes," Zach said. "My mother has kept them all these years. She never showed them to me." A dark cloud covered his expression then, and he let it stay while he moved his attention back to the box.

Kelli didn't know what to say or do. She wanted to read every word of those letters, right now. She wouldn't leave the restaurant until she did. At the same time, she didn't want to know what her father had said to his bastard son. A son he'd had with a woman while he'd been married to Kelli's mother.

She didn't have any letters from her father, and a sharp hook of jealousy caught her right behind the ribs, making her gasp. Zach either didn't notice or didn't care, because he didn't look at her or say anything.

"Kelli?" the hostess called, and Kelli turned on wooden legs and walked away from her half-brother, regretting her decision to meet him this morning. Perhaps it would be okay, and she allowed the busyness and the noise of the restaurant to enter her ears fully, distracting her enough to follow the woman to a booth by the window and sit down.

Zach put the shoebox on the seat next to him as he slid into the other side of the booth. "You don't have to see them," he said.

"It's okay," Kelli said, but she couldn't quite look him fully in the face. She picked up the menu and studied it like she had to know every single thing on it.

"I don't think it is," Zach said. He reached across the table and put one hand over hers. "I'm sorry, Kelli. I didn't even think how you would feel about the letters. I thought...well, I guess I thought it would help us get to know him better."

"I knew him," Kelli said, her tone much sharper than she even knew she could do. She felt like a completely different woman lately, and she didn't know why or what to do about it. All she knew was that her entire world had tilted with Joel's death and with finding the deed to her father's glassworks in his files. Kristen had given it to her; signed it right over. Kelli had thought about that dilapidated art studio every day since.

She'd thought about her own art, and what she might make in the same space where her father had been so creative, had done his best work, and sculpted the statue that still stood in the town square on Diamond Island.

Zach wore surprise and shock on his face, and Kelli ducked her head. "I'm sorry."

"No, it's fine," he said, lifting his own menu. "Of course you knew him."

Kelli hid behind the many types of eggs Benedict she could get, wondering if what she'd said was true. Did she know her father? She hadn't known he'd slept around on her mother. She'd known she'd loved him as a little girl, and that he'd taught her how to work with glass, a skill very few people in the world could do well.

"He was the best master glassblower in the US," Kelli said. "He made pieces for everyone in the cove, and he'd sell them to tourists all summer long in the boutiques and bazaars all over the islands." As she spoke, her fond memories pushed out the bad ones. "He'd go to Nantucket, where he'd sell commissioned pieces to the rich and famous there, and his work spread west into the Hamptons, New York City, and even the White House."

Zach wore a look of hunger on his face, and Kelli looked into his wide, dark blue eyes. "He's got a dish in the China Room there," she said. "Nancy Reagan bought it after she'd seen some of his work in a theater in New York."

"What kind of work?"

"It was a glass sculpture," Kelli said, all thoughts of eggs and hollandaise sauce gone. "Reds, oranges, even black glass. It stands thirty-four feet tall, and it's in the lobby of the Belasco Theater. They're famous for their use of lighting, and they lit his glasswork in such a unique way, it looked like flickering fire." She smiled, because her father had been so proud of that piece. "He'd tell anyone and everyone about that. In fact, he had pictures of it he'd put out on his table at the boutiques."

"He made a living here?" Zach asked. "Why didn't he go to the city?"

"He always said he'd been born in the cove, and he'd die in the cove." Kelli's mood shifted, and she tried to cover it with a smile. The corners of her mouth wobbled though, and Zach saw it all. "And he did." She cleared her throat and reached for the glass of water on the table. It was tepid and tasted like metal, but she drank it anyway.

Thankfully, a waiter arrived at the booth and asked if they were ready. She ordered the traditional plate and looked at Zach. He hadn't spent much time looking at the menu, and he didn't look down now. "Same," he said.

The waiter nodded as he collected the menus and left, and Kelli asked, "Do you even know what you just ordered?"

"No idea," he said, smiling. "But I figure if you like it, I'll like it."

Kelli marveled at him, at the easy way he took things in stride. She wondered if he got that from his mother, or if she should have those same genes flowing in her. "It's a traditional eggs Benedict," she said. "Nothing extra or frilly. And a big portion of bacon." She loved bacon, and she didn't have the occasion to eat it very often.

Her phone dinged, and she glanced at it to see Julian's name on the screen. Her pulse jumped, and she wasn't sure if that was a good thing or not. Was she excited? Nervous to read the text?

"He's your husband, right?" Zach asked, leaning both elbows on the table.

"Yes," Kelli said, turning the phone over. "He can wait." She'd signed the documents he needed for the loan yesterday. "What about you? Do you have a wife? Girlfriend?"

Zach shook his head no. "Not at the moment."

"Where are you living?" If Kelli could get him talking about himself, perhaps she wouldn't have to revisit the painful memories surrounding her father.

"My mom is in Portland," he said. "Maine. She's—" He cleared his throat. "In a nursing home there."

Surprise darted through Kelli. "She is? Is she...okay?" She hated the question the moment it left her mouth. Of course his mother wasn't okay if she was in a nursing home.

"She's had cancer for a while now," he said, picking up his own water glass. "Her sister lives there, and when she left the cove, that's where she went. I was raised there."

"Oh. I'm sorry about the cancer."

Zach looked up, flashing a smile so quickly she could barely see it. "Some days, I think I've come to terms with it. Others, I'm not sure." He drew in a deep breath. "Looks like today is one of the days I'm not sure." He looked at her again. "This latest round of treatment has been particularly hard for her. She made my aunt take her home for a week or so, and she's been cleaning out her house while I've been gone."

"Thus, the shoebox of letters," Kelli said, feeling like a jerk for her reaction to them.

"Yes," he said.

"Will you go back there?" she asked. "To Portland. You lost your job, right?"

He heaved in another breath and blew it out slowly. "I don't know. If my mom passes...there's nothing really for me in Portland. There's some great galleries, but I doubt I could get on at one."

"Wait," Kelli said. "Galleries?"

"Yeah," he said. "I'm an art curator. Or I was." He shrugged like it was no big deal, but Kelli did not think Zach being in the art scene was a coincidence. "I was blamed for something at work—a lost painting—and I doubt any of the other galleries will even look at my application." He met her eye again, something new in his. Hope, perhaps. "I'm thinking of getting back into the studio myself. Hearing you talk about Guy and the incredible artist he was...I don't know."

"You're an artist too?"

"I majored in art in college," he said. "My mother was so mad." He laughed, the sound of it carrying true happiness. So much so that Kelli smiled too. "What are you going to do with that? she'd ask me."

He leaned back as the waiter arrived with their food. The salty scent of bacon mixed with the buttery hollandaise sauce, and Kelli's stomach roared. "Thank you," she said to the man. "Can I get some orange juice?"

"Sure thing."

"And coffee," she added.

"Two coffees," Zach said.

The man knocked on the table and said he'd be right back.

"What kind of art do you do?" she asked.

"Sculpture," he said. "Mostly. I like watercolors too, but I've never been able to master them."

"Sculpture and watercolors are two completely different things," she said, picking up her fork.

"When I worked as an artist, I sculpted," he said. "And I was definitely a starving artist." He beamed at her. "So I continued my education and got a master's degree in art history, and that qualified me to be a curator. That took over my life, and I haven't done much in the studio since."

"So maybe it is time to get back to it."

"Maybe."

Kelli cut into her eggs and took a bite, her mind spinning. She owned the glassworks building now. She wasn't going to use it, but she hadn't been able to put it up for sale either. She hadn't even told her mother or Julian about it. Her husband would've only seen dollar signs, and he'd have wanted her to list it for sale immediately.

She hadn't told him about the house on Seabreeze Shore either, and Kelli suddenly had a new reason for the distance she felt between her and him. She had secrets—maybe he did too.

Perhaps she could give the glassworks to Zach. Julian was making things work with the courier business without the assets she had in her name on Five Island Cove. He wouldn't even have to know.

The very idea was crazy, and yet Kelli couldn't let go of it. She opened her mouth, but the waiter arrived with their coffee and juice. The moment broke. Her confidence and bravery fled.

Zach met her eye. "What?" he asked.

"Nothing," she said in a falsely bright tone. "Once we finish eating, I do want to take a look at some of those letters."

"Really?" Hope lit his face, and Kelli ignored the squirming feeling in her stomach.

"Yes," she said. "Really."

CHAPTER SEVENTEEN

Alice didn't leave her bedroom until she was sure the activity in the kitchen had wrapped up. The master suite sat down a short hallway from the kitchen, and Alice sat in the massage chair, listening to the adults and children talking and eating. She couldn't make out any words, per se, but the noise soothed her.

She did love entertaining, but she didn't feel fit for company quite yet. Eventually, Ginny knocked on the door and said, "Mom?"

"Yes," Alice said, reaching to press the button on the controls to stop the massagers.

Ginny opened the door, her worry plain on her pretty face. Alice smiled at her, wishing she could erase the discomfort in her daughter's life. For a while there, she'd thought she could protect her children from the harsh truths of the world with a lot of money. They did have a good life, with plenty of abundance and little to worry about.

But it wasn't enough.

She knew they didn't care about stuff; they wanted to be happy and safe at home. Alice had tried to give them that while Frank lived a completely different life. She hoped to be able to do it again, right here on Five Island Cove.

"Robin's talking about going down to the beach," she said. "She's on the phone with the jet ski rentals, and she gave me the thumbs up."

"That's a good idea," Alice said. "Charlie mentioned taking the volleyball net too."

"He's already got it loaded in the wagon." Ginny perched on the edge of the bed. "Are you okay? What was in that envelope?"

"I'm fine, dear," Alice said, using all of her strength to get out of the chair. Sitting on the beach in the warm sun would be all she could do that day. With the weekend looming, if she wanted to fight the hearing agenda Frank had filed, she'd have to do it today. She had a case number and a hearing code, and she could do it from her phone. She should've been taking snapshots of the document Frank had signed weeks ago and been uploading them for the past hour.

Alice found she simply didn't have the strength. The judge would still give her custody, and she'd still get child support. She might have to pay the mortgage on this house, and Alice wasn't sure how she could do that.

She gave Ginny another smile and gathered her daughter into a hug. "I love you, Ginny-bear."

"I know, Mom." Ginny hugged her back. "I love you too." She looked up at Alice. "I know something's wrong."

"Can you go get Charlie?"

Ginny's eyes widened, with more worry spilling into them. "Yeah." She got up and left the bedroom, and Alice took the opportunity to open the blackout curtains and let in the light. Perhaps that was all she needed to do—let in the light.

She took a deep breath, almost able to smell the sea air through the closed window. She knew this was where she was supposed to be, and she'd do whatever she had to in order to stay here and protect the twins.

"What's going on, Mom?" Charlie asked, and she turned toward her children as he closed the bedroom door. He really was devilishly handsome, and Alice had no doubt Mandie genuinely liked him.

"I have to go back to the Hamptons next week," she said, wrapping her arms around herself.

"Why?" Ginny asked, exchanging a glance with Charlie. He simply wore a frown on his mouth, his eyebrows folding over his dark eyes.

"Dad has requested a hearing," she said. "I tried to make the separation and divorce easy and amicable. He signed a document outlining what he'd pay for, and when, but he doesn't want to do that now." She spoke slowly and deliberately, trying to use the most neutral words she could. She didn't want to sway Ginny or Charlie in either direction.

"What does he want?" Charlie asked. "Will we have to live there?" He looked at Ginny, his fear plain. "I don't want to live in New York, Mom. Will the judge ask us?"

Alice held up her hand, wishing she wasn't in this situation at all. "You're most likely not going to live with him at all. We have a strong case for full custody with me. It's the house payment, the car payments, the alimony, all of that that he wants to contest." He hadn't changed the amount of child support, and she felt it her duty to tell them that. "About the only thing he didn't change was how much he'll provide for you two."

She opened her arms, and Ginny and Charlie stepped into them simultaneously. "He loves you," she whispered, though she honestly didn't know if it was true or not. "So don't worry about anything, okay? You haven't forgotten that I'm a lawyer, too, have you?"

"You should get everything you can from him, Mom," Charlie said, and the vitriol in his voice surprised Alice. She pulled away and looked at him, searching his face for clues to what he meant by that.

"Charlie?"

He looked at Ginny, who nodded. Alice flicked her gaze to Ginny too, and she looked white and like she might puke. "Tell her, Charlie."

Charlie drew in a deep breath and looked at Alice. He was taller than her now, but she felt like she still had to be the strong one out of the three of them. She did, because she was the adult, and she was their mother, and just because they were in big bodies now didn't mean they knew how to handle adult situations.

"Remember how you went to that PTA conference last year?"

"Yes," Alice said slowly.

"You were gone for maybe two days." Charlie swallowed and looked at Ginny again. "Dad had a woman over while you were gone. They stayed in the bedroom almost the whole time, and..."

Alice's heart beat against a hard stone. Or maybe her heart had become the stone. "And what?" She'd known Frank cheated on her in the city. But in their own home? With the children present?

"I had to get him to sign a permission form for this science experiment, so I went up there. I knocked, but no one came to the door."

"Dear Lord," Alice said, sinking onto the bed. "I don't want to know."

"I heard them having sex," Charlie blurted. "I'm sorry, Mom. I should've told you."

Alice pressed her eyes closed and shook her head. She would not cry in front of her children. Not over Frank and the terrible things he did. "You didn't do anything wrong," she managed to whisper.

She opened her eyes, so many things becoming clear. "Is that why you failed that biology unit?" She wished she'd never left for the PTA convention. "I thought you failed because you skipped class."

"I did skip class. I didn't have permission to do the dissection, so I didn't see the point in going," Charlie said, swiping at his eyes.

Alice's heart ached for her beautiful boy. She drew him onto the bed next to him and let him lean into her while he continued to sniffle.

"I hate him," Charlie said, his voice taking on a new strength.

"No," Alice said. "No, Charlie, you don't."

"I do," he said. "And I don't get how you don't."

"Who says I don't?" Alice squeezed her son's shoulder. "I will do everything I can to make sure we can stay together, right here on Five Island Cove. Okay?" She peered into her son's angry eyes and Ginny's scared ones.

They embraced again as Robin's voice came closer, and she said, "Yes, thank you," and Alice looked over Ginny's shoulder to see her best friend standing there, concern on her face.

"Jet skis?" Alice asked brightly.

"Yes," Robin said. "They have two, and we can pick them up in an hour."

"Great," Alice said as falsely as ever. "Let's get packed, guys. We can buy lunch at the beach today, but if you want something to drink, you better put it in a cooler and bring it."

She definitely needed something to drink, but she honestly couldn't think of something strong enough.

Ginny turned to leave, but Alice gripped Charlie's hand. "We need to talk about Mandie."

"Mom," Charlie said.

"Robin," Alice said. "Can you get Mandie? Let's get this over with so we can enjoy the day at the beach."

"Sure." Robin hurried away

Alice peered at her son. "You're a very good-looking boy, Charlie."

"Mom," he said again, ducking his head.

"We've had plenty of talks about sex," Alice said.

"Please, don't do that again. Not in front of a girl."

"How long has this been going on?"

"Not long."

Alice put her fingers under her son's chin and lifted it until he looked at her. "Define that."

"I kissed her yesterday for the first time."

"Did you even go surfing this morning?"

"Yes," he said. "We did. And it was fun. She's really nice, Mom, and she's cute, and *please* don't make a big deal out of this."

Alice shook her head, a smile crossing her face. "Charlie, you've met Robin, right? Even if I don't make a big deal out of this, you're kissing her daughter."

"Okay," Robin chirped, and she practically shoved

Mandie into the bedroom, followed her, and closed the door. "Don't just stand there," she bit out as she passed her daughter. "Come have a real conversation."

Robin shook her head at Alice, her irritation like a scent on the air. Alice tried to communicate with her silently, but Robin didn't seem to be getting the messages. They definitely handled things differently, that was for sure.

"One thing we can agree on," Alice said. "Is that we're worried about this relationship." She gestured between Mandie and Charlie.

"It's no big deal, Mom," Charlie said. "I've kissed other girls."

Beside her, Robin sucked in a breath. "I realize that," Alice said smoothly. "But this is a special circumstance, where Mandie is currently staying with us, Charlie. Living here. You realize that's a little different, right?"

"Right," he mumbled.

"Okay, so I think we need a couple of rules," Alice said, glancing at Robin. They probably should've come up with the rules together.

"Yes," Robin said as seamlessly as if they had rehearsed this conversation. "Number one, you'll still be able to see each other, obviously. But you shouldn't go off anywhere on your own, just the two of you." She looked at Alice, who nodded.

"Yes, that's a good one," Alice said.

"Fine," Mandie said, shooting daggers at her mother.

She and Charlie were definitely handling this differently too.

"But we like to go surfing in the morning," Charlie argued. "What are we supposed to do?"

"Take someone with you," Robin said. "I'm up early."

"Mom, no way," Mandie said.

"Then—"

"You'll have to figure something else out," Alice said over Robin. "Because that's the rule."

Charlie looked at Mandie, who looked back at him. "We could invite my sister."

Charlie shrugged and looked back at Alice. "What else?"

Alice glanced at Robin, hoping she'd have another rule, because Alice didn't.

"No hanging out in bedrooms," Robin said. "Each other's, empty ones, or anything like that."

"No late-night texting," Alice added. "You shouldn't be sending pictures to each other at all."

"I can live with all of that." Charlie looked one moment away from exploding, and Alice felt it wise to tie up this conversation quickly.

"So be smart," Alice said smoothly, as if they were talking about what kind of ice cream to buy at the store. "And we won't have to be on your case for the next couple of weeks."

"Longer than that," Robin said. "You guys live here now."

"You do?" Mandie looked at Charlie, who glanced at Alice.

"Oops," Robin said. "Sorry, Alice."

Alice waved her hand like it was no big deal. "I'm going to talk to everyone on Monday," she said. "So Mandie, if you could keep what your mother said to yourself for a few more days, I would appreciate it."

"Sure," Mandie said, nodding.

"Okay," Robin said. "You can go."

They both turned and left the master suite as quickly as possible, leaving the door open behind them.

"If this is how my mother felt," Robin murmured. "I owe her an apology."

Alice couldn't quite relate, because her mother had missed some of her teenage years. Her father had no doubt worried about her, but men and women were different, and there was nothing quite so strong as a mother's worry for her children.

Robin turned and hugged Alice. "I can't imagine going through this alone. Thanks for being so level-headed about the whole thing."

Alice just held her tight, hoping and praying that she could weather the storms ahead in a respectable way. Because there was definitely dark clouds on the horizon.

"Okay, got everything?" she asked Charlie and Ginny the next morning. "Grandpa is taking us out on the boat today."

"We've got everything," Ginny said, hitching her mini backpack over her shoulders.

"Sunscreen? Hats?" Alice picked up her purse, feeling torn in several directions. She'd been up for a large part of the night, going through receipts in her online credit card statements, printing documents, and putting together her case for the hearing on Tuesday.

Every time she wavered on what she was doing, she remembered Charlie's voice saying he hated his father and that Alice needed to get everything she could from Frank. Something had come alive in Alice after everyone else had gone to bed, and she had a folder a half-inch thick with evidence and proof of Frank's lavish expenditures, his mistreatment of her and the kids, and more.

He wanted to renege on the agreement he'd signed? She'd bring everything she had, and while he may have forgotten that she'd worked in a family law firm, Alice had only been rusty in her research skills for about ten minutes. After that, she knew how to pull statements, how to search accounts, and how to spin things to put her in a positive light and everything Frank had done for the past fifteen years in a negative one.

"Let's go, girls." Eloise paused in front of Alice. "I don't know if we'll be back for dinner tonight. Can I text you later?"

Alice blinked, trying to focus on her friend. "Yes. Yeah, sure."

Eloise smiled and herded Billie and Grace toward the front door. She'd brought Aaron's girls back to the house last night, because he had to work today, and they wanted to be with the other kids last night. She was taking them to her mother's today. Kelli was taking the long ferry ride over to Bell to see her mom and her new boyfriend, something everyone had gasped at last night.

Robin was taking her girls back to Diamond Island, but Alice didn't know if they had plans or if they'd just hang out at home for some peace and quiet. AJ had a date with her new boyfriend, DJ, and she was bringing him back to the house that night for dinner.

It was Alice's turn to cook, and she was planning to invite her father and Della too. She had so many plans for the day, including telling her dad about her pending divorce. Her stomach tightened, and Alice hadn't eaten much of anything for a couple of days now. Since those papers had come, she'd been subsisting on coffee, mocktails, and a few sips of a protein shake.

"We have everything," Ginny said, bringing Alice back to the present. "Let's go." She marched out the door that led into the garage, and Charlie glanced at Alice as he went by.

"She's right, Mom. Grandpa has all that stuff on his boat."

"Right," Alice said. "Of course he does."

Her father loved boats more than almost anything, and Alice loved that about him. The drive to his house overlooking the black sand beach only took ten minutes, and a half an hour later, they were all piled on the boat and setting out into the sea.

Della handed Alice a cold can of diet soda and said, "You seem good, Alice."

"Thank you, Della," she said, her voice easily sliding into the political one she used when conducting PTA meetings. "So do you." She smiled at her step-mom. "How's my dad?" She nodded to where he showed Charlie something with one of the ties.

"He's slowing down a little," Della said. "Thank goodness."

Alice chuckled with her, because she knew the drive her father had. He'd never hired anyone to do anything he could do himself. He worked constantly, either at his job or around the house, and she'd learned a lot about dedication and hard work from him.

"Have you seen Scott lately?" Della asked.

Surprised by the question, Alice turned toward Della more fully so she could see her face better. "No, but I talk to him fairly often." Her brother lived on Pearl Island, and he'd moved the family real estate business there about the same time her dad had married Della.

Alice had never quite thought of the two events in that order, and she wondered if there was more to that story. "Why?" she asked.

Della wore tightness around her mouth, and she glanced over to Alice's father. "He stopped answering your father's texts and calls about a month ago. We're awfully worried about him."

Alice frowned, her mind flying through the past few weeks. "I invited him to sit by us at the classic car parade," she said. "He said he was too busy, but he responded."

"Good," Della said. "I don't need you to ask him anything. Connor would not be happy with me if you did. I just know he's very worried something's happened or he did something to upset Scott."

"What could he possibly have done? Does he have an idea?"

Della shook her head as her husband turned toward them. He left Charlie to fish over the side of the boat and joined Della and Alice. "What are you two gossiping about?"

"Nothing," Della said with a smile as he slipped his arm around her waist.

Alice took a sip of her cola, the taste much too bitter. "I have to tell you guys something," she said. She hadn't told very many people about her decision to file for divorce. Her friends in the Hamptons had made all of their assumptions when the packing crate had shown up, and out of her real friends, she'd only told Robin.

But she'd already had two very hard conversations this morning, and she took a big breath. "I filed for divorce several weeks ago. The twins and I have moved here.

We're going to live in the house on the other side of Rocky Ridge."

She looked first at her father, unsure about what she'd find on his face.

Surprise, sure. Everything softened after that, and he drew her into a big bear hug that she'd missed so much. "It's about time," he whispered. "Praise the Lord that man can't hurt you anymore."

Alice wasn't so sure about that, but she did gain a bit of strength and confidence from her father's reaction, and she breathed in the comforting, if a little fishy, smell of the man who had never abandoned her.

It was so good to have somewhere—and someone—to call home.

CHAPTER EIGHTEEN

Kelli held Parker's hand as they disembarked from the ferry. Her mother waited on the other side of the pylons, and Kelli smiled at her. She scanned the nearby crowd for a man, but she didn't see anyone.

"Grandma," Parker said, and he let go of Kelli's hand and ducked under the rope keeping people from the ramp.

"Parker," Kelli said, nerves shooting through her. No one cared what he'd done though, and her mother laughed as she scooped him into a hug. Kelli went around the barriers and ropes the way Parker should've, and she hugged her mother too.

"It's good to see you guys," she said. "How was the ferry ride?"

"Long," Kelli said.

"But we saw a whale," Parker said.

Kelli smiled and shook her head at her mother. It was maybe a whitecap, but definitely not a whale. Her mom beamed down at Parker anyway and said, "Really? What kind of whale?"

As her son started chattering about the different kind of whales—he was obsessed with the sea—Kelli simply followed her mother out of the ferry station. She'd spent an hour going through the letters from her father to Zach at breakfast yesterday, and she had gotten to know him a little bit better.

She'd shared some things with Zach too, when he'd ask if her father always capitalized his R's, or if he always ate coffee and toast for breakfast. She'd said that yes, he'd always done both of those things. *He's a creature of habit*, she'd told him.

She'd realized then that so was she. That was why little things that didn't happen according to plan stressed her out.

"Should we head over to the park?" her mom asked as they reached her car. "The balloons are already up, but they have live demos, food, and games."

"Yes," Kelli said. "Let's head to the park." She enjoyed the leisurely drive, as her mother never, ever went over the speed limit. She twirled one finger through a lock of her hair and watched the water on her side of the car as her mom continued to ask Parker questions.

"Did you stand up on the surf board?" she asked.

"No," Parker said. "I couldn't do it, but Charlie said he's

going to take me again, and he's sure I'll get it before we have to leave."

"Hmm," her mom said. "Surfing is hard."

Kelli had been thrilled when Charlie had invited Parker to go surfing with him and Mandie that morning, because it had made Parker so happy. He was the youngest of the kids at the house, even now that Billie and Grace had come to spend a couple of nights with Eloise. None of the other girls in the house wanted to go, but Parker had set his own alarm, gotten up and gotten himself dressed, and met Charlie and Mandie downstairs.

Kelli had enjoyed a couple extra hours of sleep, as she'd had a hard time settling down the night before. Her mind never seemed to turn off.

"Are you coming, dear?"

Kelli glanced over to find her mom leaning down into the car. She'd already gotten out; they'd parked.

"Oh." Kelli quickly unbuckled her seatbelt. "Yeah." She grabbed her purse and opened the door, the sun beating down on this section of asphalt. It would be cooler on the grass, and Kelli quickly caught up to her mother and Parker.

"Look at that one, Mom," Parker said "It looks like a bear."

Kelli gazed up into the sky, the variety of balloons taking her breath away. She couldn't imagine being in one of those baskets, so high above the ground with nothing to cushion her fall. They all seemed way too close to each other too, and one big gust of wind would send them knocking into one another.

The gas in the tanks would explode, and hot air balloon parts would come raining down on Bell Island.

Kelli's anxiety could really be applied to anything.

"Let's get a drink," her mom said, leading them to a lemonade stand. She ordered for all three of them, not bothering to ask what they wanted, though they had fruity flavors and syrup mix-ins.

They got plain lemonade, and Kelli sipped hers and smiled, though it was too tart. "Thanks, Mom."

"We invite everyone to gather 'round," someone said into a microphone. "We're going to do a twenty-minute demo on how to launch a balloon. Kids up front, if they want to help."

Parker turned back to Kelli, questions in his eyes. She nodded, and he skipped ahead of them to the front of the crowd.

Kelli didn't care how to launch a balloon, so she stayed off to the side, a few rows back, her eyes on Parker and the demo at the same time. Her mother stood beside her, and Kelli found she didn't have much to say to her.

Why she didn't have much to say, she didn't know.

"How's Julian?" her mom asked.

"Good," Kelli said. "So busy at work." She flashed her mom a smile. She hadn't been back to the cove in a long time, but Julian had literally only been in Five Island Cove one time—for the island wedding reception she'd insisted they have.

Her mother had grown up here, and she had a lot of friends still. Kelli hadn't wanted to deny her the chance to celebrate with them. Heather hadn't provided that same opportunity, and Kelli had never regretted the decision to have a reception here though she and Julian had been married in New Jersey.

"The courier business must be good," her mom said.

"It is," Kelli said, though she still didn't have much cash flow. "We're buying out a company, actually."

"You are?" The surprise in her mother's voice wasn't hard to hear. Kelli also felt a little disingenuous saying "we're," as if she had anything to do with Julian's business at all.

You do, she told herself. *Your name is on the loan too.*

Her mom wanted to know all about that, and Kelli stayed on the safe topic of conversation. She didn't have many when it came to her mom—the weather, their jobs, Parker—so she'd take what she could get.

The demo ended, and they wandered through the park, looking at old hot air balloons, and watching a video on the history of their invention and uses.

"What do you think, Parker?" she finally asked. "Should we go get lunch?"

"Can we go to The Kaleidoscope Café?" he asked. "I love that tri-color shell mac and cheese."

Her mom smiled at him and ruffled his hair. "How did

I know you were going to say that?" They laughed together, and Kelli had a vision of what life could be like if she lived in the cove.

She could not fathom coming back here. Even the two weeks here, which did do something to smooth out the ragged edges of her soul, were difficult enough. She thought about why as her mom drove them over to The Kaleidoscope Café.

Julian waited at the top of the list for why it was hard for Kelli to come to the cove. Dealing with memories of her life here. Seeing people she knew in high school. The woman on the ferry when she'd arrived was a good example of the kind of treatment Kelli didn't need in her life.

She didn't like boats, and she didn't want to go back to her childhood home. Everything combined made it so much easier to stay in New Jersey.

"Okay," her mom said as she eased into a parking spot. "They look pretty busy, but I had someone come over early and put us on the list."

Kelli looked at her mother, and she seemed so different. She looked the same on the outside—her light hair had settled into a beautiful shade of gray, and she'd stopped coloring it. She had blue eyes like Kelli, and it had been a long time since Kelli had seen the sparkle in them that she beheld now.

"You're going to meet him," she said to Parker in the back seat. "His name is Devon, and he's my boyfriend."

Kelli wasn't sure if Parker understood completely the meaning of the word boyfriend, or that it was a little odd for someone her mother's age to have one. He just said, "Okay," and got out of the car.

Her mom met her eyes, a hint of worry in hers. "Are you ready for this?"

"Are you?" Kelli asked, smiling. "It's fine, Mom. You're allowed to date."

"I know," she said. "It just feels a little bit odd, introducing my boyfriend to my daughter. I don't even think I've ever used the word boyfriend before." She shook her head and got out of the car too.

Kelli followed them, choosing to fade into the background so Parker could have the limelight with his grandmother. They went inside the restaurant, and a man stood from the chair immediately next to the door.

"Sharon," he said, his voice deep and rich. He smiled at her mom and leaned down to give her a quick peck on the cheek. "You made it."

"Yes," she said, moving to his side. "Devon, this is my daughter, Kelli. The middle one."

"So pleased to meet you," Devon said, extending his hand for Kelli to shake. He had a good air about him, and Kelli liked him instantly. She smiled and shook his hand.

"And my grandson," her mom said, pride filling her voice. "Parker."

"Hey, buddy," Devon said. "Do you shake, or do the knuckle bump, or do we just say hi?"

Parker simply looked at him, then to Kelli. "Say hello," she prompted. "Bump his knuckles. Something."

Parker held out his fist, and Devon bumped it with his, a smile spreading across his face. He turned to her mother. "They said twenty minutes when I got here about twenty minutes ago."

"Perfect timing then," her mom said. "Why don't you tell Kelli a little bit about what you did on the mainland?"

"I was a real estate agent," he said. "Mostly in Long Island, but sometimes into the city and even over on the Jersey side of the river."

"That's where Kelli lives," her mom said. "Newark."

"Oh, yeah," Devon said easily. "Great town."

It was way more than a town, but Kelli just nodded. "Do you have kids, Devon?" she asked.

"Yes,' he said. "My wife died about eight years ago. I've got two sons. They both run the real estate company my grandfather founded."

"And you came to Five island Cove?"

"Yes," he said. "About five years ago now. I'd been here before; sold a couple of things back in the day. I've always liked it here."

"And you live on Bell?"

"Just around the corner from you mother," he said, grinning at her. "Took me five years to find her, though."

She smiled back at him, and Kelli wondered if she'd ever looked at Julian the way her mom was currently looking at Devon. She held so much adoration in her gaze, and Kelli figured she probably had felt like that about Julian at some point in the past. Now, it seemed like they connected better when they were apart. She couldn't remember the last time she'd been able to look straight into Julian's eyes.

Perhaps when he made love to her, she did. Even then, he usually had his closed. The only time he didn't was when he was about to reach his climax. Then he'd look her in the eye with pure passion in his gaze.

She pushed the images out of her mind, because she didn't need to be thinking about intimate things in her present company.

They waited at least ten more minutes, but Devon didn't get up and go ask why they hadn't gotten a table yet. He didn't even seem to notice that it had been longer than the hostess had said. If that had happened to her dad, he'd have marched over to the podium and demanded to be the next group taken to a table.

Kelli hated how he seemed to crop up in her memories no matter where she went. Of course, The Kaleidoscope Café was iconic on Bell Island, and they'd come here many times to eat as a family—at least before her father had lost everything.

After that, they barely had enough food at home to survive. It hadn't been for the free breakfast and lunch program offered through the school system, Kelli felt sure she or one of her sisters would've starved.

"I'm going to go see what's taking so long," she said at

the next lull in the conversation. She left her mom sitting with Devon and Parker and approached the hostess stand. She couldn't believe what she was doing

She'd turned into her dad.

Spinning away from the woman behind the podium, she headed back to the long bench where everyone sat. Devon looked at her, his dark eyes full of questions. He'd probably once had a full head of dark hair too, but now, only streaks of it remained. He seemed too big for Five Island Cove, as he was tall and broad-shouldered.

"They said it'll be soon," she said, though if they'd been watching, her mom and Devon would know she hadn't actually talked to anyone.

"Devon," a woman called, and Kelli breathed a sigh of relief. Everyone stood, and Kelli did what Kelli was best at —she went last.

"How's the gym, dear?" her mom asked once they had menus. "Kelli works as an aerobics instructor."

"Is that right?" Devon asked.

Kelli nodded and put down her menu. She knew what she wanted, as she'd been here many times before. So had Parker, and he hadn't looked at his menu either. "How did you two meet?"

Her mother giggled—actually giggled—and looked at Devon. "You tell it. It's so much better when you tell it."

Kelli focused on Devon, though she really wanted to keep analyzing her mother. She hadn't seen so much happiness on her mom's face in years. Decades. She seemed like a completely different person, one who was younger, more vibrant, and faced with a fresh outlook on life.

"It all started at the grocery store," Devon said, and Kelli settled in to listen to the tale of a missing wallet—her mother's—and the kind stranger who'd helped her find it—Devon.

"And we've been seeing each other since," Devon said. "It's been what? A couple of months now." He looked at her mom, who smiled and shook her head.

"I love that your sense of time is so bad," she said. She looked at Kelli, and once again, Kelli had that jagged hook of jealousy pulling through her.

Her mom was so happy, and Kelli wanted even one iota of that happiness for herself. "It's been a month, Kel. Our first day was actually May sixteenth, so come tomorrow, it will have been exactly one month."

With the two of them smiling at each other, Kelli almost felt like she shouldn't be there. Thankfully, Parker had entertained himself on his portable game machine, and Kelli looked at her phone, willing it to ring.

To her surprise, it did, and Julian's name came up on the screen. "Oh, it's Julian," she said to her mother. "I've got to get this." She swiped on the call and lifted the phone to her ear. "Hey, babe."

"You've got that delivery for Rogers and Roy, right?" he said, and Kelli knew he'd dialed her by mistake. "And listen, for tonight, just stop and get the Chinese you want and come over. We can go over the proposal and talk strat for the big day."

"Julian," she said. "It's Kelli."

"Kelli?" Scuffling came through his end of the line. Then a quick laugh that sounded flustered. "Sorry, hon. I meant to dial Tiff."

"Clearly," Kelli said with a plastic smile in place for her mom and Devon. She'd had to identify herself to her own husband. How embarrassing. "When are you doing the proposal?"

"Next Thursday," he said.

"Is that the big day?"

Julian didn't answer right away, and the next thing he said annoyed her. "Kel, Tiff's calling in. I have to go, okay?"

"Okay," she said, but he'd already gone. No *I love you*. No, *hey let's call again tonight at eleven-thirty*. "Sure," she said as if the conversation were still happening. "If you want to, it's fine with me."

Her mind whirred, and she realized she needed to figure out who Tiff was and what kind of relationship she had with Julian. He'd just told her to bring the Chinese food she liked, and Kelli assumed that "come over" meant Tiff would be in her house, with her husband, that night.

Her stomach boiled, but she put in her order for chicken fried steak anyway, knowing she'd probably eat four bites and be too sick to continue.

She said good-bye as if the call had just ended, and added, "Sorry," for her mom and Devon. "He just needs me to send a quick text..." Her thumbs flew over her screen as she pulled up a delivery biker she'd gotten to know while she worked in Julian's office.

Hey, Sabra, she tapped out. *Been hearing Julian talk about Tiff a lot. Who is she? One of his new assistants?*

Julian went through assistants like he went though underwear. If it wasn't just the right fit, he got rid of them. He had strong opinions and a specific way he liked things done. She could hear the tone of his voice in the call just now, and it seemed like he was sort of...apologetic to Tiff? Telling her she could come over and bring the food she liked...if she'd just come.

Yeah, Sabra said back. *She's assisting him.*

Kelli waited for more, because Sabra loved to gossip, and if there was something to know about Tiff, she'd know it and want to tell Kelli about it. But another text didn't come in.

And? she prompted. *Do we like her? Hate her? Wish we could be her?*

Sabra didn't answer, and Kelli put her phone away once the food came. The conversation was some of the easiest Kelli had ever had with her mother, and by the time she and Parker were getting dropped off at the ferry station for the monster ride back to Rocky Ridge, Kelli almost didn't want to go.

On the ferry, her phone finally chimed again, and she glanced at it. From Sabra: *You are her, Kelli.*

She frowned because she had no idea what that

meant. She asked Sabra, but the woman never answered back. Her stomach became a snake pit, and she chewed her fingernails the rest of the way back to Rocky Ridge.

Something was wrong, but Kelli was having a hard time distinguishing what, and with who. The old Kelli would've ignored it and gone on with her life-lived-in-the-shadows.

But Kelli had found her voice in the past few days, and she wanted to use it. So she thumbed out another text and sent it.

To Julian: *Who's Tiffany? I'd like to know who she is, what she does for you, and why she's bringing dinner to the house tonight.*

CHAPTER NINETEEN

Eloise watched Grace lean over the side of the ferry, wondering at what point she tried to stop the little girl. She didn't know how to be their mother, and she didn't want to discipline them or disappoint them.

"Stop it," Billie said, pulling on her sister's shoulder. "You're going to fall over."

"No, I'm not," Grace said, scowling at her sister. She glanced at Eloise, who just raised her eyebrows. Grace settled solidly on her feet and didn't lean over the side of the ferry again.

"What should we do after lunch with my mother?" Eloise asked. She'd had the girls with her since last night, and she enjoyed spending time with them.

Billie had begged Aaron to go with Eloise as they started to leave the beach yesterday afternoon, because he'd had to work most of the day today. Eloise had only said one thing, "I'm happy to take them, Aaron."

"We're just going to be sitting around at Linda's," Billie said. "It's lame there, Dad. She doesn't even let us watch more than an hour of TV."

Aaron had said that was good for them, that they should be outside or doing something more useful than staring at a screen. In the end, though, Billie had won. In a lot of ways, Eloise felt like she'd won too.

It had been quite the process to get the girls back to Diamond Island to get clothes and toiletries, as well as Grace's favorite blanket and stuffed animal. Then Aaron had to bring them back to Rocky Ridge. The whole thing had taken a couple of hours, and by the time that was done, and dinner eaten, Eloise had only a few minutes alone with Aaron on the front porch before he had to leave to catch the last ferry home.

He'd made the most of them though, that was for sure. Eloise had never been kissed quite like the way he'd kissed her last night, and her mind had taken dozens of detours in the past twelve hours.

"The beach," Grace said.

"We go to the beach every day," Billie said, taking the seat next to Eloise. "I'm sick of the beach."

Eloise glanced at the girl. "You live on a series of islands. How can you hate the beach?"

"I don't know." The girl shrugged and stared out over the water. "Do you like living in Boston, Eloise?"

"Sure," Eloise said. "It's a great city."

"I want to go to the city." Billie sighed and propped her elbow up on the side of the ferry.

"Sweetie," Eloise said gently. "What are you unhappy about?"

Billie turned toward her, her eyes widening with a bit of surprise. "I don't know. I'm sick of summer already."

"Hmm." Eloise bent down and reached into her purse. She always kept a notebook with her, just in case. Her fingers found the hard binding of it, and she pulled it out. "Maybe you need to find something you really love to do." She handed the notebook to Billie.

"What's this?"

"It's a notebook. I take it with me everywhere, just in case."

"In case of what?" Billie looked intrigued.

Eloise glanced to where Grace still stood a few feet away. She wasn't leaning over anymore, and she was listening. "In case of anything. I write down little notes in it about things that inspire me." She nodded for the girl to open it. "You won that writing contest last year, right? Maybe you need a notebook to write down story ideas."

Billie opened the notebook and started reading. Eloise couldn't remember all the things she'd written in the book —that was the whole point. When lightning struck, she wanted to bottle it. The notebook did that.

She flipped a page, and then another. "This one's practically empty," she said, looking up.

"I have dozens of them," Eloise said. "From throughout the years."

Billie started to hand it back to her, but Eloise shook her head. "You keep it. Maybe you'll get an idea for a mermaid adventure, about a little girl who leans too far over the side of the ferry, falls into the water, and gets saved by mermaids deep in the sea." She smiled at Grace, who grinned back at her.

"Do you really think there's mermaids down there?" She turned back to the railing and tipped up onto her toes.

"No," Billie said. "Don't be dumb, Grace."

"There could be," Eloise said, giving Billie a look that told her not to kill fantasies. "I mean, I've read books about mermaids."

"Fiction," Billie said.

"Sure," Eloise said. "But fiction is a great escape. It's fun to go somewhere and experience something outside your realm of normal." She kept her voice easy and light, and she caught Billie looking back at the notebook. "Do you want a pen?" she asked.

Billie just nodded, and Eloise dug in her purse for that too. After handing it to Billie, she said, "We really do need a plan for this afternoon. Otherwise, my mother will want us to come back to her house, and if you think Linda's is lame..."

Grace turned and looked from her sister to Eloise.

"Could we just gather shells? I'm making a necklace for Lily."

"Who's Lily?" Eloise asked, patting her lap as an invitation for the girl to come sit with her. She did, thankfully, because then Eloise didn't have to worry about her spilling over the side and losing her to mermaids. She wouldn't know how to tell Aaron about that.

"She lives around the corner from us," Grace said, settling onto Eloise's lap. "Her birthday is coming up, and Daddy said I could make her a shell necklace."

"If we can get Billie to the beach, we can look for shells." She glanced at Billie, but the older girl didn't even look up. "I know," Eloise added. "There's a great place that hardly anyone knows about. You have to go out in the water and around this cliff to get to it."

"We didn't bring swimming suits," Grace said, her face full of alarm. "We'll get wet."

"Yes," Eloise said, smiling. "That's part of the adventure. It's called Smugglers Cove."

"That's not a real place," Billie said, finally looking up.

"Yes, it is," Eloise said as she smiled at Billie. "I've been there. We should go. There are tons of shells, and lots of shade too, Bills." She couldn't believe the nickname Aaron used for Billie had come out of her mouth, but it just had. It felt natural, too, and neither Billie nor Grace reacted to it.

"I'll go," Grace said. "But you have to tell Daddy why our clothes are wet."

"I can handle your dad," Eloise said. "He said he'd meet us somewhere for dinner. Do we want to go to Diamond Island? Or have him come to Sanctuary? Or go back to Rocky Ridge? There will be dinner at the house, too. Alice is cooking, which means she'll probably order something." Eloise wasn't used to making group decisions, but she wanted the girls to have an amazing day, and she hoped that by them giving input to what they did that day would help.

"I thought that place AJ was talking about sounded good," Billie said, tucking the pen inside the notebook. "Can I put this in your purse?"

"Of course." She waited while Billie did that. "The bistro?"

"That too, but she said there's this restaurant up on top of one of the ridges? Lookout Point, maybe?"

"Oh, right," Eloise said. "Lookout Point. It is a fancy restaurant on the highest point on Rocky Ridge. We better call to see if we need a reservation. I think they're pretty upscale." AJ had mentioned the place last night, while they'd eaten the dinner Kelli had provided. It was a simple meal of hot dogs, cole slaw, and potato chips, but no one had complained.

Eloise was supposed to make dinner on Sunday, but Kristen had invited them all to the lighthouse for a clam bake, so she'd dodged the bullet. It wasn't really that big of a bullet in the first place. She'd just order something and have it delivered, like she'd done a few days ago.

"Can you call?" Billie asked.

"Sure." Eloise nudged Grace off her lap, and she took the seat beside her while Eloise did a quick search on her phone. She dialed Lookout Point and smiled at Billie. When a man answered, she said, "Yes, hello, this is Eloise Hall, and I'm wondering if we need a reservation to come for dinner tonight."

"Yes," the man said. "But unfortunately, we're booked for tonight. Our next available date is Thursday of next week."

"You're booked until next Thursday?"

"Yes," he said, his voice taking on an air of importance. "For dinner at least. Our lunch schedule is a little more open."

"I see." She shook her head at Billie. "I'll have to call you back." She hung up, barely hanging onto her giggles.

"What's so funny?" Billie asked, smiling too.

"He was so stuffy," Eloise said. "They're booked until next Thursday, Bills. I don't think we want to go there."

"AJ said it was good."

"She hasn't even been," Eloise said. "She said she thought she'd like DJ to take her there, because it would be romantic." AJ thrived on the romance of things, Eloise knew that. Dinner could be disgusting, but if it happened on top of a cliff, at a place that required almost a week's advance reservation, AJ would gush about it for decades.

A thought ran through her mind, and Eloise bent to get out her notebook. "I just have to write one more thing in this," she said. "We should stop by the drug store and get a couple of new notebooks too." She looked at Grace. "Do you want one?"

"Sure," she said. "I can do my drawings in them."

"Good idea," Eloise said, quickly scrawling a note about providing a dining experience at the Cliffside Inn that would have women like AJ calling for reservations weeks and months in advance.

How she could make that happen, Eloise didn't know. She put the inn out of her mind as she and the girls disembarked, because she had to face her mother soon. Somehow, her mom always knew what Eloise was thinking, and she didn't want the Cliffside Inn to be anywhere near the front of her mind.

"There she is," Eloise said when she caught sight of her mother. Sudden nerves attacked her, and she hoped her mom would be on her best behavior today. She always was, and Eloise knew that the real reason she was so anxious was because she had Aaron's girls with her.

She approached her mother, who'd obviously just gotten a hair cut. The silver on top had not been dyed black the way it usually was, and Eloise liked the new look. "Hey, Mom." She stepped into her and hugged her. "Your hair looks great."

"You think so?" She patted Eloise on the back and stepped away. "I decided not to color it anymore. It's too much upkeep."

"It's perfect," Eloise said. "I like it short too." She reached to finger he hair. "Maybe I should cut mine."

"I like yours," Billie said. "I wish I could get mine to grow longer."

Eloise looked at her and smiled. "Thanks, Bills. This is my mother, Dawn. Mom, this is Billie Sherman, and her little sister, Grace."

"Billie and Grace." Her mom beamed at them as if they were her biological granddaughters. "Aaron Sherman's girls, right?"

"Yes," Billie said. "Do you know my dad?"

"Everyone knows your dad, sweetie," her mom said. "He's the Chief of Police." She threw Eloise a look. "I don't know him, really, but I know who he is. Plus, Eloise has told me a lot about him."

Not entirely true, but Eloise appreciated that her mom had said so. She'd stayed with her mother each of the three times she'd come to visit Aaron in the cove, so she had told her mother about Aaron. Just not much about their relationship.

"I heard a rumor that you girls like pasta," she said, walking up the sidewalk. "And it just so happens that I have the best spaghetti and meatball recipe in the cove."

"You do?" Grace asked, and Eloise caught the tail end of Billie's scowl. The older girl didn't say anything though, and Eloise was glad for that.

"That's right," her mom said. "I whipped up a batch, and it's waiting for us at the house."

"Let's go!" Grace said, skipping ahead of them all. Eloise laughed, and she startled when Billie put her hand in hers. Their eyes met, and Eloise saw something there she'd never seen in the girl before.

Nerves.

She slowed her step to put a little distance between them and her mom. "What's wrong?"

"Eloise." She stopped walking completely. "Are you going to be my mom?"

Eloise blinked, the shock running through her in powerful waves. "I don't know, sweetie." She didn't know what else to say. That was an impossible question, and she thought back to what Aaron had said about not saying I-do if there were any maybe's. She still didn't have any about him, and he'd been kissing her differently this trip than any of the others, so Eloise liked to believe he didn't have any maybe's about her either.

"What do you think?" she finally asked, throwing a glance to the parking lot, where her mother had paused with Grace. "Would you like me to be your mom?"

"I can hardly remember her," Billie said, staring at the ground "And Grace doesn't at all. Sometimes...I don't know. Sometimes I miss her, and it makes no sense." She looked up into Eloise's eyes. "I think you'd be a good mom. One who doesn't leave in the middle of the night or forget to send birthday cards or—" She stopped as her eyes filled with tears. "Not want to be a mom at all." They splashed down her face, and Eloise's heart cracked right in half.

"Oh, don't cry," she whispered, pulling the girl to her chest and holding her tight. She had no idea who Carol had been and if she really hadn't wanted to be a mother. Eloise had wanted children and couldn't have them, so she'd stunted the nurturing, maternal part of her heart. But now, with Aaron's girls, it seemed to be growing and pulsing with new life every single day.

Billie finally stepped back and wiped her face. "Sorry."

"You don't need to be sorry for anything." Eloise reached into her purse and pulled out a travel-sized package of tissues. "Here you go."

"You have everything in that bag," Billie said, taking the packet.

"I've learned a thing or two in my time," Eloise said. "I never go anywhere without the essentials." She smiled at Billie as warmly as she could. "I don't know everything, Bills. But I know I like your dad a whole lot, and I love spending time with you and Grace. Maybe I'm afraid to hope I could be your mom one day, so I haven't really thought about it much."

"Why would you be afraid of that?" Billie looked at her with such innocent eyes, and she seemed half as old as her twelve-year-old self. Eloise knew it was because she'd experienced trauma, and she still needed time to heal from it. She should probably mention that to Aaron, who had said he'd put Billie in therapy previously.

"It's a big job," Eloise said. "Being a mom. And people make mistakes, and then kids get hurt, and I don't want to do that." Her own emotions wavered, but she stuck a brave smile on her face, hoping the girl would understand.

Billie finished wiping her eyes and dropped everything into Eloise's purse. "Thanks, Eloise."

"Anytime, Bills." She took her hand again, and they continued toward her mom and Grace. "I am so ready for spaghetti," she said brightly, giving her mom a quick shake of her head. She'd tell her everything later, a strong sense of forgiveness for her mom—and her dad—moving through her. They'd done the best they could, with what they knew at the time. She hadn't known it until ten seconds ago, standing on the sidewalk with a weeping Billie.

But she knew it now.

They were human too. They didn't know everything. They'd done their best—just like she was going to do.

———————

That night, Aaron arrived only moments before Alice said, "All right, dinner's ready. Start gathering in the dining area, please." Her loud voice carried into the foyer where Eloise stood in Aaron's arms.

"Hey," he said gently, putting both hands on her shoulders and moving her back. "Something's wrong. What's wrong?" He peered into her face, searching for the answer. He was a very good cop, but this wasn't something he could find a clue to.

"You have the best daughters in the whole world," Eloise whispered, closing her eyes and inhaling the scent of him. He smelled like the sea, and cotton, and his woodsy cologne. She fell a little more in love with him in that moment, especially when he took her into his arms again and held her right against his heart.

"You had a good day, then?"

"Yes," she said. "Grace wants to tell you all about Smugglers Cove, and Billie got a new notebook and she's two chapters into her first book. We ate spaghetti with my mom, and I didn't want to gouge out my eyes, and something else happened with Billie." She wanted to tell Aaron, despite Billie asking her not to. She definitely needed to mention something about getting the girl some additional therapy.

"We're eating, Eloise," Alice called. "When you're ready."

She stepped back and twisted toward Alice. "Be right there." She looked at Aaron again, who wore stern concern on his face. "Not right now. Everything is fine."

"What happened?"

"I just said I can't tell you right now."

"Daddy!" Grace came running toward her father, and Eloise got out of the way so he could scoop her into his arms and hug her. Billie entered the foyer too, much more sober though still smiling.

Eloise smiled and nodded at her, their secret code for *I didn't tell him.* Billie hugged her father too, while Grace chattered about Smugglers Cove and the "dozens and dozens" of shells she'd found.

"They're eating," Eloise said. "We should go join everyone." They did, and Eloise stood back with Aaron to take in the mass of people. Alice's house could hold them all, that wasn't the problem.

There was no problem. Eloise simply wanted to bask in the warm, accepting feeling that permeated the house. Alice had brought her father and step-mother for dinner that night, and Kelli had invited Zach. AJ had brought DJ, and he looked a little shell-shocked as Robin quipped something at her daughter, who argued back.

Aaron stepped into the fray with, "What do we have here?"

"It's a soup, salad, and sandwich bar," Alice said. "Make your own. There's room in here to eat, and tables outside poolside as well."

Alice definitely knew how to host a party, and she practically glowed under the lights in the kitchen. Eloise stayed out of the way, watching everyone as they got their food and found a place to sit. Alice joined her, and the two said nothing to one another. They simply existed in the same space, and it was calm and peaceful and perfect.

Eloise eventually filled a plate with salad and took a

bowl of clam chowder outside where Aaron and his girls had gone. She noticed that Alice didn't get a plate at all, but joined the table with a bowl of chicken noodle soup that she only took three bites of.

Something was going on with her, but Eloise wouldn't ask her in front of everyone. She would find out, though, because she cared about Alice, and she'd been nothing but supportive of Eloise and everything that had happened in the past couple of months.

"Wait, wait," Alice said, interrupting Grace's tales about the seashells. "Eloise took *you* to Smugglers Cove?" She looked at Eloise with surprise in her eyes. "She has never taken me there, even when I ask."

"It's so cool, Alice," Grace said. "You have to go."

Eloise looked steadily back at Alice, the mood playful but serious at the same time. She could see the questions in Alice's eyes, and she didn't want to answer them.

"First rights," she murmured and returned to the conversation just as Billie started telling her father about the book she'd started writing.

"Tell-All," Alice murmured back.

"No," Eloise said, lifting her head as fire shot through her.

"New truth then," Alice said.

Eloise shook her head. "I've already told all, Alice. You already know everything."

She glanced at Aaron and his girls, and Eloise did too. They seemed to suddenly be on the other side of a piece of thick, cloudy glass. The noise they made and the things they said faded into silence, though she could still see them talking, and laughing, and eating.

"I think there's more," Alice said, and Eloise heard that.

"More than me falling in love with him and wanting to be their mother?"

"And there it is," Alice said, smiling. She leaned away from her uneaten soup. "I fully expect you to take me to Smugglers Cove before you go back to Boston."

Eloise shot one more glance at Aaron. "No problem," she said. "The price for entry is the real reason why you haven't eaten in days."

Alice's face blanched, and she looked away quickly. "Kristen said—"

"This is *not* about what Kristen has to show you," Eloise said.

Alice swallowed and met Eloise's eye again. She shook her head, real turmoil on her face. Much more than Eloise had ever seen before. She folded her arms as if that would hold everything that made Alice Kelton who she was inside, as if she were deathly afraid to lose it all.

Eloise knew exactly how she felt. If she quit her job at BU and moved back to the cove, would she cease to be the woman she'd thought she was?

"When you're ready," Eloise said gently, and Alice's expression softened. She reached across the table and twined her fingers with Eloise's, and the bond between them strengthened.

"Thank you, Eloise."

"Eloise," Grace said, her high-pitched voice breaking through the barrier separating Eloise and Alice from the rest of them. "You have to tell Daddy about the mermaids."

She looked at Aaron, and he wore a sparkle in his eyes that testified of his happiness. She couldn't wait to be alone with him for longer than a few seconds, but she leaned forward and started detailing the kingdom of mermaids that existed just below the surface of the waters beyond Smugglers Cove.

CHAPTER TWENTY

Kristen made the trek up to the picnic tables for the third time in three hours, laden with a cooler full of fresh clams, crab legs, and live lobsters. She'd been down to the fishmongers that lined the shore by seven a.m. to buy the freshest seafood possible for the clambake.

Rueben, bless him, had dug the hole for her and lined it with stones, starting the fire just as she'd arrived to the picnic area for the first time. "All good?" she'd asked him, and he'd nodded.

The fire had to burn down to heat the rocks and create the red-hot coals that would then cook the seafood. Kristen had hosted dozens of clambakes in her life, and she'd get the seafood in the hole, cover it with seaweed, and head back to the house to start the steamed potatoes.

She also needed to finish the cole slaw, wrap the corn

in foil and bring it back to the fire pit, and get down to the store for more ice. Her ice maker had decided this week would be a great time to go on the fritz, and she could never look any of her girls in the eye again if she served lukewarm iced tea at her clambake.

Her nerves twittered at her, and she almost stumbled. Her girls. She hadn't seen any of them except Robin since the funeral, and she'd wondered if that would happen. Robin had always kept an open line of communication, so that hadn't changed.

The others hadn't, and Kristen supposed that hadn't changed either. She'd hoped it would, though, and she could admit she was disappointed that everything had simply gone back to normal after they'd all left Five Island Cove.

Her life had a new normal, one she was still trying to adjust to. Just when she thought she was starting to figure out how to wake up alone, or how to cook a meal for just one person, she'd jolt awake in the middle of the night, her heart pounding.

"Joel," she'd say before she realized he wasn't in the bed beside her. She'd even felt for him next to her several times.

Her devastating reality crashed around her then, and Kristen had to pick it up one piece at a time and try to fit it all back together into a brand new normal for that day.

She hummed to herself as she raked the coals out, the heat coming off of them intense. Combined with the sun overhead, Kristen could feel the arrival of summer. Nothing said East Coast summer more than a clambake, and her soul sang as she finished the preparations.

She bent to open the cooler, and she carefully placed the packets of clams, crab legs, and lobsters in a single layer, leaving room for the corn she'd bring up in a few minutes. She wanted everything in place, so when the girls arrived, all they had to do was grab a plate and eat. Alice had called again that morning, and she'd said everyone was coming, even Aaron Sherman and his girls, and someone named Zach, who claimed to be Kelli's half-brother.

Kristen's curiosity about that had skyrocketed, and she really hoped Kelli was okay. The poor woman had been scared by the waves as a girl, and Kristen smiled to herself. She found it a real nasty trick on God's part to put someone on a series of island when they were afraid of the ocean. Kelli had survived though, and she seemed to be thriving as an adult now.

Alice was bringing her father too, and Kristen had called Robin and asked if she wanted to invite her mother or father. Robin's hesitation had spoken volumes. Her parents had divorced about seven or eight years ago, long after all of their children had left home.

Robin had always had a rocky relationship with her mother, and in the end, she'd said, "I don't think so, Kristen. But thanks for asking."

"Sure thing, dear." Kristen had wanted to say so much

more, but she knew the delicate nature of families. Clara spoke to her more often now that Joel was gone, but their relationship was far from perfect. So far from it, Kristen couldn't even see a dot of perfection on the horizon.

Satisfied with the job she'd done, she layered the seaweed over the seafood and headed back to her cottage. She shucked and wrapped the corn, putting butter, salt, pepper, and garlic into each neat little pouch. The corn on the cob went in the cooler, and Kristen added paper plates, cups, silverware, and napkins to the point that she couldn't close the lid.

That done, she set a pot of water on the stove to begin heating, and she peeled potatoes, diced them, and set them to steam before she shredded cabbage and carrots. She mixed in celery seed, mayo, lemon juice, sour cream, and vinegar, and set the cole claw in the refrigerator.

Outside for one more trip up to the picnic area, Kristen paused and took a long drag of fresh air. She didn't get outside as much as she should, especially now that summer had arrived. She didn't particularly like crowds, so the big events on Diamond Island didn't appeal to her.

She liked sitting on the upper deck of the lighthouse as night fell, and watching the bright beam project out across the water. She liked it when her son came out to talk to her, and the best nights were when his wife would join him.

Jean was slowly coming around to the idea of light-house living, and as Kristen continued to clean out the extra rooms in the lighthouse, she'd taken them over, setting up a painting studio in one and a photography studio in the other.

If it hadn't been for Jean moving one of the bookcases Kristen had already cleaned out, she would've never found the videotape. When Jean had brought it to her, Kristen had simply held it and stared at it for a long time.

"Do you want me to stay with you while you watch it?" Jean had asked.

Kristen had nodded, and the other woman had come inside the small cottage. Kristen had cleaned it out—gutted it—after Joel's death, and she'd kept it as mini-malist as possible. Jean had sat with her on the single couch while the images flipped. For a few moments there, Kristen had thought she wouldn't see anything at all.

Then, Alice's face had come on the screen, and Joel's voice could be heard. "Oops," he said. Just that one word.

It was one word more than Kristen had heard her husband speak in months, and it had completely undone her. She'd wept during the three-minute improv Alice had done in high school, catching the sound of Joel's voice at the end of the video too.

"That was so great, right, love? She's just so—" The video—image and sound—had cut off then, and Kristen had turned into Jean. Her daughter-in-law had held her, patting her arm and shushing her for what felt like a long time.

Love.

How could she forget that Joel had called her that? The cancer had been cruel to him, and he'd deteriorated long before death had finally taken him.

After Kristen had gathered herself together, her first thought was to stomp on the tape until it broke into a thousand pieces. She never wanted to see it again, and she certainly wasn't going to tell Alice about it.

She now knew why Joel had been so interested in Alice's high school theatrics, and Kristen simply didn't need the reminder that her husband had cheated on her with Alice's mother.

Jean had guided her down the hall to the bedroom and brought her a glass of water and some pills. Kristen had fallen asleep, and when she'd awakened, the tape wasn't in the player. Jean had taken it.

Kristen thought that was a good solution too. Let Jean decide what to do with it. In the end, though, Kristen couldn't stop thinking about the tape, and she knew the reason was because Alice should have it.

She hoped to show her—and all the Seafaring Girls— that her husband hadn't been a total monster. Deep down, though, Kristen knew some wounds never healed. They wept all the time, for years, quietly and sometimes you thought they'd gone away, only to have them manifest themselves with a simple word, a gesture, or a random object that conjured up a memory your mind hadn't forgotten.

She reached the fire pit again, and removed all the paper goods from the cooler, setting them on the picnic tables. There were only two there, and if it were just her and her five girls, they would've fit with room to spare.

But with teenagers and children and significant others, Kristen had asked Rueben to bring up two more tables and a bunch of chairs.

As she was moving the seaweed to add the corn on the cob to the pit, she heard the engine of the side-by-side Reuben drove around the land here to make sure everything was in tip-top shape. "How's it looking?" he asked as he parked and got out. He hauled a table off the back and started setting it up.

Kristen groaned as she covered the last of the corn and straightened, a pain sliding down her spine and into her hips. "Good," she said. "You built the perfect fire."

Reuben smiled and kept unloading the things he'd brought. "You want a ride back?"

"Yes," Kristen said. "And maybe one back up. I need to bring up a few more things, but they can wait until we're closer to eating." She looked back down the path. "I need to go get more ice."

"Ice?" he asked. "You don't have enough?"

She hadn't told him about the ice-maker, so she just shook her head.

"I'll drop you off and go get it," he said. "We're only about an hour out now."

"Okay." She got in the passenger seat of the ATV and waited for him to finish with the tables and chairs. He dropped her off at her cottage, where she went inside to finish the steamed potatoes, make the lemonade and sweet tea, and cut all the fresh limes and lemons. She'd just put a literal pound of butter in the microwave when someone knocked on the door.

"Kristen," Robin said in the next moment, and Kristen abandoned all her tasks in her small kitchen.

"Come in," she said, the addition of visitors to her cottage wonderful. She embraced Robin, then both of her girls. Alice's twins came next, and she drew them right into a hug too, though she hadn't seen much of them last time they'd been in the cove.

Finally, Alice came through the door, and Kristen took her in with one look. She wasn't eating; Kristen could see that right away. She wore a lot of makeup, but Kristen had seen this bone-weary look on the woman's face before. Years and years ago, when her mother had died. And a few times since then too.

"Alice, dear." She drew her into a hug too, feeling how very slight the woman was. She wanted to remind her of something she'd once told her father—*you have to take care of yourself so you can take care of your kids.*

She suspected Alice didn't need her advice. She didn't

want it. She wanted Kristen to support her and love her, and thankfully, Kristen was very good at doing both of those things for Alice.

"Hello, Kristen," Alice murmured in her ear. She stepped back a moment later and looked around. "What can we help with? We came early to help set up."

"Oh, we're set up," she said. "We're up at the picnic tables, and Rueben just put up the extra tables."

"We should've called," Alice said, shooting a look at Robin. Robin lingered in the kitchen, because the cottage wasn't big enough to take on an addition six people in the living room. She seemed more stressed than usual, because she didn't even glare back at Alice.

She did say, "She would've just denied us anyway."

"She's right," Kristen said. "Though I will have you kids take some stuff up, if you want. Rueben's off getting ice too, and we want some of this stuff to stay cold."

"Direct them," Alice said, and Kristen did just that, sending the jars of sweet iced tea up with Charlie, and giving the cole slaw, potatoes, bowl of lemons, and container of butter to the girls.

They left, and Kristen looked between Alice and Robin. "The others aren't coming?"

"They are," Alice said. "We got the ferry ahead of them." She put a faint smile on her face. "I want to see what you have. Just me and Robin. Then we can decide if the others need to know."

Kristen nodded, though she was a bit surprised Alice and Robin would keep a secret from the other three women. They'd had their cliques in the past, but she'd been impressed by the way they'd rallied together around every single person the last time they'd been here.

"It's nothing," she said.

"You said it was a little shocking."

"For me, it was," she said, stepping around the cabinet that held her TV. "Come sit down. It's a video."

"A video?" Robin asked, moving as if underwater. "Of what?"

Kristen picked up the remote and sat right in the middle of the couch, leaving a spot for either woman on either side of her. Alice sat beside her, her expression quizzical. Robin perched on the edge of the couch, as if she might need to spring forward and block the television screen if she deemed the image something she didn't want Alice to see.

"Okay," Kristen said, taking a deep breath. "Here we go."

The same flickering, bouncing lines came up, and she felt Alice's impatience pouring off her in waves.

Alice's face filled the screen.

Joel's voice came next.

"Oh, no," Robin said.

"It's my senior-year improv," Alice said, her voice made of the ghosts of the past. They sat in silence and watched the whole thing.

When the video and sound cut off together, Kristen lifted the remote and snapped off the TV too. She hadn't broken down this time, so she'd definitely made some improvements.

"Well?" she asked. "Would you like it? Or should I throw it away?"

Alice turned her head toward Kristen, her mouth slightly open. "You were right. It's a little shocking."

"But not bad," Robin said. "I mean, Alice didn't go on to become a famous actress, but she was actually pretty good in high school."

Kristen looked at Robin, a smile spreading across her face for the first time in months. A true smile. She started to laugh, something else that hadn't happened in a while, and before she knew it, Alice and Robin were giggling too.

"I'll take it," Alice said. "Heaven knows I need something to make me laugh these days." She got up from the couch and collected the tape from the player, tucking it neatly into her purse. Out of sight. "Thank you, Kristen."

"Of course." She heaved herself to her feet too. "Thank you for coming." She embraced them both again, a feeling of warmth and love moving through her. "So, what's new?"

"Nothing," Robin said too quickly. Kristen stepped back, aware she'd just been lied to. She wasn't sure what to push and what to let go, and she ended up moving into the kitchen to look at her list.

"Just the ice," she said, turning back to her girls.

"I'm getting divorced," Alice said, her eyes looking somewhere past Kristen. "Hopefully." She gestured in the general direction of Robin. "She's worried sick about Duke. He called today, but it was almost a pocket-dial. She could hear him, but he didn't seem to know he'd called. He kept saying something about his arm hurting."

Kristen switched her gaze to Robin, who's bright blue eyes were as wide as they could go and filling fast with tears.

"I haven't been able to get in touch with him," she said. "Or with his friend up there. Or his boss."

"Oh, no." Kristen hurried back to both of them, gathering them close to her again the way a worried mother hen would for her scared chicks. "It's okay," she murmured. "It's going to be okay."

Robin sniffled and buried her face in Kristen's shoulder. Alice stood unyielding and silent, though she gripped Kristen with a fierceness that spoke of her own emotion. Kristen didn't know how it was going to be okay. She didn't have anything else to say.

She loved these women, and they loved her, and for right now, that was enough.

AN HOUR LATER, ROBIN HAD ERASED ALL EVIDENCE OF HER tears. Alice had never cried, and she put a smile on her face when her father showed up. Kristen soaked in the sun's rays and the energy of the group that had gathered to the lighthouse and the picnic area.

"Kristen," Connor Williams said. "This looks amazing."

"There's plenty of butter," she said. "So help yourselves."

"I'm not waiting," Aaron said. "If you don't act fast, guys, Alice will eat all the crab legs."

Alice likely wouldn't even eat one, but she grinned at Aaron too. Eloise watched her with keen interest in her eyes, and Kristen knew that at least one of her girls suspected something was wrong with Alice. It wasn't her place to say anything, and she was actually glad Alice had filed for divorce. It was about time, in Kristen's opinion.

No one said anything about the item Kristen had shown to Alice, and even Kelli had hugged her tight and stood back with a smile as she'd introduced her half-brother. Kristen could see Guy Watkins in him, and she'd been as polite as polite could be.

"This looks great," AJ said. "I wonder where DJ is..." She looked over her shoulder and down the path, but no one was coming. "He was on a flight." She gave Kristen a quick smile, which Kristen returned.

She didn't need all the details of these women's lives. She was just so happy to have them here with her, even for a few hours. They revived her, breathed new life into her weary lungs, and gave her hope for the future.

"Thank you all for coming," she said once nearly

everyone had a plate of food in front of them, even Alice. "I love you all so—" Her voice caught, and she pressed one palm to her chest as if that would unstop all the emotion there.

"We love you too, Kristen," Robin said, jumping to her feet. She engulfed Kristen in a hug, saying, "Seafaring Girls group hug."

Before she knew it, all five of them had surrounded her, and she started to laugh. What a freeing thing laughter was, and love, and she experienced both power-fully in that moment. Everyone laughed with her, and when they went back to their seats and looked at her again, she simply said, "Thank you for coming. It's wonderful to see you all here with your families and loved ones. Now, eat a lot. I bought enough clams to feed an army."

She grinned at everyone, feeling every one of her seventy-four years. She collected her plate of clams and crab and took the spot Rueben had saved for her at Robin's table.

"You have to come out to Alice's house," Robin said, her motherly eyes on high. "And I'm not taking no for an answer this time."

"All right," Kristen said.

"All right?" Robin's eyebrows went up.

Kristen had worried she'd be a burden, or that no one would want to see her. But she now knew differently, and she knew she'd feel like she was going home no matter where she spent time with her Seafaring Girls. "Yes," she said with a smile. "All right. Just tell me when."

"Let me make a plan with everyone," Robin said, her bright eyes getting brighter. Kristen just smiled and picked up a crab leg to dunk it in a bowl of butter. Nothing better than that—except her girls being here with her.

CHAPTER TWENTY-ONE

Alice leaned away from her laptop and rubbed her hands along the back of her neck. The clock read just after two in the morning, and she had the distinct thought she needed to go to bed. She couldn't pull another twenty-hour day. She knew the exhaustion sat heavily on her shoulders, shone from the wrinkles around her eyes, and shot straight out of her bagged eyes.

She had enough ammunition for the hearing, and her pulse blipped with a hint of panic as she thought about where she'd be in just thirty-six hours. Perhaps she should look through one more credit card statement, check one more email about a hotel reservation, or email back Charlie's principal about the dates Frank had checked their son out of school for a "fishing trip."

Her son had told her that they hadn't gone fishing. They'd gone to a cabin in the woods, sure. But there were no fishing poles, and Frank had not stayed in the cabin with Charlie. He'd stayed next door, in a second cabin he'd rented under a woman's name. She'd had trouble tracking down that rental, and the principal had given her the dates again, though she'd had them in her calendar.

She'd finally found it as an obscure charge that Frank had contested, saying he was double-charged for the cabin rental. Charlie had answered all of her questions the same the second time she'd asked him, and Alice hated with every fiber of her being that she was involving him in this battle.

"No more," she vowed to herself, closing the laptop. "It's enough. Whatever will happen, will happen." She rolled her neck and her shoulders, working the kinks out of them. She wasn't particularly religious, but she took a moment in the stillness of the house, thinking of all the people there with her.

No matter what happened, she wouldn't be left completely alone. She had a law degree, and she had brains, and she could weather this storm. She wanted to make sure Charlie and Ginny were as protected from the elements as much as possible, so she'd put her documents together, scoured emails and statements, sent emails, answered texts, and confirmed her presence at the hearing at noon on Tuesday.

She had a flight leaving Five Island Cove at six-twenty in the morning, which meant she had to be on the first ferry off Rocky Ridge, at four-fifty.

She didn't care about the lost sleep. She barely rested when she did lie down and close her eyes.

"Soon," she whispered as she leaned her head back. "Dear Lord, I need a break soon." She closed her eyes and breathed, everything in her mind spinning into a powerful sense of vertigo that had her reaching for the desk beside her. She steadied herself, her stomach clenching painfully against itself.

Eat, she thought. *Sleep.* She hadn't done much of either since Robin had come into the bedroom with that packet of papers and the news that Charlie and Mandie were to the kissing stage of their relationship.

Instead of going into her bedroom from the attached office, she detoured into the kitchen and pulled open the fridge. Kristen had sent three lobsters with Robin, as well as a nearly full bowl of potatoes. Alice could eat both cold, and she did, standing right there in the light from the fridge.

For a moment, she felt outside herself, looking down on this pathetic wraith of a woman eating in the middle of the night. She snapped back to herself and took another bite of the creamy lobster meat. It was smoky too, and the only thing that would make it better was butter.

Her stomach filled fast, and Alice sighed as she closed the fridge and went down the hall to her bedroom. Ginny had stayed in her room tonight, and Alice sank onto the plush mattress and lay down without changing out of her leisure suit. Her thoughts lingered on the videotape

Kristen had given her before the clambake for a few moments. It had been...surreal to hear Joel's voice from so many years ago.

She knew what word came after the tape had ended. The same one he'd said to her many times.

"Talented," she whispered. "Joel thought you were talented." Alice had some skills, she knew that. She hoped to put her talents to use in the courtroom where her hearing would take place, and with that hope in her heart, she fell asleep.

―――――――――

THE NEXT MORNING, ALICE FELT BETTER THAN SHE HAD IN three days. Her stomach cramped again, this time because it now knew what it felt like to be full, and it was empty. She poured herself a cup of coffee while Kelli manned three waffle makers, calling out, "Four more waffles," every thirty seconds or so.

"I didn't even know I had three waffle makers," Alice said, stirring plenty of sugar into her coffee. She hadn't even known she owned one.

"I found them," Kelli said. "So you must." She smiled at Alice, her eyes stopping for a moment. "You look better today, Alice."

"Thank you," she said, lifting her cup to her lips. "Mm. This needs cream." She stepped over to the fridge and got out the plain cream. "And can I shred up some of this lobster meat and put it in my waffle?"

She pulled the second lobster claw out of the fridge that went with the one she'd consumed last night.

"That actually sounds really good," Kelli said. "The sweet waffle batter with the savory lobster. Is there enough for me?"

"Absolutely," Alice said, cracking into the claw with her bare hands.

"Waffles," Kelli called, but no one came forward to get them. One glance out the window showed the outdoor tables nearly full, and Kelli unplugged one of the makers. "I don't think we need to keep making twelve of these every two minutes."

"Only for us," Alice said with a grin. She felt more like herself than she had in weeks—since she'd entered Frank's office with her proposal. She made quick work of the lobster and Kelli used her measuring cup to put uncooked batter on the waffle maker. Alice sprinkled the lobster all over it, and Kelli used a fork to add more dollops of batter to mostly cover it.

She closed the lid, and Alice put a quick bite of lobster meat in her mouth. "I love lobster."

"It's the food of the gods," Kelli said. "That's why."

Alice chuckled as washed her hands and joined Kelli at the counter. She stood close to her on purpose, putting her arm around the shorter woman's waist. "We're okay, right Kel?"

Kelli looked at her. "Of course, Alice."

"Good." Alice smiled at her and hugged her fully. "I don't want you to be angry with me."

"I'm not."

"I wasn't trying to micromanage you." Alice spoke softly, because she knew she could come off as brash and confident, especially to someone like Kelli.

"I know that, Alice." Kelli held her tight, and Alice breathed in the soft, strawberry scent of her hair. She was a simpler, better version of Alice that she desperately wanted to become, and she stepped back and gave Kelli a smile.

"Let's check these waffles," Kelli said, focusing her attention there. "I can smell them." She lifted the lid, and four perfectly crispy, golden lobster waffles looked back at Alice.

Her mouth watered, and she took the two Kelli put on her plate and slathered them in butter before pouring syrup over all of it.

"What is happening here?" Robin asked, stilling with her empty plate in her hand.

"Lobster waffles," Alice said around a mouthful of the very best food she'd ever tasted.

"Want one?" Kelli asked, but neither word was very defined because of the huge bite of lobster waffle she'd taken. She grinned at Alice and then Robin, who just stood there, her eyes wide.

"Who are you?" she asked, her expression softening into a smile. "And heck yes, bake me up a lobster waffle."

A COUPLE OF HOURS LATER, THE FIVE OF THEM PILED INTO one car, with Alice behind the wheel. The drive to the black sand beach happened in near silence, only the radio playing and occasionally one of them singing along to the song that came on.

Alice pulled into the extra space that ran alongside her father's house. The steps in front of her would lead them down the black sand beach, and Alice suddenly wasn't so sure she wanted to go.

"Come on," Robin said. "The beach is waiting." She got out of the car and stepped to the trunk to get her bag and her beach chair. Everyone followed her, because Robin had the type of personality that demanded as much.

Alice went last, making sure to lock her car before she started down the steps. She held onto the railing, the glittering sand below calling to her now that she could see it. She took a deep breath, almost able to smell the volcanic activity that had formed the cliffs and sand on this side of the island.

Robin marched out onto the sand, seemingly picking a spot at random to set up her chair. There was no shade here, and they'd brought one umbrella to set up. AJ got to work doing that, because she'd developed a knack for it, and Alice set up her chair and sank into it.

Everyone else did the same, pulling up a patch of shade. Kelli and Eloise started to spray sunscreen, and Alice took the container from Eloise when she handed it to her. She sprayed her arms and shoulders, rubbed it on her face, and made sure to get the tops of her feet. Her cover up would protect the rest of her.

"No one wants to start?" she asked when the silence between them continued.

"You start," Robin said, keeping her gaze out on the water.

"Okay." Alice watched a wave roll ashore, and she loved everything about this beach. It wasn't a private beach, but not many people came here, because it was on the northeast side of the island and had huge waves. It wasn't a kid-friendly beach, and the sand got hotter than other beaches around the cove.

"I'm glad you all came," she said. "I really think we should come every summer if we can." She glanced around at the others, but AJ sat in front of her, and she wasn't turning around to meet Alice's eye. "The summer sand pact meant a great deal to me as a teenager," she continued. "Like, I was going off into this great big world from these tiny islands, and I just...I knew if I needed something, you guys would be there."

Robin reached over and took Alice's hand.

"I feel like that again," Alice said. "Tomorrow morning, I'm leaving to go back to New York for a hearing with Frank. I filed for divorce, and he signed an agreement, and now he doesn't want to honor it."

Eloise pulled in a sharp breath; AJ turned around; Kelli twisted in her seat too, her eyes wide behind her sunglasses. "You filed for divorce?" she asked.

"I started drafting the agreement I wanted Frank to sign almost the moment I got home from Joel's funeral." Alice finally tore her eyes from the waves. Her throat tightened, but she pressed through the emotion. "And I have to go out into the big, scary world again, and I'm just glad to know you guys will be behind me no matter what happens."

She sounded like she'd swallowed a log, her vocal cords shredding around it and making her voice much too high. Alice hated the burning sensation in her eyes, but she didn't hate it when Eloise reached over and hugged her. "We'll be right here, Alice."

"We'll go with you in spirit," Robin said. "You won't be alone in there. Remember that."

She nodded and swiped at her eyes, settling her shades back into place. She drew in a deep breath. "Phew. Okay." She pushed her breath out.

"So summer sand pact," Robin said, taking over, thankfully. "Eloise has the first rights of refusal to talk about Aaron. Kelli called the Tell-All. We've done New Truth before, so it's not technically part of the pact."

"What is technically part of the pact?" AJ asked. "I can't even remember."

"You can't remember?" Kelli asked, gaping at her. "You're the one who named it, remember? At Friendship Inn, you said, 'we need a pact to come here every year.' Robin threw her drink at you."

"That was a pure reflex," Robin said, laughing. "We almost died getting to Friendship Inn."

"See?" Kelli asked, pointing at AJ. "I told you it was super hard to row that boat."

AJ tipped her head back and laughed. "I never said it wasn't hard. I just said you weren't in danger of dying."

"Yes, we were," Robin said. "Number one, we didn't even tell anyone where we were going. We could've easily capsized and never been heard from again."

"Lost to the depths of the sea," Eloise said, her voice quiet. "And so Alice suggested we use this black sand beach."

"I remember that," AJ said.

"And we said we'd meet there every year to make sure everyone was okay," Eloise said. "We said it was a safe space, where we could tell all, and we'd still be accepted." She looked at Alice. "I don't remember who came up with first rights of refusal."

"Again," Kelli said. "AJ."

"How am I responsible for this whole pact?" She shook her head and started gathering her long hair into a ponytail. "Why don't I remember it?"

"It was soccer season," Alice said, the connection blitzing through her brain as if someone had flipped a switch.

"Oh," AJ said, and they all stilled again.

Alice hadn't known then that AJ had just discovered Joel Shields coming on to her sister after a soccer practice. Perhaps AJ simply wasn't in her right mind when they'd rowed out to Friendship Inn for the first and only time. Or obviously, any of the stuff after that either.

"She didn't want to talk one night at the lighthouse," Kelli said. "And she said, 'this goes in our summer sand pact. First rights of refusal to talk about any given topic.' Robin picked it apart, and it was agreed to that only one person could have the rights, and only for one topic of their choosing."

"I don't need it anymore," Eloise said. "I can talk about Aaron now."

Alice looked at Robin, but she said nothing.

"We promised to come here," Kelli said. "Just us. No husbands and no kids, and, I don't know." She faced the water again. "Reconnect."

"Catch up," Alice said.

"Get help," Eloise added.

"Feel accepted," AJ said.

"Be ourselves," Robin said in a near-whisper.

The silence draped over them again, each of them inside their own heads. Alice tried to grab onto any single thought and make it the one the focused on, but they all just flitted away from her. The heat lifted off the sand, making her warm from head to toe, and she knew her strong friendship with these woman had something to do with that too.

She breathed in, and Robin did the same. "I have something too," she said.

This time, AJ and Kelli turned around before Robin said anything. "Duke got in an accident yesterday on the fishing boat." She held up one hand. "He's okay. He's fine. It was a very minor accident, I guess, as far as what could've happened. He's not coming home." She paused, her chin wobbling with the effort she put into not crying.

"Just let it out, Robin," Alice said quietly. "You do get to be yourself here."

She made a sound Alice had never heard before, somewhere between an explosion and a sob, and she ducked her head. "I didn't tell the girls, and it took everything I had not to get on a plane last night and go up there to make sure he told me the truth." She looked up and took off her sunglasses so she could wipe her eyes. "I'm okay." She drew in a series of deep breaths, and Alice just watched the waves while AJ reached over the back of her chair and squeezed Robin's hand.

"He's okay. We're okay." Robin sounded like she was trying to convince herself as well as everyone else.

After a few more seconds had passed, Alice asked, "Anyone else need the privacy and safety of the summer sand pact?"

Eloise shook her head. Kelli did too and faced forward again. AJ said, "You guys have busted open all my secrets on this trip already," and added a light laugh to it. She too turned around, and Alice looked at Robin, who was still attempting to calm herself.

"You're not alone in this either, Robin," she said. "Just like you'll all be with me in that hearing tomorrow, we're all with you right now."

"I know."

"Do you?" Alice didn't want to be rude. "Sometimes you like to be Superwoman. And you *are* Superwoman. But it's okay to rely on us too."

"It actually shows that you know when to be strong and when to let others help," Eloise said.

"I'm working on it," Robin said, and she smiled at Alice, then Eloise. "Now, is it too early for lunch? I feel like I could use a big piece of cheesecake."

"Oh," AJ said. "Remember that blackberry-lime cheesecake at Friendship Inn?"

"How can you remember that and not that you literally almost killed all four of us in that boat?" Kelli demanded, and Alice had never been so happy to be with these four women, on this beach.

CHAPTER TWENTY-TWO

AJ sat in an empty bedroom on the second floor of Alice's house, her computer on the desk, and her view out the window unparalleled. She had no idea what it would be like to have this much money, though she'd never really been in a position that she needed to worry about how she'd pay for things.

Until now.

She'd always been employed—and with a good job too—and it was just herself she needed to take care of. This spiral she'd been in for the past eight weeks had really put a dent in her savings—and her confidence.

She shook her hair over her shoulders and sat up straight and tall. "You're qualified for this job," she murmured to herself, letting her attention wander back down to the beach, where she could see the waves moving in what felt like slow motion.

There were a lot of people on the beach today, almost like they'd finally realized there was more to Five Island Cove than just Diamond Island. AJ had always known that, but even on Saturday, when everyone had split up to go see their families in the cove, she hadn't made the trip to Pearl Island.

Her father still lived there, retired now from his lobster and shrimp boat. He'd kept the clamming up for a few years, but he hadn't worked in at least a decade now. AJ should've gone to see him—at least called to tell him she was in the cove. They could've had lunch, which her father would've made for her. Something.

She hadn't. Amelia had left Five Island Cove for a few years, but she'd returned, and she lived on Pearl Island too, only a half-mile from their father. AJ should've called her too. She'd kept in touch with Amelia the most over the years, but Amy didn't understand AJ's lifestyle.

Most of the time, AJ didn't understand it either.

Their oldest brother, Paul, had left the cove after high school, and he worked on the West Coast now, out of an FBI office there. He was about as far from Five Island Cove as a person could get, and sometimes AJ envied him. At the same time, she had enjoyed her time with her friends in this house. Well, after she'd slept off her hangovers and figured out how to get through the day without being on the edge of drunk. Then she'd enjoyed her time on Rocky Ridge.

Her mind wandered to DJ, whom she'd chosen to

spend her free Saturday with. She'd finally kissed him that day while they lay on the beach on Sanctuary Island, and everyone had been so focused on Alice and Eloise that none of them had asked AJ about her day.

She was fine not talking about it. DJ hadn't made it to the clambake on Sunday due to a delayed flight, and she'd blocked off Monday for the summer sand pact on the black sand beach. She'd spoken to him once on the phone, and they'd texted a little bit.

The communication between them, though, had already started to wane, and while AJ had had the thought that if she got this new job in New York City, she wouldn't be able to keep seeing DJ, now it wasn't so much of a concern.

Bitterness crept down her throat. Her relationship with DJ was a week old today—she'd met him on the plane last Tuesday. They'd been out three times before she'd kissed him, and she hadn't seen him since.

She didn't know what that said about him. But the real problem was she didn't know what that said about her.

Was that all she was good for? A hot kiss, a quick tumble between the sheets?

And she hadn't even done that with him.

Yet, her mind whispered, and she hated that that little, three-letter word was there. She'd be in the cove for another week, and then hopefully, she'd have somewhere to send what she owned, because she'd be relocating to New York.

A week was more than enough time for AJ to sleep with a man, but as she sat at the desk and watched the undulating water in the distance, she vowed she wouldn't do that again. Not with DJ, not if they weren't going to commit to a long-distance relationship the way Eloise and Aaron had.

Her phone rang, sending her pulse straight to the top of her head, where it beat wildly, trying to get out. She sucked in a breath and looked at the screen, recognizing the number.

"Game time," she told herself, and she picked up the phone. "Alan, hello," she said in a falsely bright voice.

"AJ," the man said. "Sorry I'm a few minutes late."

"I hadn't even noticed," she said, clearing her throat. Her mind wouldn't be as swept clean as easily, but she managed to click open the document where she'd taken notes on their other calls.

"So I've got my executive team here with me," he said. "I'll let them go around and introduce themselves."

"Perfect," AJ said, and she quickly tapped the phone to speaker and put her fingers on the keyboard as the first woman started to speak. AJ had a knack for remembering names and faces, and she typed up the names as each person said them.

Six other people on the call, and the pressure on the back of AJ's neck increased. She took a deep breath as Alan took the call again.

"So that's the team," he said. "We're looking at your

photo from Atlanta Sports News, so it's almost like you're here with us."

"Oh, perfect," she said with a light laugh. At least her professional headshot from her last job was amazing.

"How long were you there?" one of the woman asked.

"Atlanta? Oh, let's see. Twelve years? Yes, just over twelve years."

"AJ, it's Ben. Your resume is impressive. Alan really likes you and thinks you'll be perfect on-air. Simon called your boss at ASN, and he had great things to say about you."

"Excellent," AJ said, smiling. She was going to get this job; she could feel it way down deep in her gut.

"I guess what most of us are wondering is why you left Atlanta. Twelve years is a long time. Surely you had contacts on the teams there, press passes you didn't have to renew, and relationships with the long-time players. Not to mention your on-air team." Ben left his words hanging there, and that something AJ felt in her gut was now sickness.

Everything he'd said was true.

"I can do all of that again in New York," she said, hoping to dodge the real question. She'd learned from players and coaches exactly how to do that. "I'm excellent with players and coaches, as I've spent my life being a player and training with coaches."

"Yes," Melissa said, as her voice had definitely been the highest on when the intros had gone around. "But

New York is a completely different market than Atlanta. There's none of that...what is it? Southern charm up here. Players are brash, and coaches don't care to impress the press. There's always someone else they can talk to."

AJ had relied a lot on her looks to get through the doors of locker rooms and coaches' offices in the past. Her chest tightened, because what if that didn't work in New York?

"I understand that," she said. "I once dated a guy who played for the Yankees, and when it was over, there was no wondering why." She gave another light laugh, but no one on the other end of the call joined her. She straightened in her seat, wondering what to say next.

"So, why did you leave Atlanta?" Ben asked again. He wasn't going to let her dodge the question, and she shouldn't have expected him to. He was a reporter, after all, same as her.

AJ drew in a deep breath and looked at the beach-goers again. Perhaps she should just stay here. Alice would let her stay in the house, as it was massive and there would be plenty of room for both of them.

She knew now that Robin had known about Alice's divorce and that she was actually living in this house now. Still, AJ could keep living in the basement bedroom and never have to see Alice—that was how big the house was.

"Personal reasons," she said, realizing she was still on the call. "I left for personal reasons."

No one said anything on the other end of the line.

Finally, Ben or Alan or one of the men asked, "Were you dating Nathan Cooke?"

"I was," she said, pain streaming through her from front to back.

"I see," Alan said. "AJ, we're going to put you on hold for a moment, okay? Don't go anywhere."

She nodded, because what else could she do? A beep sounded, and she slumped in her seat. They'd put her on hold; that was not good. That feeling in her stomach had fled, and she wondered what it meant.

"He's engaged to someone else now," someone said, as if they didn't know their speaker was on. Another woman said something too, and AJ let her attention drift for a moment. They thought they'd muted the speaker, but they hadn't.

When they realized it, they'd be mortified. "Ben?" she asked. "Alan? I can still hear you."

Alan swore, and he said, "Be right back." Another beep, and this time, their voices muted.

AJ didn't need to stick around to learn why they didn't want to hire her. Was her relationship with Nathan really going to be the thing that kept her from getting another job in sportscasting? She hadn't done anything wrong. She was allowed to date players.

She'd never benefitted all that much from her relationship with him. He never gave her an interview, and if she wanted to talk to his coach or another player, she used her own contacts and connections.

Anger grew in her, and her fingers twitched toward the phone, ready to tap the red icon and hang up. At the same time, she wanted to fight for herself and her decisions. She hadn't done anything wrong. She had nothing to be ashamed of.

Armed with that knowledge, she stayed on the call.

Probably only sixty seconds later, another beep sounded and Alan said, "Can you hear me?"

"Yes," AJ said. "And look, Alan. Ben. Melissa." She continued with the other names she'd typed into her document. "My relationship with Nathan Cooke was lasting. We lived together for a few years. I never used him to get favors from his team or from other coaches. I never did a feature on him or interviewed him. I'm a damn good reporter and sportscaster, and that has nothing to do with Nathan Cooke."

Her chest ached, and she relieved some of the pressure there by breathing in. "I understand New York City is a different market than Atlanta. Everyone in the world of news and sports knows that. I was happy in Atlanta...until I wasn't. It had nothing to do with the job, or my ability to do the job. I don't see how Nathan Cooke is relevant to this job interview at all, frankly."

"AJ," Alan said.

"But you obviously do," she said. "I'm sorry I wasted your time."

"Don't hang up, AJ," Alan said quickly.

"We don't think Nathan Cooke is relevant to the job either," Ben said.

"And we want to offer you the job," Melissa said.

AJ said nothing, because she had not expected that.

"Is she there?" Alan asked. "AJ, are you still with us?"

She blinked and looked down at the phone. The numbers on the timer for how long the call had lasted clicked by. One, two, three.

"Yes," she blurted. "Yes, I'm still here."

"Great," Alan said. "Did you hear Melissa?"

"Yes," she said much quieter this time. "I heard her."

"Congratulations," Alan said. "I'll send over the hiring packet, with our offer, and you can review it at your leisure. I know you're on vacation right now."

"Yes," AJ said again, wondering if she knew any other words.

"Perfect," Alan said. "I think you'll find the package more than fair, and I hope to hear from you soon."

"When do you think you'll be able to make a decision?" Ben asked. "Would by Friday work?"

"Yes," AJ said again. "I'll look for the email, and I should definitely have time to review the package and let you know by Friday."

Some sportscasters had agents to help them negotiate big contracts and on-air time. AJ had never seen the need for that—but she hadn't seen the package from ESPN-New York yet either.

"Thank you," Ben said, and everyone else chorused in

that they liked talking to her, and they couldn't wait to hear from her.

The call ended, and AJ sat there, dumbfounded.

"You got the job," she said, a smile spreading across her whole face. She burst from the chair and ran from the room. Her feet sounded like thunder on the stairs as she went down, and she practically exploded through the back door and into the back yard, where most people had just settled down to a poolside lunch.

"I got the job in New York City." She looked around at Robin, Eloise, and Kelli, sorely wishing Alice were there.

A moment of silence filled the air, and then cheers went up. All of her friends came over to congratulate her, and AJ basked in their love and her own happiness.

Amidst it all, she did have the distinct thought that it would be nice to have a spouse to share this moment with. Her friends were great; she loved them, and she knew they were indeed happy for her.

But it wasn't the same as having a life-partner, and AJ knew it. When she told DJ about the job, AJ fully expected to end things with him, and some of the joy inside her deflated.

CHAPTER TWENTY-THREE

Eloise bent down and pressed a quick kiss to Billie's forehead. "I'll be back in a couple of hours, okay? You listen to Robin."

Robin looked up from the magazine she was reading, a quick smile on her face. "We'll be fine. Ginny's going to make chocolate ice cream."

"She said I could help," Billie said, looking from Robin to Eloise. She wore quite a bit of concern on her face, and Eloise wondered if she should go with Aaron. All she'd be able to do was hold his hand and snuggle into his side on the ferry from Rocky Ridge to Diamond. Then she'd have to make the trip back by herself.

She hadn't had hardly any alone-time with him in days, though, and *he'd* been the one to suggest it. *He'd* arranged with Robin to watch his daughters so they could go back to Diamond Island together.

She only had one more hour with him tonight, and then tomorrow, he was off work for the whole day. The girls didn't want to go back to the house with him, though, and Eloise didn't mind if they stayed with her.

"You can," Robin finally said. "She won't leave you out." She flipped a page in her magazine, and added, "Go, Eloise," without looking up.

Eloise started, blinking. "Yes," she said. "Okay, bye, girls."

"Eloise?" Aaron asked, coming back in the front door.

"Coming," she said, hurrying toward him.

"The car is here," he said. "But if you need a minute—"

"Nope," she said. "I don't. Let's go." She put a bright smile on her face and secured her hand in his as they left the house.

"What's going on?" he asked.

"Nothing." She looked up at him as they started down the front steps together. "Just making sure Billie will be happy here without either of us."

"Billie's not happy about anything right now," Aaron said, his eyebrows drawing down.

"What do you mean?"

"I mean, she's a moody teenager, and she's already driving me nuts." He gave her a dark look. "I don't know how to deal with teenage girls."

Eloise burst out laughing, though Aaron did not join her. "Honey," she said, tipping up onto her toes at the back of the car. "No one does." She grinned and pressed her lips to his in a sloppy kiss.

He took her into his arms and growled, trying to line up their mouths for a proper kiss. Eloise ducked her head, though, because the front of Alice's house had plenty of windows, and they had a driver watching them in his rear-view mirror. "Come on."

She opened the door and slid into the back seat, leaving room for him to follow her. He did, but he took her hand instantly. "Ferry station," he said, and the driver eased away from the curb. "When's Alice coming back?"

"Tomorrow, I think," Eloise said. "She had to stay and go over some things with her lawyer." The hearing had "gone well" in Alice's terms, and she'd begged a couple of days out of the others. Eloise wanted her to take her time and do what she needed to do. So did everyone else, but she knew the guilt would be crushing to Alice. She'd wanted these two weeks to be perfect, and she hadn't anticipated being gone for a single minute.

Their group text had been full of support for her, and Alice had sent the crying emoji and then not answered again. Eloise had never seen Alice cry—or if she had, it had been a very long time ago—but she suspected her friend had probably shed a few tears in the past couple of days.

"I thought she *was* a lawyer."

"She is, and she's great," Eloise said. "But that doesn't

mean she wants to represent herself. It's emotional, a divorce."

Aaron's hand in hers tightened. "Yes, it is."

"Where is Carol?" she asked, making her voice as light as she could. She hadn't told Aaron anything Billie or Grace had said to her about their mother, though she probably should. She wanted to keep their confidence, but also help them. And that meant, she needed to tell Aaron.

"Uh, I'm not sure," Aaron said. "She doesn't exactly keep in touch with me."

"You look her up from time to time, don't you?"

He swung his gaze to hers and nodded. "Yeah," he said with a sigh. "I just want...I don't know. It's better she'd not here. Billie and Grace don't need her messing with their minds." He shook his head and returned his attention out his window. "I just don't see how someone can walk away from their life—their kids—and not even send a card or an email. Something."

"It's unfathomable to me too," Eloise said. "Aaron? Billie asked me if I was going to be her mother."

Aaron whipped his head back toward her, his eyes wide and sparking with something that excited Eloise. "And? What did you say?"

"I said I didn't know." Eloise could hear the conversation in her head. "She cried, Aaron. I think she needs someone to talk to."

"I had her in therapy for a while," he said. "The guy thought she was doing better."

"Maybe she was, at the time," Eloise said. "But she might need the extra support now, as she's getting older."

"I'll talk to her." He leaned toward her. "But, really. What did you say?"

"I told you what I said."

Aaron smiled, but the gesture didn't reach all the way to his eyes. "I know you, El. You said way more than 'I don't know.'"

Eloise put her free hand on the side of his face, enjoying the scruffy feeling of his beard against her palm. She wanted to feel it against her cheek too as he kissed her. "I asked her if she wanted me to be her mom."

Aaron didn't ask another question; he likely wouldn't interrupt again.

"She said she missed her, and she wasn't sure why. She hardly remembers her. She cried then, and she said I would probably be a good mom, because I wouldn't leave in the middle of the night or forget to send birthday cards or not want to be a mom at all."

Aaron blinked, and it was clear by the fire in his eyes that he did not like what he was hearing. "Go on."

"And then I told her I liked you a whole lot, and I enjoyed being with her and Grace, and maybe..." Eloise looked away, breaking the connection between them. Heat flared through her body, almost like she was having a hot flash. "Maybe I hadn't thought about being her mom, because it's kind of scary."

"Is it?"

"Of course it is," Eloise said, glancing back at him. He hadn't moved a muscle, but she couldn't quite look into his eyes. "Instant-mom. No time with just the two of us, before a family comes along. I don't know what I'm doing with a ten-year-old and a twelve-year-old." She let out a sigh, because she didn't want to be afraid of being a mother to his kids.

In a lot of ways, she wasn't. In a couple, she definitely was.

"No one knows what they're doing," Aaron said. "I pity the person who thinks they have parenthood figured out."

The driver coughed, and both Aaron and Eloise looked up to him. He laughed next, and nodded. "Sorry, I couldn't help overhearing. That's literally the truest thing I've ever heard someone say from the back seat."

Aaron smiled and looked back at Eloise. They fell into silence for the rest of the trip to the ferry station, and Aaron paid the guy, bought tickets, and led her onto the ferry.

"Do you think we'll have time for ice cream?" he asked as the boat pulled away from the dock several minutes later.

"I'm sure we will," Eloise said. "They run late in the summer." She stood at his side, his arm warm and comforting around her. "I do love your girls, Aaron," she murmured.

"I know you do, El. I can see it and feel it."

She nodded, wondering if he could see and feel how she felt about him. She couldn't quite decipher Aaron's feelings for her, though they'd had several talks about their future together and what they each wanted.

The sun disappeared below the ocean line, the sky still lit up in shades of rose, gold, and navy.

"I got an email back from Britta in HR," she said next. She'd been sitting on the email for almost twelve hours now, and she wasn't sure how to tell him.

"You did?" Pure curiosity rode in his voice. "And?"

"And I don't even have to go back in the fall, if I don't want to," she said. "I have twenty years at the university. I can retire now, though I won't get my pension until I'm sixty-two. I can buy up to five more years, and that will earn me twenty-five years, at which point, I do get my pension now. And more money for the rest of my life."

Aaron stood next to her, unmoving. She couldn't feel his gaze on her face, and desperation built inside her. "Tell me what you're thinking," she said.

"I'm wondering how much it would cost to buy five years," he said.

"It's a lot," she said. "I could cash out my retirement accounts and have enough."

"What are you going to do?"

"I have no idea." Eloise could not even remember

what her life had been like inside the college classroom. It felt like so much had happened since then—Joel's funeral, meeting Aaron, flying back and forth, giving her cats to her mother, coming back for this two-week trip, really getting to know his girls...

Eloise sighed. "Honestly? If I was a risk-taker, I'd buy the five years, sell my brownstone and everything I own in Boston, move to Sanctuary Island, and start fixing up the inn. I could live in the back apartment and get a business loan for the improvements the place needs."

She'd need to hire people to help with cooking and cleaning, booking and RideShare arrangements, figure out how to fix a sprinkling system and how to make sure the chlorine in the pool was at the right level, and so many other things.

The list was a mile high, and yet, Eloise didn't shy away from it.

"Who says you're not a risk-taker?"

Eloise giggled and leaned further into Aaron. "We both know I'm not." She thought of the moldy smell in the apartment too, and she might not be able to live in the inn straightaway. Her heartbeat pulsed, but she refused to let the fear choke her.

"Well, I'm not," he said. "And you're always the opposite of me."

"You are too," she said. "You literally put your life on the line every day. That's a huge risk."

"Oh, come on, El. Put my life on the line every day?" He laughed. "You know Five Island Cove better than that."

"There was some ruckus at the hot air balloon thing."

"No, there wasn't," he said dryly. "That was a sea lion that got a little too close to some people and their food. They freaked out, and then they ran into other people, who ran into traffic. That wasn't a ruckus. That was a rogue sea lion."

Eloise laughed again, and Aaron pulled her closer. "I sure do like you, Eloise," he whispered. "What did you tell Billie? That you like me a whole lot?"

"Yes," she said, her voice catching in the back of her throat. She decided to take that risk and be as brave as she could be. She turned toward Aaron, his other hand coming to rest on her hip. She looked up at him. "I'm falling in love with you, Aaron."

"Good," he said easily. "Because I'm falling in love with you too, Eloise." He lowered his head and kissed her, and this time, Eloise didn't care who was watching.

A COUPLE OF HOURS LATER, ELOISE RODE THE ISLAND BUS TO the ferry station. She and Aaron had had time for dinner and ice cream, and he'd taken her to the free line that would take her to the ferry, and he'd gone back to his house.

Eloise basked in the glow of a great date, and she

didn't notice that the bus had stopped. She looked out the dark window and then to the driver. They weren't at the ferry station yet. A laundromat sat at the end of a strip mall, the only thing open right now.

"You have to get off here," he said. "It's the last stop tonight."

"No," she said. "This line goes all the ferry station."

"The last ferry is leaving right now," he said in a gravelly voice. He had to be close to eighty years old, and Eloise wondered if he drove this bus for enjoyment or if he needed the money. "We don't go down there on the last route."

"But I have to get on the ferry to Rocky Ridge," she said, panic starting to build in her stomach. "I'll get a RideShare." She hurried toward the door, thinking she should've just gotten a ride in the first place. But the ice cream shop had been right by the free bus line, and they literally went straight to the ferry station.

"Suit yourself," he said as she passed. "But it's closed."

She said, "Thank you," and got off. Five minutes later, a car pulled up to the laundromat, and Eloise couldn't get in fast enough. If Aaron thought there weren't scary places in the cove, he'd never loitered outside this laundromat in the dark, waiting for a ride.

"Ferry station, please," she said, and the woman started driving. Feeling somewhat vindicated, because this driver hadn't told her the ferries weren't running anymore, Eloise settled into her seat.

She knew the moment the woman pulled into the ferry station parking lot that she would not be getting on a ferry that night. "They're closed," she said.

"Yeah," the woman said. "Last ferry at nine-fifty-one on weekdays."

Eloise glanced at her watch. It was just after ten. "I thought...why'd you bring me here then?"

"Lots of people leave their cars here," she said. "I just figured...you don't have a car here?"

"No." Eloise shook her head, numbness moving through her. No, she did not have a car here. She also did not have anywhere to stay on this island. She looked out over the water, and she could see the pinpricks of light, indicating the houses on Sanctuary. Over there, she could stay with her mother, or even at the inn.

Over here...

Eloise had choices. Robin's house was sitting empty, and Eloise could get the code to her garage with a simple text. She could stay at the lighthouse with Kristen. The woman would probably be thrilled to have her, and Eloise couldn't imagine her loneliness.

And then there was Aaron...

"Where would you like me to take you?" the woman asked. "There are plenty of hotels here, and it's summer, but I bet you could find a room."

"No," Eloise said, her voice hardly her own. "I have someone I can stay with." The last word stuck against her tongue, but she managed to push it out.

Her mind raced. The driver waited. Finally, Eloise couldn't sit on a decision any longer. She gave the driver Aaron's address and sat back, her fingers rattling around each other.

What would he do when she showed up on his doorstep? Would he be in bed already?

Did she want to get in bed with him?

Her skin prickled, and it felt like she'd breathed out and was a mile from Aaron's house, and breathed in, and she'd arrived.

"Thanks." She paid the driver and went toward the front door. His motion-sensor light came on, and inside, behind the door, his dog began to bark.

Eloise slicked her palms down her shorts and reached for the doorbell. She heard scuffling inside, and Prince stopped barking. A moment later, the door opened, and Aaron stood there, wearing the exact same thing she'd seen him in thirty minutes ago.

"I missed the last ferry by ten minutes," she said. "Guess we shouldn't have had the double-scoop cones." She put a smile on her face, and it wasn't hard. Because faced with him, all of her fears fled. All of her nervousness simply disappeared.

This was Aaron, and she was very nearly in love with him. "Can I come in?" she asked.

"Yeah, of course." He stepped back and let her in, closing the door behind her.

Eloise had been here before, but this was different. It

reeked of different, and she turned back to him. "I still have no maybe's," she said. "You?"

"Not a single one."

Eloise smiled and stepped into his arms, easily tipping her head back to kiss him.

CHAPTER TWENTY-FOUR

Alice disembarked from the plane, the weight of the world on her shoulders. The last three days had been made from nightmares, but Alice had only slept for twelve or thirteen hours, so she knew she wasn't dreaming them.

The hearing had gone well, and the judge had been impressed with her meticulous gathering of receipts, her proposal to her husband to dissolve their marriage, and the plethora of evidence she had for why he needed to pay for what she'd asked him to pay for.

She had ordered Frank to leave the accounts as they were, and to continue to pay for things as if he and Alice were still married. Because they were. Legally, they were.

She had not brought up his repeated infidelity, but she'd hired Susan Burmingham, and she'd wanted anything Alice had against Frank. They'd spent the better part of Tuesday afternoon and all day Wednesday together, putting everything Alice had gathered—receipts from hotel rooms, cabins in the woods, jewelry for his mistresses, all of it—into some semblance of order.

Alice kept meticulous records, and she had documents of everything Frank had paid for over the last twenty years. She knew how divorce court worked; he would not get away with paying nothing. He'd supported her and the children exclusively since the twins' birth. He would have to continue to do so.

She couldn't wait to get back to the house. She wanted fully caffeinated coffee, and some of Robin's lemon bars, and all of her friends around her. She wanted to hug her children, and hear the laughter as the kids splashed in the pool.

She stopped at a kiosk in the airport and grabbed a bottle of water, though what she really needed was wine. Chocolate. Pasta. And a lot of painkiller.

Alice could tolerate a lot of pain, and she'd wait until she could eat something better than a hot dog that had likely been sitting under a warmer for an hour before she took any pills and drank anything stronger than water.

She waited through two full ferries before she was able to get off Diamond Island, and the journey from there took a little over an hour, because she'd arrived at the height of afternoon travel, with tourists returning to their bungalows and hotels.

The line for a RideShare stretched down the sidewalk,

past the ropes that had been set up to mark where to stand. Alice heaved her carryon with her, her mood growing fouler by the moment. She took out her phone, expecting to see a text from someone.

Charlie or Ginny, whom she'd texted her flight itinerary to. Perhaps Robin, who also knew what time Alice was coming in.

She had nothing.

She tapped the phone icon to call Robin, because it might be faster if she simply got in Alice's car and came to get her. She had driven herself early on Tuesday morning, but her friends needed the car, and they'd come to get it later that day.

"Hey," Robin said, her voice light and carefree. Alice knew how much it took to make her tone sound that way, but it still rubbed her eardrums wrong.

"Hey, can you come get me?"

"Where are you?"

"I'm at the ferry station."

"On Diamond?"

"No," Alice said, frowning. She looked around like Robin would jump out from behind a car. "Rocky Ridge."

"You're back already?"

"Back already?" Alice asked. "I texted you that I'd be in on the three-fifty flight."

"That flight got cancelled," Robin said. "They moved everyone to the seven-ten."

"No, they didn't," Alice said.

"That's what their app said."

"Well, I can assure you, Robin, that I am standing at the ferry station at Rocky Ridge. Can you come or not?"

"No, I can't," Robin said. "I'm at the lighthouse."

On Diamond Island. Alice's heart sank all the way to her shiny, designer shoes. "Are the twins with you?"

"Yes," she said. "I'm so sorry, Alice. Charlie and Ginny got the notification about your flight too. We figured we'd stay here until then, and we'd meet you at the airport."

Tears burned behind Alice's eyes. "It's okay." What else could she say? Sure, her heart wasn't beating normally, and she didn't want to go another minute without hugging her children. She needed someone at her side right now, because the thought of them all being with her wasn't enough anymore.

"Do you—?" She sucked in a breath, because her voice was nasally and about to crack.

"We're coming right now," Robin said. "Come on, Mandie," she said, her voice growing distant. "Go get them. Alice is back already."

Alice felt like such a burden, and she hated that. She let Robin snap at her girls, and the activity on the other end of the line continue though she didn't need to hear it.

"Do you want to talk to Ginny and Charlie?" Robin asked.

"No," Alice said quickly. "I don't..." She didn't want them to hear her tears in her voice. She didn't have to say it for Robin to know. "Who's at the house?"

"Uh, I don't think anyone is at the house," Robin said.

"Okay," Alice said, moving forward in the line. "Bye, Robin."

"Alice—" Robin started, but Alice ended the call.

No one had been anticipating her arrival. She wondered when they would've noticed that she hadn't shown up. In fact, right now, she could wander off and get in any car or on any boat and drift away, and no one would know for at least an hour. Maybe longer.

She wondered how far she could get in a boat in an hour. They wouldn't even know which direction she'd gone.

Something seethed beneath her skin, an anger that she'd kept suppressed for many years, especially the last few days as she stood before a judge, determined not to show a single emotion. She never allowed herself to do that with Frank either, and seeing him at the other table with his fancy lawyer friend had ignited her determination to make good on her word.

He'd signed the agreement. If he didn't want to adhere to that, she'd do what Charlie had told her to. She'd take everything she could from Frank, the way he'd done to her.

When it was her turn for a car, she stepped to the podium and said, "I want to go to Friendship Inn."

"That's off the south side of the island," the teenager there said in a bored voice. He plucked something from the podium on his side. "It's a ten-minute boat ride. The inn is closed now, but the island is open until dusk." He handed her the pamphlet, and she took it with her to the waiting car.

She was delivered to the south ferry station, which was little more than a dock. She found a man there with his feet up on a desk, watching TV, and she tossed the pamphlet next to them. "How much to take me to Friendship Inn?"

He looked away from the screen. "Ten bucks there," he said. "Ten bucks back"

"Do you wait for me there?"

"You can tell me how long you wanna be there, and I'll come back and gitcha."

Alice pulled a twenty-dollar bill from her purse and handed it to him. Before she knew it, she and Clyde were the only people on his boat, headed through the choppy waters toward a smudge of earth on the horizon that Clyde believed would be underwater in another decade.

Alice said nothing, and when she stepped off the boat only seven minutes later, she asked, "How long can I have?"

"This island closes at dusk, technically," he said, glancing behind her. "Not sure why you'd want to be here at all, but you gotta do you."

Alice glanced at her watch. It was almost five-thirty. Her stomach growled. Her head ached. Her eyes burned with unshed tears she had a feeling she wouldn't be able to hold back for much longer.

"I need an hour," she said, turning away from him quickly.

"You got it," he said behind her, and Alice walked away from him, her rolling suitcase making the most unnatural noise as it scraped against the asphalt.

The guttural growl of Clyde's engine started up, and Alice kept her back straight. When she couldn't hear it anymore—when it was just her, the wind, the sun, the waves slapping against the rocks, and this empty, forsaken island, Alice let her tears fall.

She abandoned her suitcase next to a tree, and went to a nearby picnic table that probably hadn't been used in years. At least it sat in the shade, and as Alice put her head in her hands and cried, at least she didn't have to pretend to be okay anymore.

———

SOMETIME LATER, ALICE STOOD ON THE ROOF OF Friendship Inn, looking toward Rocky Ridge. She'd only cried for a few minutes. She was very good at letting everything out quickly, stuffing all her broken parts away, and smoothing everything over.

This time, though, she wasn't sure she was going to smooth anything over. Robin had texted a couple of times, saying she and the teens were on their way back to Rocky Ridge. Kelli, Alice had learned, was out with Zach, and AJ had an afternoon date with DJ, where she was expected to break-up with him, because she'd gotten the job in New York City.

Eloise was on Diamond with Aaron and his kids too, and Robin's last text had said that there was some juicy gossip with them.

Alice hadn't responded to any of the messages.

She didn't care about gossip, especially if Eloise was involved. The woman hated to be talked about, and Alice wouldn't do that to her.

She hated that she'd missed the celebratory dinner for AJ and her new job, and she hated that she had this fury and frustration boiling in her gut. No one had purposely shunned her, but her feelings still quivered, and she really just wanted to break down a door and see what the inside of Friendship Inn looked like.

She knew one thing: No one would ever find her here. For some reason, that sent a thread of vindication through her. Let them show up at *her* house and sleep in *her* beds, wondering where poor Alice had gone.

The bitterness burned the back of her throat, and she tried to swallow it away. That didn't work, and she'd finished the single bottle of water she'd bought at the airport. She'd probably be sunburned from standing out under the sun for so long, and Alice eased away from the edge of the roof and went down the metal stairs on the side of the building.

The shade did bring a measure of relief to her, but her head still pounded like someone was trying to drill their way out. She blinked, the C-shaped flashes of light in her vision signaling an optic migraine.

She hadn't had one in a while, but she hadn't been sleeping the way she should've been. It would only last fifteen or twenty minutes, and then her vision would clear.

Alice wished her vision for the future would crystalize as easily.

She pressed a couple of fingers to her forehead, almost feeling like she'd moved past her skull and into her brain. She had to take some painkiller, and she navigated away from the shady side of the inn and back to her bag.

She unzipped the top pocket and took out the pill case she kept there. She dry swallowed three pills and turned back to the building. Friendship Inn had initially been someone's private home, and it stood three stories tall, with ten-foot decks that wrapped around every floor. Every room had an ocean view, and Alice turned to that white sand on the south and west side. The east edge of the island was made of the same black rock as Rocky Ridge, and she wondered if the two islands had once been connected.

The Friend family lived in the building with their three children, and they'd hosted the most wonderful parties on their island. Alice had studied them, their fortune, and their fame after she and Frank had been married. She may have even used some of Elizabeth Friend's recipes for her first couple of dinner parties.

When she'd died, the family slid into a gradual decline, until eventually, the home was sold. The new owner named it Friendship Inn, and opened up the nineteen bedrooms, each with an accompanying en suite.

It was during those days that rental companies rented kayaks and canoes for people to row from Rocky Ridge to Friendship Inn Island. Alice had come to the island twice, one of which was with her Seafaring Girls, where their summer sand pact had been made.

She lost track of the inn after she'd left the cove, but it had been closed for years now. Probably at least fifteen or sixteen.

Alice went down to the beach, and she could see her eighteen-year-old self lying on her back on the hot sand, looking up into the sky. Robin had been to her right, Eloise to her left; Kelli and AJ on the other side of her. They'd laughed about their row across the channel, and then Robin had asked what they were most worried about.

Alice could not remember what she'd said, nor could she remember what Eloise or AJ or Kelli had said. She only remembered what Robin had admitted to.

I'm worried I'll end up just like my mother.

Alice wondered why she was thinking about that right now, of all things. She wasn't sure, but she sat down on the sand, wishing she had a big, wide-brimmed hat, a beach chair, and a cardboard tray of crab cakes from the little concession stand that had operated out of the ground-floor of the inn.

She ran her fingers through her hair and let out a breath. She drew in another one through her nose and lifted her hands above her head, using the air to push all the negativity out of her mind and soul. She'd taken up meditation and yoga within a few months of her marriage to Frank, because she was managing an insane schedule and so was her new husband.

After a few minutes, she started to feel more like herself. Thankfully.

Her phone rang, and her son's name sat on the screen. Alice actually hesitated, because she just wanted to be left alone.

She answered, because an hour ago, she'd wanted to be surrounded by the people who loved her and whom she loved. For some reason, her wounded feelings had taken her in the complete opposite direction.

On the third ring, she swiped on the call. "Hey, Charlie."

"Where are you, Mom?" He sounded like he was walking on the beach, the wind rushing across the receiver of his phone.

"Where are you?" she asked.

"We just docked at the ferry on the Ridge. Did you make it back to the house?"

"No."

"No?"

"Are you okay?"

"Yes."

"Is Ginny okay?"

"Um, yes?"

"Tell Robin thank you for looking after you. I'll be back...sometime tonight."

"Mom," Charlie said, definitely irritated with her now. "What's going on?"

"What's going on?" Alice said, a flip switching inside her. "I'll tell you what's going on. I've been in New York dealing with literally the most stressful thing of my life, and I get back after letting everyone know when, and everyone's off on their own, enjoying their vacation. From *my* home. But does anyone really care about me? No, I don't think they do."

Charlie didn't answer, and the next voice that came on the line was Robin's. "Alice, we're getting off the ferry now. I know Eloise and Aaron are bringing a couple of trays of pasta and garlic bread from Diamond for dinner."

"Great, enjoy it," Alice said, her voice as cold as ice. She hated this pettiness in her, but she'd held so many things back for so long, and she didn't want to do it anymore. She was tired of stuffing her own feelings and her own needs back down into her stomach, and she had simply been silent for long enough.

"Alice," Robin said. "I don't know what to say."

"Then don't say anything," Alice said. She caught site of Clyde's boat chugging toward her, and she added, "I have to go, Robin. Thank you for taking care of the twins. I really will be back tonight to relieve you."

"They're fine, but—"

"Bye, Robin." She didn't want to hang up on her best friend again.

"Okay...bye."

Alice ended the call then and let her phone fall to her lap. Regret lanced through her, and she hated that she'd been cruel to her friend and snapped at her son. A sigh leaked from her mouth, and she got to her feet to brush the sand from her slacks.

She hated that she was even wearing slacks. She just wanted to wear jeans like other people, and cutoffs in the summer. She wanted to throw away her flowing, white pants, and her sparkly tops, and all of her strappy sandals.

Alice would do anything for a pair of flip flops right now.

She met Clyde at the dock, got back on his rusty boat, and returned to Rocky Ridge. A few minutes out, she tapped to call a RideShare, and the car waited for her by the time she bid adieu to Clyde.

"The shops on Driftwood," she said. "Please."

"You got it." The kid behind the wheel barely looked old enough to drive. He delivered her to the shops without incident, and Alice faced the quaint shops, each one in a little house of its own. The area had a lot of trees, and some of the stores were out on the beach, where a wooden boardwalk had been constructed for shoppers.

The shops were busy for a Thursday night, and Alice realized it was the Ridge Two-for-One Weekend, and tonight was the first night.

She walked into a shop she'd been in several times in the past, but not in the last twenty years. The space inside wasn't huge, but the racks held as many clothes as they could. The hangers were wood, with metal clips holding the skirts and pants. The clothes were high-end, but casual at the same time.

Alice didn't need new clothes, but she did enjoy retail therapy and she was so very tired of being Alice Kelton, the perfectly put-together woman who never let anyone know precisely how she felt.

She plucked a pair of denim shorts from the rack, an item she hadn't worn since leaving Rocky Ridge twenty-five years ago.

She was ready to find herself again, and she wasn't sure if that woman would wear denim shorts, but she was going to try them on and find out.

CHAPTER TWENTY-FIVE

R obin paced from the kitchen, past the dining room table, and toward the couch. "What are we going to do?" She'd asked the same thing three times, and no one had answered her.

She'd sent out a mayday text to the other ladies, and Eloise had immediately called. She couldn't drop everything and come, because she and Aaron were waiting for the food.

AJ had said she'd be back in five minutes, but it had been fifteen. Kelli had walked in with Zach five minutes ago, but she'd run into the bathroom a moment later.

She came out, and Robin spun toward her. "What are we going to do?"

"I don't understand the whole situation," Kelli said.

"My mom is mad," Ginny said. "No one was here when she got back, and she feels abandoned."

Robin looked at Alice's daughter, surprise moving through her. "Is that how she really feels?"

"Yes," Ginny said, her brown eyes wide and worried.

"Okay, where would she go?" Robin asked, her phone chiming. She yanked her attention to it, her heart leaping. Maybe Alice had calmed down enough to see reason.

Guilt gutted her. She should've been at the airport the moment Alice stepped foot in the cove. She'd been gone for three days—three very, very stressful days—and Robin knew better than the others how Alice functioned.

She was so strong on the outside. She hid everything. Eventually, all of that pressure and stress built up, and built up, and then she'd literally collapse. Robin had seen in several times as she'd grown up with Alice, and she'd felt it coming since she'd arrived in the house.

"I don't know," Ginny said. "We haven't come to the Ridge much in the past couple of years."

"I'm here," AJ said as she came in the entrance from the garage. "What's going on?"

Robin looked at her, wondering if AJ had been upset about her break-up with DJ. She didn't seem to have bloodshot eyes or tear-stained cheeks. She did carry concern in her expression, and she came directly to Robin.

"Alice is AWOL," she said. "She was on the three-fifty flight, and no one was here to greet her." She glanced at Ginny. "She feels abandoned, and we have to find her as soon as possible."

A sense of panic gathered in Robin's chest, and it grew and grew until a band of pressure started squeezing the breath out of her lungs.

"What about tracking her phone?" AJ asked, glancing at Kelli and then Robin. "Where's Eloise?"

"She's picking up dinner." Robin spun to Charlie and Ginny, who both sat at the table. They didn't look happy, and Robin wished she knew what to say to them. "Can we track her phone?"

"She can track ours," Charlie said. "I don't know about hers."

"How do we find out?" Robin would call Frank if she had to. That was how desperate she was to find Alice quickly. She should not be out there alone, as Robin felt sure she was in a downward spiral, and the landing would be an explosion.

Alice wouldn't want to hit in public, and Robin regretted that she hadn't texted Alice to confirm that her flight had been delayed. Now that she thought about it, Alice would've definitely texted or called to say her flight was delayed.

She'd been enjoying the afternoon at the lighthouse, and she'd just pulled a pan of brownies from the oven when Alice had called.

It had taken forever to find Charlie, because he'd been hiking down on the cliffs, and the ferry station had been packed. Robin remembered what tourist season in the cove was like now, and that she didn't normally travel between the islands when there were thousands more people here.

"I'm logging on to our cell phone provider," Charlie said.

Robin pulled out the chair and sat beside him, not wanting to pressure him but unable to keep herself away.

He said the last four digits of Alice's phone number as he tapped. "It has it on it."

Robin wanted to rip the phone from his hands, because he seemed to be moving like molasses.

"How do I tell where she is...?" His voice trailed off, and Robin's fingers twitched.

"Let me look," Ginny said.

Charlie handed her his phone, and Robin clenched her teeth together. Her phone rang, and she flinched as she looked down. Eloise.

"Hey," she answered, keeping both eyes on Charlie and Ginny, who both leaned over his phone.

"Where is she?" Eloise asked. "We have the food, and we're headed to the ferry. Have you spoken to her?"

"Yes," Robin said. "And she didn't hang up on me this time, so that's something, right?"

"I feel so bad," Eloise said. "We should've been there."

"We should've," Robin said, meeting Charlie's eye as he looked. "We're trying to locate her phone to find her. I have to go. I'll keep you updated." She'd no sooner ended the call with Eloise when her phone rang again.

Duke's name sat on the screen this time, but Charlie said. "We have an address."

"Let's go," Robin said, practically dumping the chair over she stood up so fast. She answered Duke's call with, "Hey, babe. I don't have much time right now." At the same time, she really needed to be able to talk with him. He was supposed to have seen a doctor that day, and she wanted to know if the gash on his arm would keep him from working for the rest of the summer.

"Okay," he said. "Just wanted to report that I got the all-clear for work."

"That's great," Robin said, relieved he wasn't injured so badly that he couldn't work. At the same time, she'd almost hoped he wouldn't be able to, because then he'd come home. She honestly didn't know how Aaron had been taking care of his girls alone, or how Alice would do it with the twins once her divorce from Frank was final.

She's been single-parenting the whole time, Robin thought as Duke continued talking about his doctor's visit.

"What's going on there?" Duke asked. "Are you running?"

"Sort of," Robin said, getting behind the wheel of Alice's car. "It's a long story, but we have to go get Alice."

"How did her hearing go?"

Irritation flared in Robin. She wanted to talk to her husband; she did. But she'd told him she didn't have much time. "I'm going to have to call you back."

She started to back up, but Charlie called, "Whoa, whoa, whoa," and she slammed on the brake.

"What's happening?" Duke asked.

Robin couldn't hold the phone and drive and think and panic. "I have to go," she said, and she ended the call. She flexed her fingers on the wheel and pressed the button to open the garage.

Checking now, she saw she could back up without hitting anything. "Give me the address," she said, infusing some calmness into her voice.

Charlie read it off, but Robin wasn't as well-versed with Rocky Ridge as she was with Diamond Island. Even on Sanctuary, she'd be able to find her way around without much help. "Can you map it?"

He tapped and tapped, and finally a voice said, "Continue on Sandy Shores Drive for one mile."

The closer they got, the more Robin suspected Alice was at the shops on Driftwood Beach."

"You have arrived," the map said, and Robin started looking for a space. There were people everywhere, and she had no idea why. Whatever was happening here had probably been the reason the ferries had been so crowded, and she got out of the car, feeling hopeless as person after person walked down the sidewalk.

"How are we going to find her?" Ginny asked.

"Call her," Robin said, not about to give up now. "One of you call her. If she doesn't answer, the other one will call." She looked at the twins and they looked back at her, expecting her to know what to do. She didn't, but she was going to act like she did. "And we'll do that until we hear her blasted phone ring."

Ginny nodded and made the call. Robin started walking down the sidewalk, taking in the celebration and all the racks out on the sidewalk. They were having a big sale, and Alice would be in heaven here.

Help us find her, Robin prayed, and Ginny said, "Mom, where are you? We came to the shops, but there are so many people here."

Robin's hopes lifted, and she watched Ginny nod and turn away from her. "Yes," she said, though she'd lowered her voice as if she didn't want to be heard. "All right." She hung up and faced Robin and Charlie. "She's at Livingston's, trying on shorts. She wants us to come help her decide."

Confusion sat in the girl's eyes, and Robin's emotions warred with one another. "Fine," she said. "Let's go do that." She marched ahead of the twins to the map. She found Livingston's, which was a little shop only two houses down from where they stood.

She went that way, her heartbeat crashing against her ribs. Several racks had been set outside the shop, but Robin went inside. Cool air conditioning blew, and a tall, lithe woman stood at the other wall.

Alice.

Robin strode toward her as Charlie said, "Mom."

Alice turned toward them, and she stepped out from

behind a clothing rack. "What do you think?" She wore a pair of denim shorts that were far too short for her long legs, especially at her age.

Robin stopped short, her first reaction to snap at Alice for the worry she'd caused. For being so silly about not having someone there to greet her. At the same time, she had no idea what Alice had truly been through in the past twenty years, and she couldn't judge.

"No," she said. "Those are not you."

Alice cocked her head at Robin, her eyes narrowing. "Ginny?" she asked, switching her gaze to her daughter.

"They're...kind of short, Mom."

"Charlie?"

"I mean, I guess," he said, clearly uncomfortable.

Alice turned back to the mirrors as if the four of them were just enjoying a regular night of shopping together. "I suppose you're right. I don't really like them."

"Alice," Robin said. "Aaron and Eloise are almost back with the food, and it's time to come home."

"No," Alice said. She didn't look at any of them as she went into the dressing room.

Robin's exasperation reached the boiling point. She marched right over to the door and managed to twist the knob before Alice could lock it. "Yes," she said, crowding into the small space with Alice. "Listen. Your children are scared, and they're worried sick about you. I am too, and I'm sorry we weren't there when you got off the plane, but it was an honest mistake. You have to come back to the house."

Tears filled her eyes, and though Alice was taller than Robin by quite a bit, she did not back down.

"I can't," Alice said, her voice wavering. "I don't know who I am anymore, and I need some new clothes to help me decide."

"No." Robin said, shaking her head. She gathered Alice into an embrace as she fell the last few feet of her downward spiral and hit the ground. "No, you don't."

Alice sobbed into Robin's shoulder, the pain echoing from her horrible and causing Robin's own tears to pool and slide down her face. "You're Alice Williams," she said. "And she is strong, and smart, and beautiful. She can weather any storm, and she is not going to let Frank Kelton beat her." Robin stroked Alice's hair as they cried together. "You're Alice Williams, and you have never liked short shorts—or denim for that matter—and you told me once that I better not let them bury you in a dress either."

Alice half-laughed then, but she did not lessen the grip she had on Robin's shoulders. She didn't mind, though Alice's bony fingers were like knives in her shoulder blades. Robin could be the strong one this time. Robin could hold Alice upright until she could do it for herself again. Robin, though she felt one breath away from a complete collapse too, was needed and necessary, and she craved that feeling.

"Ginny," she said. "Charlie. Come in here."

The twins entered the dressing room too, and Robin expected Alice to turn away, compose herself, and then face them, calm, cool, and collected. The way Alice always did.

Instead, she grabbed onto them and the three of them embraced while Alice continued to cry.

CHAPTER TWENTY-SIX

E loise stretched toward the end table near her and set her coffee cup on it. Hours had passed since Robin had returned to the house with Alice and her twins, and Alice had disappeared into the master suite for twenty minutes and come out wearing a black sweatsuit with pink pinstripes down the sides of the legs and the outer arms.

With bare feet and her hair damp and tousled from the shower she'd taken, she looked stunningly human. "Sorry I made everyone wait to eat," she'd said, and that was all.

They'd eaten, and the kids had enjoyed the night in the pool while Robin kept Eloise busy in the kitchen making mocktails.

Aaron had taken his girls and left a few minutes ago.

Kelli had put Parker to bed, and then she'd stepped outside to say goodbye to Zach.

"We're going to clean up and go to bed," Charlie said, stepping over to his mother. She stood from the hearth where she sat and embraced him, her eyes closing as she did. In that brief moment, Eloise saw and felt her emotion, though Alice had been trying to box it up behind a stone mask.

Ginny hugged her mother too, and Robin said, "I'll be right back," and followed her girls upstairs. Eloise looked at AJ, who stared into the depths of her coffee cup as if the liquid there held a great secret she needed to riddle through.

Alice sighed as she sat back down, and Eloise looked at her. "Come sit on the couch," she said. "It's too hard over there."

Alice did so without argument, which was something to Eloise. Alice sometimes prided herself on doing the hard things no one else wanted to do. She smiled at Eloise as she sank onto half of the loveseat kitty-corner to where Eloise sat.

"I don't want to tell it twice."

"I wasn't going to ask," Eloise said. She hadn't invoked her rights of first refusal when Robin had started to question her about Aaron, but she hadn't come right out and asked if Eloise had slept with him. So Eloise hadn't answered. She didn't want to drag something special to her through the mud, and it was really none of anyone's business anyway.

She reached out her hand, and Alice put hers in it. They squeezed together, and Eloise's felt like the whole sky could crack open and rain down, and it wouldn't matter. Alice would be there for her, and she'd be there for Alice.

"I'm sorry I wasn't here to pick you up," she said.

"Please, don't," Alice said, but not unkindly, as she removed her hand from Eloise's. "I already feel so stupid."

"Why?" AJ asked.

"Because I basically threw a little hissy fit that my friends have their own lives?" Alice sounded like she was guessing.

Eloise studied her, trying to find the right things to say. Robin came down the steps, a sigh leaking from her mouth too. "Is Kelli back?" She glanced around, a look of displeasure crossing her face. She started for the front door just as it opened.

"Bye," Kelli said, and then she came into the living room too. They all sat down and looked at one another, and it was clear no one wanted to speak first.

Eloise had been in situations like this before. Not with friends, but with students. Once the ice was broken, things could improve.

She'd always looked to Alice or Robin to lead out in times like these. But Alice was in no shape to do that, and

Robin honestly looked a little lost. Like her thoughts lingered somewhere far away.

Eloise knew where—Alaska.

"How's Duke?" she asked. "Wasn't he going to the doctor today?"

Robin swung her head toward Eloise, her blue eyes widening. "Yes, he was."

"And?" Eloise reached for her coffee cup like this was exactly what they should be talking about.

She shook her head, and Eloise's stomach dropped. "Robin," she said. "Is he okay?"

"He's not coming home," she said, her voice beyond tight. She closed her eyes and then swiped at them quickly. After drawing in a long breath, she said, "So yes. He's okay. The doctor cleared him to go back out on the boat. He just has to keep his arm dry, and he has to have Bryan check the dressing every night, and he's on some antibiotics so he doesn't get an infection."

"He got stitches, right?"

"Yes." Robin looked at Eloise again. "Eight. He's okay."

Eloise understood the secret code Robin used from time to time. This time, she was saying, *drop it, Eloise.*

So Eloise dropped it, but she had to pick something else up. She looked at AJ. "How did DJ take the news?"

She finally looked away from her coffee, blinking out of whatever trance she'd fallen into. "It went okay," she said.

"Did it?" Robin asked.

AJ shrugged and handed Eloise her coffee cup as if Eloise was her mother and would have a purse to put it in. She set it on the table next to hers, a bit of irritation slinking through her. AJ sagged into the couch behind her and closed her eyes. "I'm never going to meet a decent guy."

"I thought DJ was decent," Alice said.

"Yeah, well, even the nice ones can fool you," AJ said.

"What happened?" Robin asked.

"Nothing happened," AJ said. "That's the problem. He literally chuckled and shook his head. He said, 'you've got to do what works for you, AJ. It's not like we were serious.'" She sat up and opened her eyes. "No one is ever serious about me. Do I put off some sort of vibe or something?" She wore agony in her expression as she looked around at everyone.

Eloise recognized the desperation in her, because Eloise had experienced it plenty of times in her life. Usually when everyone else in this room had a date to the prom, and she did not. When they got asked to go on hayrides and to beach bonfires, she went to the lighthouse so she wouldn't have to admit to her mother that she once again didn't have a date on a Friday night.

"You don't put off a vibe," Kelli said, patting AJ's leg. AJ looked at her for a few seconds and then sagged into Kelli's shoulder. Kelli said something else to her, but Eloise couldn't hear what.

"Things are going well with Aaron?" Alice asked Eloise.

Her heart beat out two beats in the space of one, but Eloise managed to nod normally. "Yes, I think so."

"He thinks so too," Robin said. "I saw him watching you with his kids tonight."

Eloise ducked her head and tucked her hair. "I might have told him I loved those girls."

"That'll be important to him," Alice said.

Eloise could only nod. "I'm going to need a lot of help with them," she said, looking around at everyone. "I've never been a mother."

"You think you two will get married then?" AJ asked.

Eloise didn't want to say anything else. She didn't want to hurt AJ, and thankfully, AJ said, "Of course you will. It's only me who can't find a freaking guy like Aaron Sherman." She got to her feet and started to round the couch.

"AJ," Eloise said.

"Don't go," Robin said at the same time.

"I need a sec," AJ said, striding through the kitchen and out into the garage in a matter of seconds. Her legs were so long, and Eloise envied her in that moment. Ironic, considering that AJ probably envied Eloise for her relationship with Aaron.

"I didn't mean to make her feel bad," Eloise said.

"You shouldn't have to apologize for having a great relationship," Robin said quietly. "Though I understand how you feel." Their eyes met, and a strong sense of understanding flowed between them.

"I have something to say," Kelli said. "But I really don't want to say it twice."

"She'll be back," Alice said. She stood and gathered the coffee cups on the table. "You done with this, Eloise?"

"Yes," she said. "Thank you." She looked at Robin as Alice passed in front of them. She lifted her eyebrows as soon as Alice had her back to both of them. Robin just shook her head. Exasperation streamed through Eloise. "I'm not good at this," she whispered.

"You're doing great," Robin whispered back.

"I'm having ice cream," Alice called from the kitchen. "Who wants some?"

"Me," Robin said. So did Kelli.

"I'll pass," Eloise said. Her stomach couldn't handle the dairy and the confrontation. AJ returned before Alice brought three bowls of ice cream into the living room.

"AJ?" she asked.

"No," she said. "Sorry. I just—I'm happy for you, Eloise." She looked at Eloise, and it seemed like her whole face might crack if she tried to move any part of it.

"I know you are," she said. "I'm sorry DJ was such a moron. I just think he said that to protect himself."

"We needed more time," AJ said. "But I want the job in New York."

"Yes," Alice said. "Tell me about the job in New York."

"It's a great job," AJ said, growing more animated now.

"It's not on-air yet, but it's prep for the live segments. Lots of interviews and opportunities for me to build relationships with players and coaches and other media personnel." She continued to talk about the station, as well as the apartments she'd been looking at, and the pay.

"I'm so glad," Alice said. "Though I was sort of looking forward to having a roommate." She put a pretty smile on her face, and Eloise saw the girl she'd been the day after her mother had died.

Fresh-faced, casual clothes, in so much pain but still able to smile, despite everything.

Eloise wanted to be like that one day. So strong that she could smile through anything.

"All right, Alice," Eloise said. "Your turn. Pretend we were all at the airport with balloons and flowers and that we welcomed you home right."

"You guys," she said, ducking her head. "I feel bad. I overreacted."

"No," Eloise and Robin said at the same time. " And even if you did," Robin added. "Your feelings have merit."

"I just... The hearing went pretty well, actually," Alice said. "I haven't slept or eaten properly in a long time, and I'm so tired." She put a weary smile on her face that trembled against her lips. Tears filled her eyes, but she didn't try to hide them. "I worked with an old friend of mine from law school to get everything else we needed for the case, and we burned the candle at both ends."

She shook her head, her expression growing distant,

almost like it was flying back across the water to the Hamptons. "The judge told Frank to abide by the agreement he signed, but ultimately, it's his choice. She did put a freeze on the accounts. He can't move money around and he has to keep paying the bills he normally would until a decision is made, so that's good for me."

She looked up, first to Robin, who'd taken her place on the hearth. Then Eloise, then AJ, and finally Kelli. "I wanted these two weeks to be a safe haven for me. You guys are the only absolutely safe place I have left." Her tears splashed down her face. "And when I found out no one was here, I don't know. I just, I felt..." She shook her head. "It doesn't matter."

"Abandoned," Robin said. "You felt abandoned."

Alice nodded. "It's silly, but I thought of how hard I'd worked to get everyone here, and all the schedules for meals and activities, and no one could even take a few minutes to make sure I had what I needed? It felt like the last twenty years of my life with Frank, all condensed into that ten minutes, and I was angry. I was lost. I was so hurt. And honestly, I was not strong enough to accept that I had no one." Her voice broke, and she did wipe her face then.

She put a bite of ice cream in her mouth next, and Eloise took that as a sign that she was done. She looked at Kelli, who just shook her head. "I'm good for tonight."

"You sure?" Robin asked. "You said you had something to tell us."

"Well..." Kelli started. "It's about the Glassworks."

Eloise knew what she was going to say before she said it, and by the way Alice lifted her head, suddenly dry-eyed, she did too.

"I'm going to offer it to Zach," Kelli said. "He's an artist, and—"

"Kelli, the Glassworks is easily worth half a million dollars," Alice said. "That's not something you *give* to a man you met a week ago."

Eloise didn't pipe in, but she agreed. Kelli had said only a few days ago during the Tell-All that her husband was buying a business with money they didn't have.

"I don't want it," Kelli said.

"Then you *sell* it," Alice said. "There are plenty of people on this island that would love that land. The building is in great shape."

"I agree with Alice," Robin said gently, and Eloise nodded.

"I wasn't asking for your opinions," Kelli said, her eyes shooting lasers, particularly at Alice.

"Okay," Alice said, holding up one hand and crossing her legs. She took another bite of ice cream, but Kelli had already finished hers. Robin stirred hers in her bowl, but Eloise had not seen her take a single bite yet.

"Anything else?" Robin asked.

"Yes," Eloise said, looking around at the other four women. "We're okay, right? The five of us?" She took an extra moment to meet Alice's eyes. "I'm really sorry, Alice. Truly."

"I am, too," Robin said. "We were just waiting for your flight to come in, I swear. Kristen was going to come with us too."

Alice nodded, her tears appearing again. "I know, you guys. Like I said, I feel stupid."

"Please forgive us," AJ said.

"Already forgiven."

"We love you, Alice," Kelli said, and considering the daggers she'd just shot at the woman, that was a big statement.

Eloise got up from the couch and hugged Alice. Before she knew it, all five of them huddled together in the living room, with Eloise right in the thick of them. "I love you all," she whispered, her voice one of the quietest among the other affirmations being said.

When they broke up and stepped back, Eloise noticed there wasn't a single dry eye in the room.

AJ went downstairs, and Kelli went up while Alice and Robin took the ice cream dishes into the kitchen. Eloise lingered by the kitchen table, her thoughts far too tangled to just go to bed now.

"I know you don't want to make a big deal out of things," Robin said, meeting her eye. "I promise I won't push for details." She exchanged a glance with Alice.

"I missed something," Alice said.

"Do you want to tell her?"

"I missed the ferry last night," Eloise said. "So I stayed with Aaron."

Alice's eyes widened, and she looked at Robin again. Then they both looked back at Eloise. She just smiled and shrugged. "It was a nice night." She stepped around the peninsula and embraced them both. "Thanks for letting me stay here, Alice. It has been a wonderful vacation."

"Anytime," Alice said, and Eloise knew she meant it. She left Robin and Alice in the kitchen, and she did go downstairs then, so many decisions to be made in the next few days.

Eloise reminded herself she didn't have to make them all by morning, and that alone allowed her to finally fall asleep, her mind still rotating around the possibility of retiring right now, moving to the cove, and starting work on the Cliffside Inn.

CHAPTER TWENTY-SEVEN

K elli had chickened out yet again. She managed to put Julian's excuses out of her mind for long enough to fall asleep. But they were right there, taunting her, the moment she woke up in the morning.

She kept her eyes closed as she came to consciousness and realized the brightness of the light beyond her eyelids.

She couldn't hear Parker either, and he'd probably left the bedroom to go downstairs and get something to eat or hang out with Charlie. Kelli had enjoyed seeing him break out of his shell a little bit, though it did make her mother heart a little sad.

Julian had been telling her for years that she couldn't cry every time Parker had a first day of school, and Kelli had wept in private the past two years. She enjoyed spending time with her son. It wasn't a crime.

She opened her eyes, the thought that she and Parker might be all the other had if her suspicions about Julian and Tiff were true. She'd asked him last week who she was and why she was bringing Chinese food to her home, and Julian had taken his sweet time to respond.

Hours later—after midnight, in fact—he'd said she was his assistant over marketing, and they had a long to-do list for the acquisition of BusinessBike, the company Kelli had signed her name to a loan to purchase.

They wanted to make the announcement at a specific time, with specific graphics and videos. They'd been working around the clock on that, and he'd still had all the regular stuff he did for Thompson Transport.

His text had been curt and harsh, and he'd basically told her to stop bothering him with ridiculous insinuations about him and his assistant. He insisted nothing improper was going on, and Kelli had felt about two inches tall.

She had actually apologized to him. As the days went by, she grew angrier and angrier about that. She had every right to ask him who this other woman was, especially if he was spending almost twenty-four hours a day with her.

She hadn't texted or called him since Sunday, and he'd gone silent too. She knew he was busy, but she still sighed as she sat up and stretched the kinks out of her muscles.

"You should've told them last night," she muttered to herself as she bent over, feeling a satisfying pull in her lower back. She'd said she had something to tell everyone and she didn't want to do it twice.

She did—but it wasn't about the Glassworks. She'd actually thought that was the safer of the two topics.

Divorce or the Glassworks.

Alice had turned into Mama Bear in the blink of an eye, and Kelli wasn't surprised to see Robin and Eloise agree with her.

Perhaps she should simply put the Glassworks up for sale. She'd been thinking about it for a couple of months now, since Kristen had signed the deed over to her on the last day before she'd returned to New Jersey.

For some reason, she didn't want to. She wanted Zach to have it. "Someone in the family should have it," she told herself as she walked into the bathroom. She hadn't planned on showering—until she saw her hair. She'd forgotten she'd gotten in the pool last night after dinner, and her honey blonde hair held a bit of a green tint now.

The hot water further relaxed her, and she let her mind wander now. Maybe she and Zach should go tour the Glassworks together. She could judge his reaction to it and ask him some more questions about how serious he was about picking up his art again.

She would still have the house on Seabreeze Shore. No one would ever take that from her, and she thought about taking Zach there too. Just to show him where his father had lived, once upon a time.

She wasn't sure if she was ready to share that with

him, though. Only AJ knew about the house, and she should probably tell Robin, Alice, and Eloise before a man she'd met a little over a week ago.

Alice simply didn't understand the bond Kelli felt to Zach. They'd both craved their father's approval and attention, just in two different ways. She never ran out of things to talk about with him, and some things she'd longed to mention to Heather or Sabrina, she couldn't bring up. All it did was inflict hurt on her sisters, and Kelli wouldn't do that.

Talking to Zach had healed some of the weeping wounds inside her, closed them up so she could breathe again.

Upstairs, she found Parker eating a toaster pastry with the teenagers. All of them looked sunburned and wind chapped, her son included. "What time did you guys go out?"

Kelli wasn't even sure what time it was right now.

"Six," Charlie said. "The waves are huge right now." He grinned at her like huge waves should be celebrated, but a sliver of anxiety ran through Kelli. She glanced at the clock to see it was almost ten-thirty, and her heart skipped a beat.

"Where is everyone else?" she asked.

"My mom wanted to go shopping," Ginny said. "Eloise and AJ went with her, because when AJ came down, you were in the shower. Robin said she'd wait for you, but I'm not sure where she went." She looked around the dining room, kitchen, and living room, as if Robin might be hiding behind the love seat. She shrugged. "We're going to Smuggler's Cove this afternoon, they said."

"Okay," Kelli said, a pinch sending a shock through her lungs. What if she didn't want to go to Smuggler's Cove? No one had even asked her.

She didn't care what they did with their day. She had four more here, and then she'd head back to New Jersey to really find out what was going on with her husband and his assistant.

Her stomach writhed as if she'd swallowed live snakes, and any thoughts of eating breakfast vanished. At the same time, perhaps if she ate, she'd could get those snakes to settle down. She moved into the kitchen and pulled out the container of leftover spaghetti from last night's dinner.

With it whirring in the microwave, she sent a text to Robin. *Sorry you had to wait for me. I'm eating real quick, and then we can go.*

She didn't answer, and Kelli shoved her phone in her back pocket when the microwave beeped. She sat down with the kids, who were talking about some app on their phones she didn't understand. Parker seemed interested, and he laughed with them, though he had no phone and couldn't possibly know what they were talking about.

She met his eye and smiled, and his face straightened. Kelli wasn't sure what that was about, and she wasn't going to ask in front of the others. She finished her spaghetti, cleaned up her dishes, and stood in the kitchen.

She felt like an island, like she could see everything and everyone who'd come through this house over the past ten days, streaming by her in super speed. AJ stomping out last night. Alice coming in once they'd found her. Robin and her girls making seafood pot pie, Kelli herself making the waffles, the mocktails they'd enjoyed over the evenings they'd spent together, AJ sitting at the bar, looking like she'd just lost her dog after the others had poured out her wine coolers.

Life simply passed Kelli by in those few seconds, and then she blinked, and all of that disappeared. She left the house through the garage exit and found the door had been raised. A car sat in the driveway, so Robin hadn't left.

She went out into the sunshine, closed her eyes, and took another breath. That was when she heard, "I know that, Duke. I'm allowed to be worried, though."

She turned toward the sound of Robin's voice and found her sitting on the steps, her phone stuck to her ear. Kelli walked that way, and Robin lifted her head a moment later. She did not look happy, and she stood up too. "I have to go. I'll call you back tonight, okay?"

She nodded, her eyes growing harder and harder with each thing Duke said. Kelli wanted to tell her that she wasn't even speaking to her husband, but she kept that information locked down tight.

"Okay," Robin said. "Love you too." She hung up and let out a frustrated sigh. "You ready to go?"

"Everything okay?" Kelli asked.

"Yes," Robin said, her voice almost a falsetto. So, that was a no. Kelli knew how she felt, because she wasn't okay either. Neither of them would say why, though, and for Kelli that was just fine. For now. That was fine for now.

"YOU DIDN'T TELL ME I HAD TO WADE OUT INTO THE ocean," Zach said later that afternoon.

Kelli watched Eloise march right into the surf. Alice had only hesitated for a moment, and then she'd kicked off the ugliest pair of flip flops Kelli had ever laid eyes on and followed Eloise.

Even Robin was rolling up her pants, as if that would do anything. They had to wade out to about waist deep. Her pants were going to get entirely wet.

Kelli hadn't minded the few hours of shopping at the Driftwood Beach. They were having some great sales, and she bought Julian's mother a few tea towels that had lobsters and the lighthouse on them—very quintessential Five Island Cove symbols.

"I didn't know," Kelli said. She wouldn't have dressed differently, because she'd only brought shorts and tanks, and the sun seemed hot enough today to steam dry her cotton shorts in only a few minutes. But Zach wore denim shorts, and she felt bad for him as she watched Robin and AJ meet the waves.

AJ started to run, and in the next moment, she dove

right into a wave. Robin's peal of laughter floated on the breeze coming off the water.

Kelli sighed. "Are we going or not?"

"I think so," he said. "Are you sure it's okay I'm here?" He looked at her, but Kelli kept her gaze on her four best friends.

Alice had eyed Zach like he'd brought a horrible, sulfuric smell with him when he'd shown up at the house mere moments before they'd left. "Yes," she said, but her voice now sounded a lot like Robin's had earlier.

She didn't care what Alice thought, and that was something brand new for Kelli. He was her half-brother, and she wanted to ask him about the Glassworks. She kicked off her sandals and picked them up. "Let's go."

She led the way into the water, gasping when it reached her thighs. "It's cold," she said.

"Yeah, this is weird," he said. "There's a very cold vein of water right here."

"Listen," she said, because it would be easier to talk to him when she couldn't see his face. Navigating the waves while walking in water dominated her attention, and she took a few seconds to speak.

"I can get us into my dad's old glassworks building. Do you want to go with me?"

"You can?" Zach asked.

"Yes."

"Yeah, of course I do," he said. "When are you leaving?"

"Tuesday," she said. "So tomorrow, Sunday, or Monday." She'd need to talk to the others and see what their plans were. It was her turn for dinner that night, and she'd decided she'd stop at the grocery store on the way back from this little adventure on Sanctuary Island. She could get hot food from the deli, a few bags of rolls, a case of soda, and call it good.

"Any of those work for me,' he said. "Though I do have a job interview on Monday."

"You do? For what?"

"Part-time art teacher at the high school," he said. "I guess the teacher they have now has a daughter who's pregnant, and she's anticipating taking a lot of time off, so they want like, a permanent sub."

"Oh, that's great," Kelli said.

Behind her, Zach chuckled. "A part time substitute teacher is great?" He laughed fully now. "I'm going to be so popular with the ladies."

Kelli smiled, but she couldn't argue. She needed to focus so she didn't die on her way around this cliff, and she started cursing Eloise, then Alice, then Robin, and then AJ with every slow, heavy step she took.

They were always trying to kill her in these waves that surrounded the cove. Always.

As she came around the corner, the most magnificent cove of calm water greeted her. Her friends all stood on the shore, gazing at something different. Kelli didn't know where to look either.

The greenery growing right out of the rocks, as if this island had been transported from somewhere much more tropical? The dark brown sand, so different from the white, sandy beaches everywhere else?

The perfectly, clear, teal water?

"This is amazing," Zach said, her awe sounding in his voice. She sloshed her way out of the water and went to stand next to AJ, her safe place, her anchor.

"Isn't this awesome?" AJ asked. "I didn't even know this was here."

"It's beautiful," Kelli said, still trying to take everything in. "Look, there's a waterfall up there." She pointed, but AJ didn't even look. Kelli let her arm drop, and they just stood there in silence together, drinking in the magnificence of Smugglers Cove.

Finally, Alice said, "This place is magical. I really do think the mermaids live here, El."

Everyone laughed, Kelli included, and she almost forgot that the ocean had tried to end her life by body-slamming her into a vertical sheet of black rock.

Almost.

AJ took Kelli's hand in hers and squeezed, and Kelli squeezed back. She knew she was in the right place, with the right people, at the right time. And she couldn't ask for more than that.

CHAPTER TWENTY-EIGHT

Alice knew it was time to get up and go. Her back hurt from lying on the sand or sitting on a rock for the past few hours, but she couldn't make herself move. This place was as magical as Eloise had always promised it would be.

She looked up into the sky again, so grateful for sunglasses and summer, waves and water, blue sky and best friends.

"I can see the inn," she said. "It's so odd it's right there. This place feels like it's off the map."

"It's time to go," Robin said. "Kelli left fifteen minutes ago, and she needs to get to the store."

"She's acting weird, right?" Alice asked, lifting her hand to allow Robin to help her stand. She groaned with the effort, and so did Robin. They laughed as they stumbled in the sand, and Alice finally righted herself.

"A little," she said.

"No," Eloise said. She stood with both feet in the water, ready to wade out. "She's not acting weird. She's acting like the woman she should've been for the past thirty years. The one that died when her father lost everything." She looked over her shoulder. "We just don't remember her, but Kelli had a lot of fire, and a ton of opinions she wasn't afraid to share, and a lot of drive."

Alice marveled at the wisdom in Eloise. "You know what? You're right."

"She's just uncovering all of that," Eloise said. "Think about last time she was here. She was a nervous wreck. She's not even close to that now, and it's only been two months." She stepped out into the water, and Alice wanted to be the last one out of Smugglers Cove.

She waited for Robin to go next, and then Alice finally followed them, telling herself to set a reminder on her phone to come here once a month. The twins would love it too, especially if they could pack in some sandwiches and something to drink.

"I'm glad this is a rental," Robin said as they loaded into the car soaking wet. "Kelli must've gone with Zach. I didn't think of that."

No one said anything, and while Alice wanted to know how they felt about her always inviting him along, she didn't ask. Perhaps Duke would've come had he been on the islands. At the same time, Alice didn't think so. Eloise hadn't invited Aaron. Why were children not allowed to come, but Zach was?

She tried to shake the thoughts out of her head, because it was none of her business anyway. Kelli had obviously grown close to the man in a short time, and whether or not Alice liked that would only drive a wedge between them. A wedge she didn't have the strength to pick up and deal with.

AJ rolled the back window down, and that made the air in the car thump through the space strangely. Robin yelped, her hand immediately going to her window button in the front to equalize the pressure.

"Sorry," AJ said.

"It's too cold to have the windows down," Alice complained. They were all soaking wet, for crying out loud.

Everyone waited for AJ to put up her window, and Alice finally looked across the back seat to her. "Fine," she said. "I just needed some fresh air."

"We literally just spent four hours in fresh air," Alice said, relief kissing her skin as AJ put up her window and Robin did too, almost simultaneously.

AJ said nothing as she looked out the window, and Alice sensed something wrong inside her too. She didn't have to guess at what it was, though, and that was the difference between AJ and Kelli.

Eloise pulled into the line for cars to get on the ferry and showed the attendant her reservation. He peered inside to note how many people rode in the vehicle and waved her through.

Alice enjoyed the comfortable silence all the way back to the house. AJ had fallen asleep sometime on the ferry, and Alice had closed her eyes too, though sleep had never claimed her. Her mind didn't circle as much as it had even a few days ago, and Alice could only feel relief and gratitude for that.

She felt different too, and she wondered if the change in her had been as dramatic as the one Kelli had been going through. As Eloise pulled into the driveway, parking alongside the beat-up pickup truck Zach had shown up in on the road where they'd parked to go to Smugglers Cove, Alice asked, "Do you think she's really going to give him the Glassworks?"

"I hope not," Robin said.

"Let's just support her," Eloise said.

"I'll talk to her about it," AJ said. She gave Alice a weary smile, and they went into the house together.

"There you are," Kelli said with a certain level of acid in her voice. "We're ready to eat."

MONDAY NIGHT, ALICE SAT IN THE LIVING ROOM WITH HER four best friends for one last evening together. She'd made a new assortment of mocktails, and she'd drank three too many already. It was late, but she couldn't stand the thought of going to bed. Then morning would come, and everyone would leave.

It would just be her and the twins in the house, and nothing to fill any of their time. Well, that wasn't entirely true, as Charlie had already asked Alice if he could ride the ferry by himself to get to Diamond to see Mandie and meet her friends.

Alice hadn't known what to say. He had plenty of reasons why it would be good for him, and Alice saw so much of Frank in him. At the same time, she recognized herself too. She saw her son weeping at her side when they talked about the things his father had done, and she knew he had a good heart. Much better than Frank had ever had.

They'd ended evenings with tears, some with laughter, some with tension. Alice just wanted them to stay forever, and she got up and hurried into the kitchen while Robin started detailing a bride she'd worked with that had ordered four different sets of announcements and delayed the event by six months to do so.

"As long as you don't do that, Eloise," Robin said. "I can help you with your wedding."

"He needs to ask me first," Eloise said. "And besides, I don't think we're quite to that stage."

Alice poured herself another drink and turned to face her friends, feeling stronger now that she had something to focus on. "How long do you think it'll take to get there?" she asked.

Eloise looked over her shoulder. "I'll take the orange ginger one, Alice."

She nodded and turned to get another glass while Eloise said, "And I don't know. We haven't talked about marriage."

"What are you going to do about your job?" Robin asked.

"I don't know." Eloise took the glass of orange liquid from Alice with a smile. "I don't know a lot of stuff right now, so I'm not trying to be difficult." She lifted her drink to her mouth. "Mm. I love this stuff."

Alice took her spot in the recliner again and settled in, though she was ready for bed.

"I think that's it for me," Kelli said, getting up. "Parker and I have to be on the eight o'clock ferry, and I haven't packed yet."

Alice jumped to her feet and hugged Kelli. "You guys will have to come back before school starts in the fall."

Kelli gripped her tight, but she didn't confirm or deny that she'd return to the cove before autumn. Hugs and embraces went around, and Alice did what she'd always done. She started picking up glasses and napkins, stirring sticks and other bits of trash. Finally, she was alone in the kitchen, and she paused in front of the sink, her eyes out the window. The pool glinted with teal lightning in the darkness, and Alice remembered one of the first times she and Frank had come to the vacation house to entertain several of his clients.

How perfect she'd been. How white her beach-combers. How pristine her makeup, with every eyelash perfectly in place, along with every strand of hair. She hadn't been unhappy with her life then, because she hadn't understood what happiness was at the time.

She knew now that there was much more than dinner parties and the right brand of shoes, and that quartz countertops could make her smile but they didn't make her happy.

Alice was still working on what true happiness looked like for her, but she felt like she'd taken the first step in the right direction. Perhaps she'd taken three or four by now, and she sighed as she turned away from the window.

Frank had agreed to let her know if he was going to honor the agreement he'd signed within seven days of the hearing, and that was tomorrow. He'd probably wait until the very last minute, but Alice checked her phone anyway. She'd set it on silent when Charlie had started texting why he needed to get a summer job on her father's shrimp boat from his bedroom while she was trying to enjoy her last night with her friends.

She had four more messages from him, but none from Frank. Her mood sufficiently soured, she turned off all the lights in the main part of the house and went into the bedroom. She couldn't make Frank text just by looking at her phone. In fact, Alice had never been able to make Frank do anything, so she wasn't sure why she'd thought she could now.

In the morning, Alice brewed the coffee and set out the packages of chocolates she'd put together for her friends. Kelli was the first to leave, and Alice helped Parker with his suitcase as they went down the front steps. Alice handed them each a little bag filled with blue confetti and chocolates, and she hugged them both fiercely with everything inside her.

"I love you, Kel."

"I love you too," she said, her voice strained. She stepped back a moment later, and she looked right at Alice. "I didn't give him the Glassworks."

Surprise moved through Alice, and she tried to cement her stone mask in place so she wouldn't react. She was tired of wearing that mask, though. It was so heavy, and she hated that she couldn't just feel what she felt. She let it slip away, and Kelli smiled at her. "Don't look so surprised."

"I am surprised," Alice said.

"You were right," Kelli said, looking toward a silver car as it pulled up to the house. "You know how I like to romanticize things."

"Only a little." Their eyes met again, and Alice smiled at her the way she would a younger sister.

"Come on, Parker," Kelli said, and just like that, they loaded up and they left.

AJ left next, and Alice sent her off with the same python-like hug and bag of chocolates. Robin was taking Eloise to Diamond Island, where Aaron would take her to the airport later that afternoon, and as Alice watched them drive away in Eloise's rental car, she felt like crying.

So she did—right there on her front lawn, where anyone could see her.

"Mom," Charlie said, coming down the front steps. "Ginny and I want to go to a movie. Can we go over to Diamond?"

"Yes," Alice said, not wanting to argue with her children. They'd been good sports for the past two weeks, always doing what she dictated to them, and she added, "There's money in my purse."

"Will you drive us to the ferry?" Ginny asked.

"Yes."

"How late can we stay on Diamond?" Charlie asked, exchanging a glance with his twin.

"I'm old," Alice said. "And it's been a very busy two weeks. I'll be at the ferry station at ten, and I'm not negotiating."

"Ten?" Charlie looked like he'd been told he'd get an extra birthday that year. "Great. That's great, Mom. Thanks." He hugged her, and Alice melted into her son's embrace.

Ginny joined them, saying, "Will you be okay here, Mom?"

"Yes," Alice said, inhaling strength into her bones and body with her breath. "Believe it or not, I used to be alone a lot."

Ginny didn't return her smile. "That doesn't mean you liked it."

How wise she was. "I'll be okay," she said. "You guys go." She stayed on the lawn, hugging herself with her arms while they ran inside to get her purse. She dropped them off at the ferry station and returned to the house.

It still held some of the life her friends had leant it, and Alice simply stood in the foyer and basked in it.

Her phone chimed, and she expected to look down and see a text from Charlie, telling her they'd made it onto the ferry and were disembarking now.

The message was from Frank, and Alice's heartbeat rippled like a flag in a stiff wind as she swiped to open the text.

I'll honor the agreement I signed.

With that, relief soared through Alice, and she sank onto the nearby bench, allowing that emotion to stream down her face in the form of tears.

She only cried for a few seconds, and then she stood up. She could finally face the future without being chained to her past, and she felt lighter than she had in two decades.

With a new bounce in her step, she went into the kitchen and collected a bottle of water from the fridge. At the desk in her office, she started flipping pages in her planner. She needed to get the dates for next year's summer sand pact on the calendar now, so everyone could make arrangements to return to Five Island Cove.

Read on for the first couple chapters of **The Cliffside Inn, the next book in the Five Island Cove women's fiction series,** for more secrets, more romance, and more great friendship and sisterhood fiction that brings women together and celebrates the female relationship.

THE CLIFFSIDE INN, CHAPTER ONE:

Eloise stood and shook the dean's hand. "Thank you, Donald." She wasn't sure what she'd just done, but as she left his office, she knew she'd left her keys behind.

She wouldn't be able to get in her office again. It wasn't her office anymore.

Eloise walked down the hall, a path she'd tread many times over the past twenty years. She remembered the first time she'd made the trek from the human resources office on campus to Dr. Donald Travis's office. He'd been Dean of Life Sciences for two years before Eloise had started, and he'd hired her, fresh out of Harvard, no other teaching experience.

They'd always worked well together, and Eloise's mouth turned down into a frown as the bright rectangle of light up ahead signaled the exit from the building. Once she left...she wouldn't be coming back.

Her steps slowed as her mind sped. What had she been thinking? She'd just quit her job.

She'd made a terrible mistake.

She slowed further, refusing to let herself stop. She looked over her shoulder, as if everyone she'd come in contact with other the past two decades would be there, suddenly lining the halls and applauding as she walked out of the biology building for the last time.

There was no one there. No one clapping.

Eloise did stop then, and she turned back fully, her heart taking on a new brand of courage. She began a slow clap for herself, a smile filling her soul as it took over her face.

She'd done it.

She'd quit her job to move to Five Island Cove, date her serious boyfriend full-time, and restore the Cliffside Inn, a building she'd owned for about as long as she'd been a professor here at Boston University.

Her self-applause sounded loud in the summer silence of the building, and Eloise knew that in just two weeks, these halls would be full of students and teachers, aides and secretaries. She always called these last couple weeks of August the calm before the storm, and she took one last moment to envision this building, her office, her classroom, the way she always wanted to think of them— full of life, chattering students excited to learn, and the energy only a college campus could possess.

Then she turned and walked out the doors.

The heat of the season hit her straight in the chest, but she took a deep breath of the too-hot and too-muggy air anyway. As she blew it out, she heard the voices she'd spent every day talking to over the phone or video chat since she'd left Five Island Cove in June.

"She's probably not done," Aaron said. "She said it could—"

"Eloise!" Grace said, catching sight of her first. She skipped toward Eloise, who grinned down at the girl. She laced her fingers through Eloise's when she arrived and said, "I knew you wouldn't take long."

"How could I?" Eloise asked her. "It's your birthday, and we have some very important celebrating to do." She smiled at Grace and lifted her eyes to Aaron as he approached. He swept one arm around her waist and pressed a kiss to the soft, delicate spot on her throat just below her jaw and ear.

"Hey, sweetheart," he said, his voice already throaty to go with the deep quality.

Eloise giggled at the way his hand moved up her back, and she stepped sideways to greet Billie too. "Wow, Billie," she said, taking her all in. "You talked your father into the mascara."

"I told you she'd notice," Aaron said.

"Is it too much?" Billie asked, shooting her dad a dirty look.

"I don't think so," Eloise said, bending down to peer at the girl closer. She was a stunning child—and Eloise knew she wouldn't be a child for much longer. Billie started seventh grade this year, and that meant junior high. No single teacher in charge of her, and multiple classes, and all those boys...

No wonder Aaron didn't want her to wear makeup. The mascara made her eyelashes look a league long, and since Billie was somewhat of a sober child, she had the starving model look down pat.

"You look very pretty," Eloise added.

"I told you it wasn't too much," Billie said to Aaron, who seriously looked like he might stick his tongue out at her. She'd certainly used that sassy tone of voice with him.

"Billie," he warned. "Watch your attitude."

Eloise looked back and forth between them, the battle silent but raging. "Am I going to have to separate you two?" She did step between them, taking Aaron's hand in her free one and releasing Grace's so she could hold Billie's. "Come on. Let's make a pact that we won't fight today. It's Grace's birthday, and she's turning eleven. I have eleven of the *most* fun things to do in Boston planned for us, and eleven movies to choose from for tonight, and eleven different kinds of ice cream bars."

She first looked at Aaron, who she could count on to be the most mature. He still wore a storm on his face, but he nodded. "I can commit to that," he said.

Eloise looked at Billie, who stood nearly as tall as Eloise now. "Bills?"

"Yes," she said, though plenty of surliness rode in her tone.

Eloise smiled at her and drew her into a hug. The girl relaxed then, and Eloise whispered, "Hey, he let you wear it."

"I know." Billie sighed and stepped back. "Do you really think it looks pretty?"

"Yes," Eloise said. "You did just what I said too. Not too clumpy on the bottom." She looked over her shoulder for Grace, who'd wandered off after a butterfly during the battle of the wills. "Come on, Grace. If we don't get going, we won't be able to do everything for your birthday."

She'd shown Billie how to apply the mascara over a video chat several days ago. She'd bought Billie the mascara, along with an excellent makeup remover wipe, and had them both shipped to Aaron's house the next day. Billie had called her when she'd opened the package, and Eloise swore it was one of the only times she'd heard Billie laugh.

"What's the first thing?" Aaron asked as they strolled toward the parking lot. "And are we taking my car or yours?"

"Yours won't be full of residual cat hair," she said. "And it's an SUV." She knew the red vehicle parked next to her car in the lot was his, because the only other one belonged to Dr. Travis. "Let's take yours."

Aaron clicked the button on the fob to unlock it, and everyone piled in. "All right," Eloise said. "I have a few ground rules for today." She surveyed the group, twisting as far as her spine would allow to meet Grace's eyes. "Okay?"

"Okay," they all said.

"First, not everything we do will be everyone's favorite. I know that, but I still expect everyone to have a good attitude and not to complain. I went to a lot of effort to find the things we're doing, and I expect you to be kind and thoughtful of my feelings."

She glanced at Aaron, who simply looked at her with wide eyes. She wondered if anyone had ever spoken to him like that—or to his girls. "Of everyone's feelings."

"Yes, ma'am," Aaron said, reaching for and taking her hand in his.

"Second, you have to eat some real food today, or you can't have any of the birthday cake and ice cream I have at my house." Eloise smiled, raising her eyebrows at Grace, who giggled. Billie nodded, taking everything super seriously.

"Third, let's have fun today," she said. "You've never been to Boston, and it's a fabulous city." She nodded and looked at Aaron. "We're ready, Captain."

"I don't know where we're going," he said.

"Oh, right." Eloise sprang from the SUV and opened her car's back door. She pulled out her giant bag that she took everywhere with her and turned back to knock on the window. "Pop the back," she said, through the glass.

Aaron got the message, and she began to move the

eleven gifts she'd bought for Grace from her trunk to the back of the SUV.

"El," Aaron said, his voice halfway between disapproval and awe.

"Can I open one now?" Grace asked, as she'd knelt up on the seat and had seen what Eloise was doing.

"That's going to be rule number four," Eloise said. "You don't get to ask for the presents. I will give them to you when you should have them."

Grace's face fell, and Eloise's heart rebounded too. She picked up the gift she'd wrapped in pale pink paper and took it Grace's side of the car. "You get this one right now."

"Thank you, Eloise," Grace said, and she opened the present with the light of joy in her eyes. She took out the stuffed terrier and looked up at Eloise.

"That's Rhett the Boston Terrier," she said. "He's my school's mascot." The stuffed animal wore a BU jersey, but he was snarling like he might rip someone's face off if he came to life. "You have all those stuffed animals in your room, and I thought you might like one to remember your trip here."

"I do." Grace reached for her and wrapped her skinny arms around Eloise's neck. "Thank you, Eloise."

"Of course, Gracie-Lou." Eloise squeezed her tight, closing her eyes the same way as she hugged the girl, and then stepped back. With the door closed, she took a moment to clear her throat and shake off the emotion.

When she got in the front seat again, she said, "New England Aquarium, here we come."

Several days later, the high from a grand adventure for Grace's birthday had worn way off. Eloise had been working like a dog, getting everything she owned packed, thrown away, or donated to the Salvation Army.

Aaron, Billie, and Grace had helped every single day, and then she'd taken them to one of her favorite restaurants in town.

She stretched the tape over another box and took it into the front entry of the brownstone. She seemed to have come miles already, and yet, she still had many more to go. She put the thought out of her mind, because if she focused too hard on what she had left to do, she'd give up right now.

Aaron came through the front door and picked up the box she'd just set down. "Morning, El." He grinned at her, switched the box to the side and leaned in to kiss her.

"Hey." She kissed him back, glad to see him here so early. "Just you?" Usually, Billie and Grace crowded into the house behind him, and she didn't hear their footsteps or their voices.

"I told the girls they could sleep in and stay at the hotel if they promised not to leave the room or call me until noon." He grinned at her. "I'll get this loaded and come help you keep packing. Getting close?"

"I think so," she said, turning to survey the hall that led into the living area and kitchen. She had to be getting close, because they were all leaving Massachusetts tomorrow morning, on the same flight. Alice had been a great help to her in arranging to have the things she'd accumulated in the first forty-five years of her life moved across the water to the cove.

Eloise owned way too much to keep in the carekeeper's apartment at the inn, and she'd already arranged for a storage unit on Sanctuary Island. She'd be staying with her mother just down the cliff until she cleaned up the apartment enough for her to live in, and Eloise knew she wouldn't have a day off of packing—or unpacking—and cleaning for a while.

For a brief moment, she couldn't believe she'd traded her gorgeous brownstone and her prestigious job at BU for a moldy, one-bedroom apartment at an inn that likely wouldn't open for many months.

By then, it would be the off-season, and Eloise didn't expect a lot of business to come pouring through the doors of the Cliffside Inn.

She turned when Aaron set the box down, surprise flowing through her veins when he took her into his arms and kissed her like he meant it. "I just realized we're alone for the whole morning," he said, his lips sliding down the curve of her neck.

"Mm." She melted into his touch and didn't protest when he took her upstairs to her bedroom.

The next morning, Eloise did indeed have the brownstone ready to be vacated. She, Aaron, and the girls had worked until just after ten last night, and all she had to do this morning was shower, get dressed, and take her suitcase downstairs to her car. With that done, she sat on the steps and waited. She needed to drive her car to the dock, where she'd actually park it in a shipping container. That, and the one she'd filled with boxes and furniture, would arrive in the cove on a boat in ten to fourteen days.

She'd fly to Five Island Cove with Aaron and the girls, and she'd live out of her suitcase and use RideShare until her vehicle arrived.

Her stomach knotted, because Eloise Hall didn't do things like this. She stood as a couple came down the sidewalk. The man, Jacob, lifted his hand, his face already set in a permanent smile.

"Eloise," he said as he passed the gate and turned down her sidewalk.

"Hey." She embraced him and then Millie. "All right." She exhaled heavily and took the key out of her pocket. "Here's the key. She's cleaned out and ready for you."

She hadn't sold the brownstone, because they were extremely valuable, and she hadn't wanted to. She practically owned it, and she'd found a research assistant and his wife who were willing to sublet it from her.

"Thank you, Eloise," Millie said, and she hugged Eloise again. "This has been such an answer to our prayers."

"Mine too," Eloise said, nodding. She had to cling to that, otherwise, she might not be able to get herself to walk away.

Aaron rolled up to the curb in his red SUV, and Eloise felt like the sunshine broke through the clouds in her whole life. "Let me know if there's anything you need," she said. "Or if something breaks down or anything like that." She lifted her hand to let Aaron know she needed another moment. He did the same, and she focused on Jacob and Millie again. "Really. It's a good place, though."

"We're very excited," Jacob said.

"The shipping container will be gone on Saturday," she said. "Maybe sooner."

"No problem."

"Okay." Eloise turned and looked back at the thick, black door, and then faced Aaron, Billie, and Grace. "Okay." She nodded, tucked her hair behind her ears, and went down the sidewalk.

Aaron rolled down his window and said, "All good?"

"All good," she repeated. "So you'll follow me to the dock?"

"Yep." He chin-nodded to his phone in his cupholder. "I have it on the maps, and Billie is my navigator." He smiled at his daughter in the passenger seat, and Eloise couldn't wait to be in this car with them.

"Perfect," she said, and she went to her car, got behind the wheel, and drove away from the house she'd lived in for twenty years.

THE CLIFFSIDE INN, CHAPTER TWO:

Kelli had just set a bowl of macaroni and cheese with seared hot dogs in front of Parker when her husband walked in through the garage entrance. They couldn't park in the garage, because Julian had stacks and stacks of things he needed for the courier business. Bike chains, and boxes, and tubes for papers. Backpacks for his riders, bike racks, a few filing cabinets, and literally everything else under the sun.

"Hey," he said, anxiety instantly present in his expression.

"Hey." She turned away from him, coaching herself to stand straight and tall. She did not need to cower under this man's gaze anymore. She picked up the wooden spoon she'd used to stir the dinner she'd made, and one Julian would never approve of.

Well, in Kelli's opinion, he could ask his girlfriend to

make the type of dinner he wanted. Kelli wasn't going to do it, she knew that. She wished she had someone she could tell about this situation, but she hadn't been able to bring herself to put anything on the group text from her friends in Five Island Cove.

She didn't share things like this with her mother, and Julian had asked her not to say anything to his mother.

For a few weeks after she'd returned to Newark, she and Zach had communicated regularly, but their texts and messages had dwindled to only a few each week now, if that. She felt completely alone in a city of hundreds of thousands.

She spooned herself some of the macaroni and cheese and joined her son at the table, refusing to look at Julian. "What are you doing tonight?" she asked.

Since he'd had his assistant—Tiffany Mullinax—over to the house, and they'd revealed the fact that yes, they were a couple. They were dating. They were together, Kelli was trying to figure out what her evenings looked like. What her life was supposed to look like.

Julian and Tiffany didn't want Kelli to leave. He wasn't asking for a divorce. He wanted both of them.

The word that had come out of his mouth had sent Kelli into a tailspin. She hadn't even known what it meant.

Throuple.

He wanted the three of them have an open, emotional, close, and sexual relationship.

The *three* of them.

Julian put his messenger bag on the sideboard and eased past Parker and into the kitchen. Kelli had never minded the small house where they lived—until now. She'd never minded how much Julian worked—until now. She'd never minded how his whole life and what he wanted had dominated her entire existence—until now.

"I don't know," he said. "What are you doing?"

"I think Parker and I are going to go to the park," she said.

"Tiffany wondered if she—" He cut off as Kelli lifted her head and glared him into silence. "Okay." He lifted his hand in surrender, something she'd literally never seen him do. At least not to her. "You need more time."

"You sprung this on me six days ago," she said, glancing at Parker. He wasn't a baby, and he listened to every word his parents said. "So yes, Julian, I need more time." She looked down into her bowl, her appetite gone. She glanced at Parker. "Finish up, bud," she said. "We'll go to the park and maybe a movie."

If she left the house, then Julian could have his other woman over. She'd suspected he'd been cheating on her since her last trip to Five Island Cove, but he'd been denying it for two months. He denied it when he met her at the airport. He denied it when she'd walked into his office and found "Tiff" leaning over him as they both looked at something on his computer.

The way she'd been standing, and the look on her husband's face... Kelli had asked. Julian had denied it.

Over and over, he'd denied it.

Until six days ago.

Kelli was still reeling from the conversation, and it had literally lasted fifteen minutes from beginning to end. She'd left the house immediately afterward, and she hadn't come back until after midnight. Julian had put Parker to bed himself, and Tiffany hadn't been in the house. Kelli had stood in the darkness, the light above the stove the only way she could see anything in the room.

She'd felt outside of her skin, outside of her own reality. She still did.

"Okay." Julian put a couple twenty-dollar bills on the table. "Text me if you want us to come."

Kelli bristled at the word *us*, and she took the money and stood up in a fluid motion. She stuffed the bills in her pocket and left her nearly-full bowl of food on the table. "You ready, Parker?"

"Yeah," he said. He left his bowl on the table too, and Kelli was glad. Julian's eyebrows drew down, but Kelli didn't want to have this conversation right now. Kelli put a protective arm around her son and walked out the door her husband had come in only five minutes ago.

The stress and tension in her shoulders deflated the moment the door closed behind her, and then the tears came. She wasn't sad, and she wasn't nervous, and she wasn't anxious. Crying was simply her way to release all of the negative emotions she had. Positive ones too.

She put on a brave face, complete with a smile, and opened the passenger door for her son.

A few hours later, she reached for the half-empty bucket of popcorn she and Parker had shared, and the weight of the world started to descend on Kelli's shoulders. Home used to be a place of safety for her, and if she didn't have that, she didn't have anything.

Her lungs quivered, because she really didn't want to go home. "Want to take this?" she asked her son.

"Can you make caramel popcorn with it tomorrow?"

"Sure," she said. "And we get a refill, so let's have them fill it up on the way out, and we'll have lots. We can take some to my friends at the gym, and you can take some to your party."

Parker grinned at her. "I forgot about the party."

"You did?" Kelli stood as the lights started to come up. "I can't believe that. You've been so excited about it."

"Yeah." Parker didn't say anything else, and Kelli knew he had to be thinking something. She had no idea how to get his thoughts out of his head, and she often got one-word answers from him and not much else.

She stopped by to get the extra popcorn, and she herded Parker through the teenage crowd loitering in the lobby to the parking lot. Her phone rang, and she juggled the full popcorn bucket and her purse to get her phone out.

Her mother's name sat on the screen, and Kelli's heart sent out a few beats.

She managed to tap the call open and put the phone to her ear while holding onto everything. "Hey, Mom," she said, nodding for Parker to keep going.

"Hey," her mother said, her voice sounded small and very far away. Kelli could never judge the mood her mom was in, because she said everything in about the same, even tone. "What are you up to?"

"Just leaving a movie," Kelli said, walking through the twilight. School started in a few weeks, and the days would get shorter and shorter until it would be full dark at this time of night. She mourned the passing of summer already, and she still had more time to enjoy it.

"Okay," her mom said.

Kelli gestured for Parker to come get the keys out of her purse. "Mom?" she asked. "Are you still there?"

"Yes," her mom said. "I just—" She cleared her throat. "I have to ask you something, and I'm a little nervous." She gave an anxious chuckle, and Kelli's stomach tightened. Her fingers ached as she pinched the very edge of the popcorn bucket.

"Just say it, Mom," Kelli said as Parker unlocked the car and got in the front seat.

"Have you heard from Zach at all this summer?"

"Yeah, sure," Kelli said, her voice automatically

moving into a false zone. Truthfully, her last few texts to her half-brother had gone unanswered. She missed him, because they'd really connected in Five Island Cove in June, and she'd thought she meant more to him than just a couple of weeks of interaction.

"He's been coming by the house," her mom said.

Kelli froze. "He has?"

"Yeah, a few times." Her mom sounded stressed, and Kelli didn't like that.

"Well, what does he want?"

"Money," her mom blurted. "He keeps asking me for money, Kelli, and I don't have anything to give him." She spoke in a huge rush of words now. "Last time he came, the only reason I didn't just give him what I had in my purse was because Devon was with me." She let out a breath that shook over the line.

Kelli didn't know what to say or do. Her first instinct was to rush home, pack a bag, and get on the first flight to Five Island Cove. She could comfort her mother and confront Zach about his behavior. Didn't he know that her mother wouldn't want to meet him, ever? It would be like looking into the face of her husband's betrayal.

In that moment, Kelli knew exactly how her mother felt. Back then, when her husband had cheated on her, and now, as she had to deal with the aftermath of it many years later.

Kelli did not want to be that woman. She didn't want to walk through her front door after a morning at the gym and see Tiffany sitting at the table. She didn't want another woman in her family, in her marriage, in any of it.

She hadn't wanted to lose Julian, and he claimed to love them both. He wanted them both. He said lots of couples did things like this, because it kept things interesting at a time in their marriage where things sometimes got stale.

Kelli didn't understand that. Her life with Julian hadn't been stale. She'd felt distant from him, because he'd started sharing parts of himself with another woman.

"I'm coming to the cove," she said, making up her mind on the spot. She moved toward the car and put the popcorn in the back seat. It would probably spill all over the place by the time she got home, but that wasn't her primary concern right now.

"I'll call him too," she said. "Don't worry, Mom. I'll take care of Zach."

"Okay," her mom said, her voice shaky. "Sorry, Kelli. I know you two are friends."

"Yeah," Kelli said, climbing into the front seat. "Okay, bye, Mom. I'll keep you updated." She hung up, her fingers shaking. Friends.

She didn't think she and Zach were that close of friends anymore, despite her best efforts. She didn't want to call him in front of Parker, as her son had really liked Zach.

She also didn't want to wait. Her fingers flexed around the wheel, and she forced herself to wait, because the last thing she needed on top of everything else was a citation for using her phone while driving.

At home, instant annoyance shot through her when she saw Tiffany's car still parked in her driveway. "Go on inside," she said. "Tell them I have to make a call, okay?"

"Okay," Parker said. "You can get the popcorn?"

"Yep." Kelli painted a smile on her face and watched her son go through the garage and inside the house. She quickly dialed Zach then and listened to the phone ring and ring.

He didn't pick up, and Kelli ended the call. Immediately, she dialed him again, muttering some choice words for him under her breath. When he didn't answer the second time, she barked into the phone, "Zach, it's Kelli. How dare you go to my mother's house and ask her for money? Stay away from her."

Her mind raced as fast as her heart. What was she going to do about it from so far away? Zach would likely scoff when he got the message.

Kelli's mind cleared, and she zeroed in on one thing: Aaron Sherman.

"Remember that I know the Chief of Police," she said, much smoother and much quieter. Much more deadly. "If I hear that you've even visited Bell Island, I will have you picked up and held in jail until I can get to the cove and figure out what you're doing and what you want."

She was surprised by the vitriol inside her. She hadn't asked him if the allegations were true or what he needed money for. She knew her mother wouldn't call her and lie about that, and Kelli didn't have any money to give Zach anyway.

"And call me back," she said. "I'd love to hear a good explanation for why you did this." She hung up then and almost tossed her phone in the cup holder.

Another ray of light touched her mind, and Kelli got out of the car before she lost her nerve. It had been sticking around longer and longer, and for that, Kelli was grateful.

She marched into the house, where the kitchen sat in darkness, as did the living room and dining room. She expected to see Julian and Tiff on the couch, possibly holding hands, while they watched a movie.

They weren't there.

"Parker?" she asked, heading for the stairs. Up she went, and she found her son in his bedroom, already in his pajamas. "Ready for bed?"

"Yeah," he said. "I can help with the popcorn in the morning."

"Sure," Kelli said, smoothing back his hair. She'd let it grow long in the front, and she smiled at him. "Maybe we should go get haircuts in the morning."

"All right," Parker said.

"Then it won't be too short when school starts."

He nodded and climbed into bed. She tucked him in and kissed him goodnight. In the hall, she looked toward the guest bedroom and the bathroom. No sound. The master suite was downstairs, but she was terrified to go inside.

She knew how Julian made love, and she did not want to see him do it with someone else. Her lungs felt like someone had cast them in plaster when they were empty, and she couldn't get enough air.

Her feet simply moved, her muscle memory taking her from tucking in her son to her own bedroom, where she normally changed into her pajamas and went to bed, intending to wait up for Julian, and only making it about half the time.

She pushed open the door to the bedroom, and sure enough, Tiff and Julian were there. They both lay in bed —*her* bed—fully clothed, the TV flickering against the lamplight. Both lamps on either side of the bed were lit, and the three of them looked at one another.

Tiffany was on the edge of Julian's side of the bed, and he lay closer to the middle. He looked at her, begging her. Kelli could feel it from across the room. "There's room over here," he said.

Kelli could not fathom climbing into that bed with the two of them and giving her permission for this outside relationship to be brought inside. How would she explain it to her friends and co-workers? Her mother? Her son?

Herself?

She shook her head, decisions being made left and right in the few moments she stood there. "Tomorrow,

Parker has a birthday party. We're making caramel popcorn for him to take."

"Okay," Julian said. "I can probably give him a ride. Or Tiff can." He looked at the brunette, and Kelli wondered what he'd seen in her that he hadn't found in Kelli. Did it really take two women to satisfy a man like Julian?

"I'll do it," Kelli said. "On Saturday, I'm going to teach my last class at the gym, and Parker and I are going to Five Island Cove to visit my mother."

Julian's eyebrows shot toward the sky. "Really, Kel? Your mother?"

"And Eloise needs help with the inn," Kelli said, refusing to let him mock her and make her second-guess herself. She'd done that for far too long in her life, and she was ready to take the reins and direct the horse where it needed to go.

She gazed evenly at Julian, her eyes flickering to Tiff for only a second. "I can't do it, Julian," she said. "I'm sorry, but I can't do it." She started to move toward the master closet, where her luggage was.

"Parker and I are going to the cove, and we aren't coming back."

The Cliffside Inn is coming this fall! Preorder your copy today to continue the journey with the women in Five Island Cove.

BOOKS IN THE FIVE ISLAND COVE SERIES

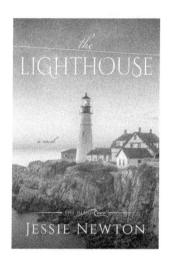

The Lighthouse, Book 1: As these 5 best friends work together to find the truth, they learn to let go of what doesn't matter and cling to what does: faith, family, and most of all, friendship.

Secrets, safety, and sisterhood...it all happens at the lighthouse on Five Island Cove.

The Summer Sand Pact, Book 2: These five best friends made a Summer Sand Pact as teens and have only kept it once or twice—until they reunite decades later and renew their agreement to meet in Five Island Cove every summer.

BOOKS IN THE FIVE ISLAND COVE SERIES

The Cliffside Inn, Book 3: Spend another month in Five Island Cove and experience an amazing adventure between five best friends, the challenges they face, the secrets threatening to come between them, and their undying support of each other.

Christmas at the Cove, Book 4: Secrets are never discovered during the holidays, right? That's what these five best friends are banking on as they gather once again to Five Island Cove for what they hope will be a Christmas to remember.

BOOKS IN THE FIVE ISLAND COVE SERIES

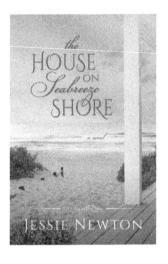

The House on Seabreeze Shore, Book 5: One last trip to Five Island Cove...this time to face a fresh future and leave all the secrets and fears in the past.

ABOUT JESSIE

Jessie Newton is a saleswoman during the day and escapes into romance and women's fiction in the evening, usually with a cat and a cup of tea nearby. The Lighthouse is her first women's fiction novel. Find out more at www. jessienewton.com.